THE SPIES OF ZURICH

RICHARD WAKE

MANOR AND STATE, LLC

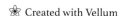 Created with Vellum

To Rich and Casey,
Wonderful children, even better adults, you are an endless source of
love and pride.

PART I

1

The heart of Zurich -- the heart and maybe the soul, too -- were at the Paradeplatz, a vast expanse just off of the Bahnhofstrasse where about 10 tram lines converged. The lake and all of its beauty, and Switzerland really is a beautiful country, was off to the right. The temples of conspicuous consumption and commerce that made this country go more than any place I had ever been, dotted the street to the left. That street led ultimately to the train station and the transportation links to still more commerce. But what held it all together was in the Paradeplatz, because that was where the banks were.

It was two banks, two substantial buildings, stone fortresses, staring at each other across the expanse. Kreditanstalt was on the north side, and Bankverein was on the west side. Those two ran everything. The truth was, they ran the country. There was plenty of money to be made by the minnows, the small private banks tucked into the side streets between the Paradeplatz and the Grossmunster -- different churches, yes -- thanks to the Swiss secrecy laws. But the whales on the Paradeplatz made the biggest decisions, funded the biggest developments, and controlled their smaller competitors by throwing them morsels of side work, or not.

That was the dynamic on a beautiful September day in 1939. It was still more than a month away from the sun's autumnal retreat, and three months away from the cold and miserable gray that descended upon the city every winter. It was bright and blue and much too nice to be inside, but the massive fourth-floor reception room in the Kreditanstalt building was filled that day with that great oxymoron, the smiling banker. One of the bank's directors, Gerhard Femmerling, a miserable prick even by Swiss bank director standards, was retiring, and we had all been summoned with engraved invitations to wish him well at a noontime reception. Looking around at the assembled dozens, grins plastered in place, I did a quick head count, and it appeared that everyone had RSVP'd in the affirmative. It was just business, after all. You had to retain your place in the queue for when it was morsel time again.

I had two rules at these kinds of things. The first was to make sure to be seen by the person or people who needed to see me and to do it quickly. There was nothing worse than waiting your turn for an audience. So I took a direct line to old Femmerling as soon as I walked into the room, and barged in on the group surrounding him, and offered a random sampling of pleasant conversational nothings, and was done with the work of the day in five minutes. That allowed me to attend to my second rule, which was never to be out of direct contact with the bar.

This was a rarity, seeing as how Swiss bankers didn't drink at lunch, except for maybe a glass of wine -- one glass, and not drunk to the bottom. But it was a full bar this day, and the scotch was really from Scotland, and the bartender was pouring my second when I received a nudge in the ribs followed by, "Bon-jour, Alex. I see that Zurich has not changed -- that there are almost no women in the banking business, and that they have never been seen in public without every button of their blouses buttoned all the way to their eyebrows."

Freddy Arpin had made the trip up from Geneva, where his family owned Banc Arpin, a little private joint whose principal customers, in Freddy's words, "were either French pseudo-Fascists or outright Fascists, hedging their bets." We had met at a conference in Basel and immediately hit it off, mostly because we were clearly oddballs in the banking business in that we didn't give a fuck. Or, as Freddy put it, "My father and brother are in the sharp pencil and green eyeshade business. I am in the cognac and silk stocking business." We got along fine.

"Long way to come for this, huh?"

"My father insisted," Freddy said. "It's OK, easy to kill the time on the train. There's plenty to read in the papers."

"Anything new?"

"No. Warsaw is still holding out, but --"

"Poor bastards," I said. "Any sign the French or the Brits are getting off their asses to help?"

"Nope."

"Useless fucks."

Some variation on this conversation was happening all over the room, no doubt. The Germans had invaded Poland two weeks earlier. The British and French had declared war on Germany a couple of days after that, but sat and watched as the Wehrmacht went about its business. The conversations -- and I had participated in my share as president of my own little bank, Bohemia Suisse -- were all about the sober calculation of the effects of war on European business in general and Swiss business in particular. I could do sober calculation if the social or business setting demanded it.

But this was a little more personal for me. My adopted home, Austria, had been seized by the Nazis in March of 1938. My real home, Czechoslovakia, had been gifted to them, bartered away a couple of months after that by Chamberlain and Daladier. So, yes, useless fucks.

I asked Freddy, "Are you guys seeing an increase in deposits?"

"You might say that. We actually had a guy show up last week from Lyon in his car, and he had the driver get out and carry in a picnic hamper stuffed with French francs. We sold him Swiss francs --"

"At an obscene markup --"

"That is getting more obscene by the day. Or, as my brother says, 'Add a point for every drop of piss you see dribbling down their legs.' So his deposit is in Swiss francs. Then we had a guy drive the French francs back to Paris and bought gold coins -- at a markup, yes, but not yet obscene. Then he brought the gold back, and it's in our vault."

"All in the same picnic basket?"

"The very same."

Freddy was saying that his father was calculating that they wouldn't be able to accept French francs at all in a couple of weeks, the way things were going -- unless, that is, the bank wanted to get into the business of using them to buy French real estate.

"If the little corporal keeps going, we could probably get houses in Paris at knockdown prices," Freddy said. "But that's a really long game. Maybe buying artwork is the way to go."

He stopped as if he were hearing himself for the first time, then said, "You think we're shitheads, don't you?"

"I don't know who isn't a shithead anymore, me included."

I went to grab two more drinks and returned to find Freddy talking to the only woman in the room with her top button undone. Her name was Manon Friere, and she was a trade representative from the French consulate, and she was more than a pleasure to look at. In this room, her red lipstick was like a beacon in a gray flannel night. She apparently had been working out of the consulate in Geneva but now was stationed in Zurich.

I waved my arm toward the windows to point out the expanse of the Paradeplatz, lit by the sun. "So how do you like our fair city? Freddy hates it, but you probably already knew that."

"You mean Tightassville?" Freddy said.

"Freddy is a Parisian at heart, trapped in a Swiss hell," Manon said

"Hell?" I said. "All of it?"

She shrugged.

Hell it is, then.

"Are you a tiny banker, like Freddy?"

"No one is as tiny as Freddy."

"That's pretty much what I hear --"

"Your vengeance is unbecoming," Freddy said. He pointedly turned away from Manon and looked at me. "Here's the story. I was dating a friend of Manon's in the consulate. At the same time, I might have also made an attempt to date Manon. It was honestly a mistake."

"You're honestly a pig."

"And my penance is her indiscriminate use of the word 'tiny' in conversations such as these."

"If the name fits," she said.

"I think it's more like when I was in high school," I said. "We had this buddy who was about 6-foot-4, and we called him Shorty."

"Exactly. Alex Kovacs, you are a true friend," Freddy said.

"No problem, Tiny," I said.

She snorted. Freddy made a face. I was smitten but also in a hurry. I had a 1:30 appointment that I couldn't miss. So I said my goodbyes and walked out into the Paradeplatz. I'm not sure I had ever been there without stopping on the way home at Confiserie

Sprungli, on the south side of the square, for a small bag of something sweet and rich and decadent -- although, as everyone knew, the truly rich and decadent things happened on the north side and the west side. Anyway, I stopped, collected my little stash, and began the 10-minute walk back to Bohemia Suisse.

As I turned onto Rennweg, I looked ahead and saw a small crowd had gathered outside of Gartner, a little restaurant that I had walked past about 500 times and never once thought to enter. As I got closer, the crowd grew, and I could see the frightened looks on the faces and hear the cries and the shouts for help. Then, in the distance, I heard a police siren.

I got to the edge of the crowd and shouldered my way through it. Finally, to the front, I looked down and saw that I suddenly wasn't in a hurry anymore. Laying on the ground was my 1:30 appointment, his head framed by a puddle of blood. He had been shot through the left eye.

A few blocks away, on Fortunagasse, was Bohemia Suisse. The bank was tucked in amid a row of houses, each with a ground floor and four floors above. It could have been just another residence in the hilly line of homes, but for the small gold sign on the door that identified the bank and said, "By appointment only." I always thought that it seemed to be more of a warning than a statement of information.

I moved slowly away from the crowd surrounding the body. I walked for five minutes in the wrong direction and did my best to check behind me while looking in the reflection of shop windows. I turned and walked in a circle around the Fraumunster and actually said a little prayer to myself somewhere behind the church, although I wasn't sure, in retrospect, about the effectiveness of a prayer that included the phrase, "Please let this not be completely fucked." Only then, when I was sure no one was following me, did I start walking toward the bank.

Even I couldn't let myself in during business hours -- such was the show of security required for private banks in Switzerland. And it was a show. At night or on the weekend I just used my key, but at 1:30 in the afternoon I rang the bell and was greeted after about 30 seconds by Anders, the security guard. He was dressed in a blue blazer and gray slacks. He was dressed that way every day, the coat specially tailored to smooth the line of the pistol he carried beneath it. He was a retired captain in the Swiss army, which I always thought was a hoot. I had fought in Caporetto for the greater glory of Austria-Hungary, for the emperor and his whiskers, while Anders oiled his gun on weekends in some barracks beneath an Alp. I made a joke about it when I first met him. His reaction, not in words but in the more powerful language of the body, made it quite clear that there would be no need to make the joke a second time.

"Herr Kovacs," he said.

"Anders," I said.

This was pretty much the extent of our conversation most days. He returned to his desk in our small lobby. What he did all day was beyond me, seeing as how most days we had no appointments. I never even saw him read a newspaper. He would let himself in. He would let me in. And he would let in Marta Frank, the office manager. She handled everything when I wasn't around, which was often. She could authorize cash deposits and withdrawals. She could, in the presence of Anders, open the vault and assist customers with their safe deposit boxes; she knew the lock's combination while he held the required key. Only I could open it by myself.

Marta had heard the police sirens. She said, "What is going on out there?"

I told her that a man was dead outside of Gartner and that he had been shot. And just as she got done gasping about that, I told her the dead man was Michael Landers, our 1:30 appointment, at which point she pretty much collapsed into the chair beside my desk, clutching my diary to her bosom. The diary was always either open on her desk or open in her hands.

She pulled herself together and looked down at the diary. "Landers. You wrote this one in. Who is he? Did I ever meet him?"

She knew very well that she had never met him, and I knew that she knew. We had only about 50 clients, most of them ancient Czech expats, so it really wasn't tough to keep track.

"He's one of the nephews in the Kerner Trust."

"Rich fool setting his money on fire," Marta said. She had been disapproving of the setup from the first time I explained it to her.

"But it's his money, and he pays his fees, so as far as I'm concerned, Bohemia Suisse will always be happy to supply Herr Kerner with all of the kerosene and matches that he requires."

The Kerner Trust was the fiction that had been created during my first months at the bank. The original depositor was a 40-year-old who had, with the aid of some stage makeup, a hunch, a limp, and a cane, passed himself off as an 80-year-old when he made his one and only appearance at the bank. It was important that Marta and Anders saw he was a real person, living and breathing. There was no way, after all, to hide a mysterious account from them, and especially from her, seeing as how the client base was so small and she kept the books.

The deposit he made was sizable, 200,000 francs. The money could be withdrawn by any of four of his nephews, all of whom I was to meet personally later that evening at Herr Kerner's home. There were no restrictions on the withdrawals. I would bring the required account identification materials on the home visit and distribute them so that a withdrawal could be made if I wasn't around.

Marta actually snorted and said, "The whole thing is ridiculous. And what are you now, his butler? Going to his house?"

"Look, it's a lot of money, and it's a service business, right?

And you're acting like he's the only eccentric on the client list. What about Herr Lutz?"

Rudi Lutz was one of our wealthiest depositors. He never made a withdrawal but, once a month, he came in and asked to see a full accounting anyway. Then he inspected the contents of his safe deposit box. This did not make him eccentric in my book, just untrusting. The eccentric part was that he showed up for every visit with a chauffeur whose job, besides driving the big black Daimler, was carrying in a small fish tank, and the several fish swimming inside, and placing it on my desk as we went through the accounts, and then on the table in the room where deposit boxes were examined in private.

"Ah, he's just an animal lover," Marta said, conceding the point with a smile.

"He's batshit is what he is," I said. "But we're happy to have his money, and we're happy now to have Herr Kerner's money."

That seemed to satisfy her. She usually said something snide when she took note of the withdrawals on the accounts that I had posted -- they tended to be at night or on weekends and handled by special appointments with me -- but that was it. "Shiftless" was her favorite word to describe the nephews. She did meet one of them once and handled his transaction, and told me later that "he had obviously been drinking at lunch." That also was by design, to assist in keeping her suspicion level low.

Marta was going to meet a second nephew that afternoon. Until, well.

She pulled herself together pretty quickly and asked, "Are you going to inform Herr Kerner?"

"No, I don't think so. It's not my news to tell. I'm sure the police will get to him soon enough."

Of course, Marta did not know how right she was. I was

going to have to tell somebody else -- not Herr Kerner, but Herr Kerner's handler.

Because Herr Kerner was actually Fritz Blum, the man in charge of an espionage network working in Switzerland, Belgium and Holland on behalf of the French, the British, and my old bosses, the Czechs, whose spies had fled to London along with the leaders of the government after the Nazi takeover in 1938. My Czech bosses, who were actually running the operation, shared everything with their hosts. My job was merely to be in charge of this sleepy bank and to distribute funds for operations to the spy network on demand. The truth was, it was the easiest and best-paying job I had ever had.

Well, it was until that day. As Marta got up and went back to her desk, I was wondering how quickly I needed to contact London, and pretty much immediately was my conclusion. But the contact information was back in my house, the return address on a random postcard currently being used as a bookmark in a book I had never read, "Dante's Inferno." And while I contemplated precisely what circle of hell I was about to enter, Marta poked her head into my office.

"There's somebody to see you," she said.

"Is there an appointment I forgot about?"

"Nope. He says he's a police detective."

I stood, and buttoned my jacket, and batted a flake of dandruff off of my shoulder, and walked out to fetch him. What circle of hell indeed?

3

Anders and the cop were talking as I approached. They were laughing, in fact.

"You guys know each other?" I said.

They stopped laughing. Anders said, "Army training together."

Perfect. That Anders did not like me had been made pretty plain over the prior 16 months. I'm not sure I had seen him laugh -- or, if I had, I didn't remember. But here he was, laughing with the cop. The two of them had probably been drunk together more than once, because what else do you do during Swiss army training but march and drill and...drink? And what do you when you're drinking but tell each other endlessly, in some variation, "Fuck them -- we are so real soldiers."

I stuck out my hand and introduced myself. The cop's name was Peter Ruchti, and he was a detective. He said his goodbyes to Anders and suggested we head into my office. The look on Anders' face indicated that he knew all along that I was a pickpocket or a pervert or something, and that I was about to be found out. In his heart, Anders was likely hoping for pervert.

Ruchti sat down, didn't want anything to drink. I tried small-talk, which is about the only professional skill I possessed. "So, were you in the army long?"

"Just two years -- I didn't make it a career like Anders. That was enough time for me to make the world safe for democracy and the bankers."

Great. Just great. "So what can I do for you?" I asked.

"Do you know a Michael Landers?"

In the minute or so I'd had to think, I had played this question out in my head. Would I admit it or not? There were upsides and downsides to both answers. Telling the truth is always best when dealing with the police, and there would be no harm in admitting that I knew the guy other than having to endure a series of follow-up questions. But then, the more I thought, there was a problem. There was no way Ruchti could find out that Landers was able to draw on an account at the bank because the Swiss banking secrecy laws were pretty much impenetrable. And there was no self-respecting Swiss banker who would ever identify one of his private clients. So if I told Ruchti that I knew Landers, I would have to invent some other context for knowing him, and that lie would be more complicated.

The alternative was to deny knowing him. Again, the banking secrecy laws protected me there. But it was a lie, and if Ruchti could ever put Landers and me in the same place at the same time, it could be a problem -- and we had met for a drink once, and he had made a previous withdrawal on a Saturday afternoon, and who knows who on the street might have seen us together.

So there were risks either way.

I went for the lie.

"No, I don't think I know him. Why?"

"He's dead. Murdered about three blocks from here. Shot

through the head. You must have heard the sirens and the commotion."

"It is pretty quiet in here," I said, pointing to the leather padding on the walls behind him, and on the door. "That's official, standard-issue private bank wall paneling, gracious soundproofing. It really works pretty well -- but I did hear a little something. I thought it was maybe an ambulance siren."

"You mean maybe 10 ambulance sirens. I think the whole police force is on Rennweg. This would be a great time to rob a bank."

I shrugged. Maybe I was going to get out of this after all. "So you're just asking everybody in the neighborhood?"

"Street cops will get to that in the next few hours," Ruchti said. "I came to you because the deceased had your business card in his wallet. When I saw that and saw how close you were, I took you for myself. Besides, I'd had enough of the crime scene. Puddles of blood turn my stomach."

He removed the card from his breast pocket and flipped it on to my desk blotter. It was, indeed, my business card.

"You sure you don't know him?"

"Pretty sure."

"So how did he get your card?"

"Beats me."

As soon as I said it, I was pretty sure I was going to need more than "beats me" to end this conversation. Flippant doesn't work with these guys. So I started to tell Ruchti how I spent my time. When I wasn't in the office, I was going through the motions of drumming up business -- and being seen drumming was significantly more important than actually signing new accounts. So besides lunching with prospective clients, mostly wealthy friends of friends who lived to have their asses kissed and their lunches paid for, I attended banking conferences and trade shows and sat through boring speeches at arts festivals and municipal project unveilings and whatnot. The truth was, I gave out 50 business cards a month, easily. For all I knew, the next random dead guy they found would have my card, too.

If Ruchti was swayed at all by my explanation, he wasn't letting on. He had that cop face perfected, that vaguely-smelling-shit-on-your-shoe look. I didn't know if I had made any progress, but I was out of things to say and didn't want to start babbling. So I just shut up.

He stared back at me, three seconds, four seconds, five seconds. Silence like that can be better than thumbscrews sometimes, and it took everything I had to match him, wordless second for wordless second. Finally, Ruchti gave up.

"Okay, we'll be in touch," he said, standing and shaking my hand and heading for the leather-padded door. I scrambled to follow him, but he stopped me. "I can show myself out."

I sat at my desk and grabbed a stack of letters to sign and a pen, playing over that one phrase in my head: "we'll be in touch." About what? I said I didn't know the guy. There should be no need for any other questions, no reason to be in touch. Maybe he didn't mean anything by it. Maybe it was nothing.

I began signing the letters and, after each signature, took a quick peek. One letter. Two letters. Three letters. Four. And Ruchti and Anders were still talking as they stood near the bank's front door.

4

One of the privileges of friendship, when the friends you are talking about are the owners of a cafe, is your own personal stammtisch. Mine was a tiny booth in the back corner of Cafe Fessler, where I could see the whole place. The table was designed for two people, max, but the space was big enough that I could spread out a couple of file folders stuffed with paperwork, and there was a decent light overhead.

I had never been an office guy, and much preferred a more comfortable environment when I was wading through the black-and-white avalanche that came with my job, as it did with a lot of jobs. Order forms and delivery schedules back when I was a magnesite salesman in Vienna had morphed into legal compliance forms and weekly deposit reports in my bank job, but it was all just shitwork, there to remind you that your job was, indeed, a job. And in my experience, it tended to go down easier with a beer or two.

Cafe Fessler usually did an early dinner business, as it was a family kind of place and an old guy kind of place. I was 40 and single, and there was precisely zero chance of me finding a date in the cafe most nights, this one included. It was 8 p.m., and we were already down to what I liked to call the "fossil collection." They were all over 70, all men. Their conversations were dominated either by jokes that traveled another mile along the rutted road from risqué to raunchy with the consumption of each successive round of drinks, or by spirited-beyond-all-sense arguments about the FC Zurich vs. Grasshoppers football rivalry.

I was plowing through the latest compliance schedule and half-listening to an anguished debate about the substitution patterns employed by "that fucking Bohm," the FC Zurich manager, when Henry sat down.

"Shouldn't you be massaging your wife's feet or something?" I said.

"She's out at dinner with a couple of girls from work."

"What do you think librarians talk about at dinner?"

"I think they rage on about the Dewey decimal system."

"Or they talk about the male librarians," I said, and Henry shrugged. Henry was one of my dear friends from Vienna, and also one-half of the Fessler empire. He ran the cafe during the day while his wife, Liesl, was working as a librarian at the Central Library, the biggest in the country. Henry's father, Gregory, was the other Fessler, still automatically Mr. Fessler to me. He took over in the afternoon and closed up at night. They both lived above the shop in enormous apartments -- it really was a big building -- with Gregory on the second floor and Henry and Liesl on the fourth.

Henry stood up almost as soon as he sat down. "I'm just getting my drink," he said. I hadn't seen Henry legitimately drunk in a while, probably years. He was on a one-Manhattan-per-day plan, a regimen from which he rarely deviated.

"Besides," he said, with a quick flick of his head toward the circle of fossils that included his father. "You know how he gets."

How Gregory got was angry if he perceived that Henry was

hanging around because he thought the old man was letting things slide. Henry ordered the provisions and the alcohol, supervised the deliveries, scheduled the staff, kept the books, and made sure to go upstairs when Liesl got home from work. Gregory was the central presence in the cafe from lunch till closing -- pinching babies, telling tales, very much the charming rogue. And if he tore up a few checks now and then, well, Henry would just have to understand.

Alone again, I got back to my pile. At the bottom was the note to write the letter to London, which I was saving for last. I felt into my breast pocket, and the postal card with the return address was there. I had stopped at home long enough to scoop it up before coming to Fessler's. This was going to be only the second contact I'd had with Czech intelligence in the 16 months I had been in Zurich. The first had been to alert me to the mechanics of setting up the spy account. Now, this, the matter of the dead client.

A knot of the old men was grabbing their coats. Henry was still by the bar, and he was talking to his father and shaking his head, and Gregory was smiling and shrugging and heading toward the kitchen. Henry walked over.

"None of those guys paid a franc," Henry said. "The old man's going to ruin us. Sometimes I think we just should have stayed in Bratislava."

"Yeah, maybe you could have bought Cafe Milos."

"And smelled like goulash forever."

"And I could have married the accordion player."

"And smelled like goulash forever," Henry said.

We had escaped to Bratislava in March of 1938 when Herr Hitler decided to add an addition onto his country and nailed Austria to the back of the house. We had to leave for different reasons. Henry had gotten in trouble with a Vienna police captain who was about to be given a free hand by the Gestapo, so he had to go, and Liesl was going with him. Our other great friend, Leon, had to go because he had two blots in his official Nazi copybook -- he was not only Jewish but a Jewish journalist besides. Then there was me. I had to go because I had been recruited by Czech intelligence to act as a courier during my sales trips to Germany, and had tangled with the Gestapo along the way. So all of us slipped into Bratislava on the night of the Anschluss and tried to figure out what was next.

The answers came pretty quickly. The Czech intelligence people owed me, and they knew it. This was handy as we needed some favors in return. Leon had no passport because, in the hurry to escape, he forgot to bring his. Henry wanted to be able to get full-time resident status in Switzerland, where his father had settled in 1936 -- Gregory had seen Hitler's moves coming even back then and wanted to beat the rush to the exits, a rush that never happened. Liesl wanted to go to Switzerland with Henry, whom she was to marry, and also wanted an introduction at the library.

So we made a deal. Leon received a Czech passport and a plane ticket to Paris, where he knew a guy who knew a guy who could get him a job on one of the newspapers. Henry and Liesl received their Swiss paperwork, two plane tickets to Zurich, and a letter of introduction at the library. I received a Swiss passport to go along with the Czech passport of my birth, along with a high-paying job as president of Bohemia Suisse. In exchange for all of this, I had to agree to keep working for Czech intelligence by becoming the banker for their network based in Zurich.

It was impossible to make the deal without everybody knowing the details, or at least most of them. With the three of them sworn to secrecy, we embarked on our new lives. They really were pretty good lives, too. As Henry walked away, I thought about how happy he was. He could be a moody guy, but

Liesl had pushed most of that out of him. The truth was, he was even kind of happy when he was bitching about his father.

It really was a good time, if you could find a way to ignore the Hitler drumbeat that was never far below the surface.

I got through my stack and was left with the letter to write to London. I had been made to memorize exactly one thing by my Czech handler, and it was the title of the book I was to request if I needed an in-person meeting. So I wrote to the Smedley Bookshop on Charring Cross Road in London:

Sirs,

I am in search of a copy of "Northanger Abbey" to complete my Jane Austen collection. Please inform me at your earliest convenience if you can obtain a copy, as well as the cost. My request is urgent, as I hope to present the collection as a gift on a special family occasion upcoming soon.

Thank you for your consideration.

The addition of the sentence containing the word "urgent" was meant to tell London just that. As I was sealing it and copying the address from the postal card, Gregory began making his way toward my booth.

5

"Mr.--"

"Goddammit, Alex."

"Gregory," I said, recovering.

"You're 40 years old. I can't believe I have to remind you."

The truth was, I couldn't help it and would never change. Henry, Leon and I met in the army and stayed friends after the war in Vienna. We were a pretty mismatched threesome. Leon was a crusading journalist and a crusading womanizer. I was a traveling salesman for the family magnesite mine, a job I shared with my uncle. And Henry, well, he was the son of Gregory, a small-time mobster who made his money through illegal gambling, loan-sharking, a little bit of protection work, and the family restaurant, which was actually a bar, a restaurant, a night-club, and a series of rooms in the back whose purpose was, in Gregory's words, "for shared company and a few moments of relaxation amid the tumult of the modern world." The shared company charged by the half-hour.

"The schnitzel was good tonight," I said. It was a small lie, a just-making-conversation kind of lie, but Gregory would not tolerate it.

"No, it wasn't. It's nothing like we made at home."

"It's pretty close."

"It's nowhere near as good, and you know it. I don't think the veal's as good, and the cooks here, they just can't get it crisp. Is it really too much to ask? I mean, how hard could it be?"

Gregory had a couple in him, and it was going to be that kind of conversation. His wife had died about five years earlier, and it took a lot out of him. It's why he worked the late shift and gave Henry the mornings. As he said, "The nights are too long if I'm not doing something."

He left Vienna in 1936, only months after Hitler marched back into the Rhineland and France sat on its hands and watched. He was the first one who I remembered insisting what everybody in Austria was insisting a year later, that we were next on the corporal's to-do list. He had been quietly shipping money to Switzerland for years anyway, and in a matter of weeks, he sold the gambling, loan-sharking, and protection businesses to his under-boss, gave Henry the restaurant to do with what he wanted and bought a train ticket to Zurich. Within two years, he had picked up the former Cafe Mortimer when Morty Spiegel died. Now it was Cafe Fessler, on Oberdorfstrasse in the old town, where the narrow, cobbled streets were crowded with small specialty shops and apartment houses, many in converted hotels from the 1700s.

Gregory pointed at his last two customers, besides me. "You know them?"

"No. Tell me."

"The guy on the left owns the coin collecting shop on Krug-gasse. The other guy owns the stamp collecting shop across the way. You know how narrow that street is -- if you're sitting on the toilet in one of the apartments upstairs, the guy across the way can read your book along with you. So these two guys stare at each other all day with pretty much nothing to do but dust their inventory. I bet they don't have five customers a week. But look at them, happy, laughing. But how can they be happy? It's so fucking dead here."

And then, Gregory delivered the line the same way he always did when this was his mood:

"It's true that I always figured I would die here. But I didn't think I would be dead when I was still living."

This was not a conversation that Gregory ever had with Henry, and it was understood that I was not to share it. Fathers and sons have tricky relationships when things are simple and, well, let's just say that having a father who was a mobster was not simple for Henry. Gregory was not Al Capone or anything like that. He had no involvement in drugs, and he did not want his guys doing anything permanently disabling to someone who got behind on his payments. He did not even want his guys allowing their customers to get too far underwater. His theory was, "What good is this guy to me if he loses all of his money and his family? I want regular, happy, return customers -- no broken legs, no busted marriages."

But Gregory did carry a gun, and he had used it in his younger days. He taught Henry to shoot and wanted him to carry, too. But Henry could barely rough up a guy who was behind on his payments -- he punched a guy in the face once, and it made him physically sick -- and at a certain point, he told his father that the only part of the business he would consider working in was the restaurant. Gregory told me once that he respected Henry for standing up to him, but that's something else the father never told the son. So when he was younger and drinking more, Henry would often come to this conclusion: "He just thinks I'm a pussy."

But that was in Vienna. Now Henry had Liesl, and now his father wasn't a mobster anymore. Zurich was simple for Henry. Zurich was happy for Henry. But for Gregory, oddly, the only time he seemed happy was when he was talking about the thing he hated most -- Hitler.

"You hear the radio today? The Poles are barely hanging on. Poor bastards."

"I know," I said. "Brave and doomed is a tough two-step."

"You know, I knew it from the minute they went in the Rhineland."

"I remember."

"It was so fucking obvious -- first Austria, then Czechoslovakia, then Poland. Anybody who could read a map could see it. At least the Poles are fighting back."

"Brave and doomed," I said.

"Better than laying back and throwing their skirts up," Gregory said. "Austria never had a chance. But if your people had fought, Hitler might have backed down."

This was true. It was at least part of the information I brought back from my trips to Germany as a courier, that the German army was more of a figment of Goebbels' newsreels than anything. But that was about a year and a half earlier, a long time in Krupp years.

"It's too late now," Gregory said. "You know they're much stronger now. It's only a matter of time."

"What is?"

"He's coming this way. He'll finish off the Poles, take a little rest to digest, belch once, and head in our direction."

"To Switzerland?"

"No," Gregory said. "France."

"What about France?" It was Liesl's voice. She was hovering over the table after her night out. At her side was a friend. It was Manon Friere, whose top button was still unbuttoned.

I stood. "Miss Friere, twice in one day. The gods must be telling us something."

"Only that Zurich is a small town," she said.

"Still, what are the odds?"

"I'm sure a statistician would come up with a calculation that would leave you quite disappointed."

If this was flirting, it was a bit on the chilly side of normal. Seeing as how there wasn't really room for four in the booth -- there wasn't really room for three, to be truthful -- Gregory got up to get the women a drink and then joined the stamp guy and the coin guy. As it turned out, Manon had been at a banking reception at lunch and a booksellers' reception at 5, where Liesl and the librarians had gone for a couple of free cocktails before their dinner. They were introduced to Manon there and brought her along.

The conversation over the drink was entirely forgettable. I said a couple of witty things, for I was nothing if not a witty motherfucker, but Manon barely cracked a smile. Oh, well. But as Manon stood and began sliding into her coat, Liesl kicked me under the table, then stared at me and offered a quick flick of her eyes in Manon's direction. I had not sensed an ounce of interest on her part, but Liesl was watching the whole thing with a woman's eyes. What the hell.

So I said, "Dinner sometime? I'll show you that it's a bigger city than you think."

Manon leaned over, grabbed my pen from the table and scrawled her phone number on one of my folders. That was it. Liesl grabbed her arm and walked her to the door, the two of them giggling the whole way.

6

The tram ride to Uetliberg started in the Bahnhof and lasted about 20 minutes, give or take. I wore an overcoat, knowing how cold it could be at the top. In the wintertime, even when there was no snow in Zurich, there would invariably be a few inches on the ground surrounding the tracks as you pulled into the station. In mid-October, with the temperature forecast for the high 40's downtown, it would be 30-something on the mountain.

I didn't know who I was meeting. The return postcard from the Smedley Bookshop in London had been succinct:

Sir,

We have located a copy of "Northanger Abbey," as per your request. We will put it in the mail on the 2nd. Please remit 1 pound, 15 schillings upon receipt. As a favor to us, if you could include a picture postcard of Uetliberg along with your remittance, it would be most appreciated. I told my grandson about your beautiful city mountain, and he is desperate to add the picture to his collection.

Cheers,

Giles Hadley

So, 1:15 p.m. on October 2nd at Uetliberg. Unless he meant 1:15 a.m., but that seemed unlikely -- there were no trains out there in the middle of the night, and no lights besides. Daytime would be much less conspicuous than nighttime. It had to be 1:15 p.m. And if it weren't, well, whoever it was would have been stood up, figured out my confusion, and come back again in the afternoon.

There were a handful of people on the tram -- an old couple, a single old man, a mother attempting to corral a pair of 4-year-old boys, and another woman with a pram. It would have been different on a summer weekend when the trams were packed, and the whole menagerie would alight, mostly families, most with small children, many with prams that required a complex geometric negotiation with the doorway of the tram.

The path off to the left was paved, and it was about a 15-minute walk straight up the hill if you were alone and persistent, a bit longer if you were involved in a leisurely conversation with a companion, a bit longer than that if you were wrangling two small children who were alternately racing ahead or complaining that they needed to be carried.

In winter, the macadam would be covered by layers of ice and then a thin carpet of packed, dirty snow, all of it topped by a healthy dressing of rough gravel. It was the gravel that prevented most pratfalls. But in the summer and early autumn, before wet leaves turned the path into a slalom, the walk was nice and comfortable and smooth. The forests along the sides had been thinned recently by workers, the felled trees hewn to precise lengths and stacked immaculately along the route. This was Switzerland, after all.

At the top, especially in the summer, the reward was an unparalleled view of Zurich and its environs -- the river, the lake, the rooftops looking down as if seated in an amphitheater.

The view and the gentleman selling cold drinks and wurst from a grill were the reasons to go on an October afternoon. Unfortunately, on this day, the view was largely obscured by low cloud, and the gentleman had not fired up the grill and had only hot chocolate on offer, and it wasn't even that hot.

I sipped it, though, and waited. I had taken a place on the far side of the viewing area, a couple of hundred feet away from the public binocular things that the kids were all climbing on and attempting to see the roofs of their houses. After about 10 minutes, I began calculating how long I had to wait before abandoning the meeting. A minute or so after that, Groucho arrived. I didn't know his real name, but he had been my Czech intelligence contact when I was recruited in Vienna in early 1937.

"Wait a minute," I said, pointing. The mustache was gone. "What happened? What will I be calling you now."

"You can call me 'Sir,' asshole."

He laughed. We had an odd relationship -- although, to be fair, I didn't know what a healthy relationship between a spy and his handler was supposed to look like. Groucho had recruited me by arguing that, given the stakes, only a coward would refuse. It worked, but it left us in an odd spot. He needed me, and I knew it, and he knew it, yet he spent most of his time giving me shit. The shared experience, though, had worn off some of the roughest edges.

"I thought you were getting out of the business," I said. In his real life, Groucho had been some kind of banker or financial guy in Vienna.

"They kept me in Vienna for a while, but it's not like there was a lot of covert information to be gleaned. Hell, they fucking bragged about how badly they were treating the Jews -- they put it in the newsreels, for Christ's sake. I was wasting my time. I was back in Czechoslovakia in a couple of months, right after you left. I became a full-time intelligence officer, and we all left for London after they fucked us at Munich."

"How's London?"

"Let me put it this way: everything they say about the food and the dentistry is true."

"But at least the Gestapo isn't in your pockets," I said.

"Well, there is that."

Groucho already knew about Michael Landers getting shot, which I expected. In the couple of weeks since it had happened, things had settled down. There was a big splash in the newspapers on the day after the murder, and then the story was on the bottom of the front pages the second day, and then on an inside page the third day, and then gone by the fourth. Nothing at the bank changed. Marta asked me if I was going to the funeral, and I made up something about it being a private service. She never asked again. And, most importantly, Ruchti had never returned with any additional questions.

Still, I was worried. I told my story to Groucho and asked what he thought.

"I can see you're concerned, and I am too," he said. "It's a complication we were hoping to avoid. We can deal with it, but it is a complication. But there's something else I want to talk to you about."

This "something else" had been my fear since I had first agreed to the whole me-running-the-bank scheme, that they were going to want more. And I wasn't going to do it. I wasn't going to spy for them again. Babysitting the bank was one thing. Actively spying was something else. They had screwed me the last time, and I wasn't going to get screwed again. They used me as bait in a scheme to frame a Gestapo officer who had uncovered their prized informant, and only through sheer luck did I survive. They swore it wasn't luck, that they always had my fate under their control, but I was convinced they were lying. The cynical bastards had used me, and I wasn't going to be used again.

I had all of that bottled up in me, and when Groucho said, "We want you to get back in the game," I exploded with a "FUCK NO!" that was loud enough to startle a couple of the kids running around nearby.

"Calm the fuck down," Groucho said.

"I'm not fucking doing it."

"Just hear me out."

"Fuck you. This wasn't part of the deal."

"First of all, I didn't make the deal," he said. "Second of all, if you've read a newspaper lately, things have changed a little bit in the last month or so. Things are getting serious."

"Getting serious?" I said. "Getting? First, he swallowed the country where you and I lived, then he swallowed the country where you and I were born, and only now you think it's getting serious?"

"Look. When Hitler made the deal with the Russians, everything changed. You can admit that to yourself or not, but it's the truth. And once they get done squeezing the life out of Poland, Germany from the west, Russia from the east, well, you know."

"No, I don't know," I said, lying.

"Yes, you do. While Stalin guards his ass, Hitler is coming this way. And I love my country as much as you do, but this has become way bigger than Austria or Czechoslovakia. If we're going to have any chance to stop him, it's when he goes into France. And on-the-ground intelligence could make the difference."

"Fuck you. I'm not doing it. I might just quit the bank and get the hell out of here. You can't stop me."

I stopped talking. He stopped talking. We both looked out into the distance, the view obscured by the low cloud.

"Can't see shit," Groucho said. "Kind of a metaphor."

We talked some more, quieter now. I agreed not to quit the bank. Groucho said he would be in town for a bit and would be in contact again if necessary. I left first. What was a 15-minute walk on the way up the hill took less than half of that on the way down.

7

"When's the date?" Liesl said.

"Date? With who?" Henry said.

"Is it the French one from the other night?" Gregory said.

And so went the ritual dissection of my love life. We were in the cafe, near closing time. Henry and Liesl had come down from the apartment for their nightly drink. Gregory was tidying up or appearing as if he were tidying up, mostly for Henry's benefit. Two of the fossils shared a table up front by the door. It was just a Wednesday night in October.

Manon and I had both been busy -- she had traveled to Lausanne to a convention of fabric manufacturers or some such thing -- but we were going to have dinner Friday night. It would be my first actual date in nearly six months. I really had no expectations, even as Liesl was talking her up to Henry and Gregory and making it seem as if I had a shot, and that it would be my fault if it didn't work out. The two times I had met Manon, it just had not felt right. But, well, whatever -- it clearly beat the alternative.

As I sat there, trying to change the subject, the door opened. I didn't hear it as much as feel it, because it was a chilly and windy night, and wind could sometimes chase up Oberdorfstrasse from the Grossmunster and fill the narrow, cobbled street, almost creating heightened pressure that would burst through a release point, such as an open door. I felt the cold and looked up and saw a man wearing a dark overcoat and hat and carrying a portfolio. He looked around and then fixed on our little group and headed toward us.

His face brightened as he approached, and brightened was followed by grinning when he arrived. He opened the portfolio pulled out a pen and began pointing at us as he spoke.

"I think this is my lucky day. You are Gregory. You are Liesl. You are Henry and Alex, in some order. I think I have hit the jackpot."

That the man was presumptuous went without saying. That he was unlikeable besides also was plain -- hair slicked down, suit just so, perfectly knotted necktie, a well-kept weasel. It took a second for us to digest the fact that he knew who we were and that he had yet to introduce himself.

"And who would you be, exactly?" Gregory said, finally. "And what are you doing with our names in your goddamn leather notebook?"

With that, the grin was gone, replaced not by anger but by a kind of hurt puppy kind of look. He was getting more unlikeable by the second. He said his name was Ernst Meissner, and that he was some kind of junior assistant bullshit attache stationed at the German legation in Zurich.

He positioned the portfolio under his arm and held his hands up, as if in surrender. "I am nothing more than the humble census taker. As a service to our citizens, we attempt to keep track of all expatriates from the Reich and to offer them contact information and social opportunities with their brethren."

"None of us are German so you can go," Liesl said. Her rudeness was more than a little sexy.

"You hold a Czech passport, according to my records. So do Alex and Henry. Gregory holds an Austrian passport. That makes all of you citizens of the Reich."

"But we're not Germans." Gregory this time, angrier. "And what right do you have to come into my place of business and--"

Meissner held up his hand, stopping the rant.

"I am sorry you are upset. Let me assure you that there is nothing nefarious about this cataloging of our citizens. Each of our legations in Switzerland has an office in charge of just such record-keeping. That is all it is -- paperwork designed to benefit you and our other citizens living abroad. In Switzerland alone, we have located thousands just like you -- tens of thousands. We keep their contact information on file. If there is ever a need to speak to someone, because of some kind of emergency back home, God forbid, or maybe to offer a business contact or a social opportunity, we have the means to get in touch. That's all this is."

Of course, anyone who knew the Germans knew that nothing was quite that innocent. I had no doubt that they were organizing little Nazi hit squads, in case the Wehrmacht ever came calling on the Swiss border and needed a little help with their entrance. I also had no doubt that the names in Meissner's portfolio, and in other portfolios around the country, were encouraged to keep their eyes and ears open and report any interesting morsels of rumor or gossip to the legation. You know, just like back home. Because while you couldn't openly wear the swastika or go all pro-Nazi in this country, there was no way they could tell what was written on your heart.

The fact that the four of us had so clearly identified

ourselves as non-cooperators was also to Meissner's benefit. If the Germans ever did invade, grabbing all of the gold and the chocolate, they would already have a list of potential enemies. Which, I guess, was why Meissner uncapped his pen, ticked a couple of boxes on his paperwork, and clapped shut his portfolio. Then he stopped for a second, re-opened it, and removed a sheet of paper that he left on the table.

"My apologies for interrupting your evening," he said. "I assure you that no one else will be visiting your cafe. Participation in our expatriate program is strictly voluntary. I hope to see you again someday, but that is entirely your decision."

We all watched him walk out and felt the rush of wind again as he opened the door. The creepiness of the whole episode was palpable. We had gotten out of Austria and Czechoslovakia ahead of the Nazis, so Henry, Liesl, and Gregory only had the knowledge provided by newsreels, and newspapers, and by their imaginations. But I had been to Germany many times before the Anschluss. I had seen the Gestapo raid someone's home and bundle a man off to who knows where. I had spent a few hours naked in a Gestapo jail cell, consumed by my worst fear -- electrodes attached on one end to a car battery and on the other end to my balls. I never experienced it, but I dreamed it enough times that it seemed more than real. Just thinking about it now had me involuntary raising my ballsack from the bench in the booth in a quick motion, only an inch. I don't think the rest of them saw me.

Here in Switzerland, we were allegedly protected, safe from Nazi invasion, swaddled in a golden security blanket. Herr Meissner, though, had just offered an unsettling vision of what might be.

"One more?" Henry said, and everyone nodded in the affirmative. He was breaking his one-Manhattan rule.

I looked down at the piece of paper that Meissner had left

behind. It was a flyer advertising a night of German music and dancing at a social hall on Forrlibuckstrasse, over by the Hardturm stadium.

Liesl caught me reading it. She said, "It's on Friday. You should take Manon and make a night of it."

8

The sun shone through the curtains and woke me. I reached for the watch on my night table. It was 7:15. The other side of the bed was empty, but her scent was still on the pillow.

I scanned the room for bits of her clothing, listened for running water in the bathroom, then for a teacup's clinking in the kitchen or footsteps in the living room. Nothing. But there was the smell on my pillow, and my fingers. I closed my eyes and remembered.

What was the last thing she said before I fell asleep? Yes, this: "Not French, but not bad."

The night had not begun well. We agreed to meet at the restaurant, Orsini, which was at one of the entrances to the plaza in front of the Fraumunster. It was my favorite, from the look outside -- a black iron gate guarded the entrance, along with a corner turret on the second floor painted a kind of salmon color, one you didn't see much on the outside of a building -- to the classic menu. It was old Zurich, old Switzerland, and I enjoyed going inside and shutting out the Hitler headlines on the newsstands. If only I had known how much Manon detested the Swiss.

Or, as she said after the waiter had taken our orders, "You've been here longer than I have, so you might know the answer to this question: Are they born with the stick up their ass, or is it inserted at the christening."

I laughed and said, "Oh, they're not that bad," defending them for no apparent reason other than to make conversation. "The Swiss bankers are a little, uh, Swiss, but ordinary Swiss people seem like people everywhere to me."

"And you know a lot of ordinary Swiss people?"

I thought for a second. The truth was, I had very few friends other than the people who came with me from Vienna. Part of it was because I flitted around pretty consistently because of my work. Part of it was because I was at an age where making new friends was simply harder than when you are in your 20's. But part of it also was because I was still my late Uncle Otto's nephew. I took on so many of his characteristics, for better or worse -- and his worst attribute was his reluctance to make lasting bonds outside of his small, established circle. I was still like that.

And so, I said to Manon, "Come to think of it, I don't have a lot of ordinary Swiss friends. So let's agree that they're all assholes and talk about the weather or something, what do you say?"

"The weather? Cold and gray, followed by gray and cold. The perfect Swiss metaphor."

"But what about the two glorious weeks of sunshine in the middle of July?"

"The tease," she said. "Another perfect Swiss metaphor."

"Are you talking about Freddy?"

"Don't insult me. He never had a chance."

Finally, a smile. This was much harder work than I had

hoped. Eventually, though, I was able to get her to talk about her background. She was from Lyon, the daughter of a silk manufacturer who could never understand why she would join France's foreign service as a trade rep, even if she were promoting industries like silk-making.

"My papa always said, 'But why would you want to leave?' When I made the decision, it was obvious -- I had lived in the same place my whole life, never out of earshot of the clattering of the looms. Why did I want to leave? Wasn't it obvious? But now I can't wait to go back."

"Have you told him?"

"Too late," she said. Her father had died two years earlier.

I offered up my story, the one that was appropriate for public consumption. Mother died in the Spanish flu epidemic after the war. Father ran the mine from near Brno with my asshole younger brother. Uncle Otto and I lived in Vienna and handled the Austrian and German clients. Then Otto died. Then Hitler came, and I fled with my friends. Then, Zurich. I left out the part about being a spy, and the identity of the most important customer at Bohemia Suisse. That was still need-to-know, even if it was my whole life.

Which hit me as I was talking: what kind of a future might I have with Manon, or with anyone, if I couldn't talk about the most important part of my life? Still, I kept on. Talking is what I did for a living, what I always have done. She asked me what I missed about my old life, and I went on an extended riff about the trains that I loved, notably the Orient Express, which came through Vienna a couple of times a week and often took me as far as Cologne. Again, I left out the part about Otto getting murdered in Cologne by the Gestapo, his body thrown off of a bridge into the Rhine, and my subsequent attempt to kill the Gestapo captain who was responsible. More secrets. So many secrets.

Manon asked if I had ever taken the train from here to Jungfraujoch. "I think it's the highest Alp, and it's truly breathtaking," she said, and then caught herself. "It almost makes you forget how cold and calculating the people are."

Jab.

"Their only emotion is greed."

Double jab.

"I'm not sure greed is an emotion," I said.

"But it's a way of life for them. A governing principle. A physical law, like gravity."

We walked around after dinner, vaguely in the direction of my flat, but only vaguely. It was a beautiful night and a clear night, and the moon reflected brightly off of the lake. The boats were tied up along the piers, not yet tarped and shut down for the winter. There were a lot of people out and about, it being Friday night. At a certain point, she took my hand.

We talked about her job for a while. She was a trade rep, which meant she talked up French industries and products in all kinds of settings -- trade shows, business conferences, private one-on-ones with businesses and government officials.

"Last week, I got to talk about silk, which I could do all day," she said. "I got into an argument at one point with a Swiss silk manufacturer. I was really trying to be polite--"

"Really?" I said.

"Well," she said. "The man went on about the quality of silk manufactured in Zurich, which is second to Lyon in the size of the business. I pointed out that Lyon was first. He said, 'Quantity is not the same as quality.' So I said, 'You are correct, sir. But even a blind man would tell you that Lyon silk is superior to any Swiss product.' It degenerated from there. We actually drew a crowd of other exhibitors from the show. He turned on his heel and stormed off at a certain point -- I think it was right after I used the term 'tight-assed fraud,' but I'm not sure. The crowd applauded. I bowed."

All I knew about silk was that I enjoyed how it felt in a darkened bedroom -- as it did, maybe an hour later. And proving that I am not a complete idiot, after gently removing her silk underpants, I rubbed them on her cheek, and then on mine and whispered to Manon, "From Lyon. Definitely, from Lyon."

9

Cafe Tessinerplatz, a pretty big place across from the Enge train station, ran a promotion they called "First Thursday." Once a month, the drinks were two-for-one and a free buffet was set up, a table laden with bread and cheese and little wursts and other assorted shit. They got a good crowd, and my guess is that they broke even on the night but maybe made a profit on return visits. Me, I'd never been back except on another first Thursday.

The first time I came, about eight months prior, had been as a specific attempt to make a couple of actual Zurich friends -- not another emigre from Vienna or Prague, not another banker or a potential client whose ass needed kissing, but an actual, no-strings-attached human being. As it turned out, I met a guy the first night who was a major in the Swiss army, Marc Wegens. We had become legitimate friends. I had met his wife and kids. He had met the Fesslers, which was as close as I had to family. But mostly, because of his travel and mine -- he was a kind of roving inspector who checked on whatever a roving inspector in a fake army checked on -- we were limited to first Thursdays at Cafe

Tessinerplatz. We both actually scheduled our business appointments around it.

So when I walked in at 6:30 on Thursday evening, Marc was already there. He was drunk enough already that I could tell he had been there for a while. Drunk or sober, unlike Anders, he didn't mind a little kidding about the tremendous Swiss military machine. Or as he said himself, "When they promoted me to major, they told me it would be twice as much work, and they were right. Now I have to work on Monday and Tuesday."

With the kidding out of the way, and my first drink beginning to take hold, we settled into a minute of comfortable silence. As it turned out, the place wasn't that busy. The waiter guarding the buffet table appeared to be even more bored than the waiter's guild required of its members. The tables of twos and threes were hushed enough that the phonograph music playing in the background seemed too loud. My mind drifted for a second to Manon, and then Marc snapped me out of it.

"Your face," he said. "I can see it. You met somebody. You're fucking somebody."

"You must be in military intelligence."

"Just human fucking intelligence. So give."

So I told him. He congratulated me in the typical male fashion, with a pat on the back and an "about fucking time" and an order of two shots of schnapps.

"But seriously," he said. "It is about fucking time. Miriam has been hinting around that she wanted to introduce you to one of her friends, Myra, who isn't tough to look at but is a horror show of a person. Miriam made her brother go out with Myra for a while and he calls her the shark because you spend a little time with her and you just know she's going to end up biting off either your head or your dick, you just don't know which. I've been putting her off but, to be honest, I was starting to lose the battle -- and, you know I love you, but my marriage comes first. Now I can call her off with a clear conscience."

"I'm touched. But this might not last that long. We both travel a lot, and she could get recalled to France or posted somewhere else."

This was the truth. I had no idea what I was into with Manon. Part of me wondered what it would be like to live a life with a person who had such a strong personality. I had spent a good portion of my life avoiding all manner of controversy, especially in my personal life. And while she was funny and physically attractive, a life with Manon would be a life of controversy. She wouldn't be able to avoid it. She seemed to have no filter.

I was telling some of this to Marc, and parrying his attempts to find out some details of the sex, when I sensed a hulking presence over my shoulder. Marc said, "Herman, Herman, sit down. Alex, this is Herman Stressel."

"I don't mean to interrupt," Herman said. The accent was German, maybe Alsatian.

"Please do," I said. "You can assist me in changing the subject."

"Alex, I'm an old married man. Just a few details to warm my night."

Herman said, "Maybe I should leave."

"You're staying," I said. "Marc's nights are warm enough. Tell me about you. What do you do for a living? Are you German?"

Stressel was indeed an emigre, a magazine publisher. I was worried I was going to have to watch my mouth, just as a matter of politeness -- because you never knew where people stood until you knew. This dance had been all the rage in Vienna before the Anschluss when you didn't know if somebody hated the Nazis or was ready to welcome them with a smooch. It was the same thing in this part of Switzerland, where -- emigres aside -- there were so many people with a German heritage or a love for German culture, and you just didn't know if that love extended to the maniac with the mustache. So you spoke carefully until one of you hinted where he stood, and then you took the hint. Delicate did not begin to describe the process.

But Stressel wasn't 30 seconds into his abbreviated biography when he made a reference to "that shithead Goebbels," so we were going to be fine. Marc and I had done the Nazi dance the first night we met, and while he represented all that was proper and neutral when he wore his uniform, he could motherfuck Hitler with the best of them after a couple of pops. So it was going to be a relaxed evening.

As it turned out, Herman left Germany in 1936. "I wasn't exactly one step ahead of the Gestapo, but I wasn't a mile ahead, either. I couldn't publish what I wanted, and I couldn't sneak enough of my true beliefs between the lines of what I could publish. They confiscated one of my editions because of a story where, if you looked only at the first letter of every paragraph, it spelled out "FUCK YOU ADOLF." Sophomoric, I know. And then there was a mysterious fire that would have destroyed my printing press if I hadn't been in the office late one night because I was fucking my secretary."

He could see my eyes widen. "True story," he said. "We were both stark naked throwing buckets of water on the fire. But, anyway, that's when I decided to get out. Now I publish what I want here."

"And what about the secretary?"

"Now she's my wife," he said. "True story."

Marc had apparently heard the tale before. I caught him checking his watch and asked if anything was wrong. He said that Hildy, his 3-year-old, was sick with the croup. He wanted to get home and see her before it got too late.

"Next month," he said, gathering his coat and his hat. "And then, I want details. No excuses accepted."

10

I offered Herman my bare-bones biography, leaving out the spying part and the business about how I came to be running Bohemia Suisse. If you don't know all the details, the story is a little bit thin. Seriously, how does a traveling salesman from a Czech magnesite mine suddenly find himself parachuted into Switzerland as the president of a private bank? Most people, though, just let it go, either because they weren't listening, or they didn't care, or if they did care, they didn't want to get involved. Because that was one thing about the Swiss -- they were buttoned-up tight, and that was true, but the melange of cultures and languages and the emphasis on banking and money seemed to leave everyone with a secret or two.

Herman, though, was less complicated, and he saw through my story. Or, as he said, "Do people actually believe that bullshit when you tell them?"

I tried to act offended, then confused by his question. He literally laughed in my face.

"I'm a lot of things," he said. "But I'm not a fucking idiot. You're connected, somehow, and you're going to tell me."

"And why would I do that?" I said.

"Because we're both half-drunk, on the way to three-quarters. And because I already told you my true story, and you owe me."

For some reason -- because I was, indeed, half-drunk, and because he was a friend of Marc's -- I trusted Herman. But I offered a caveat.

"Marc doesn't know, and you can't tell him," I said.

He agreed. And I told him the story -- again, not all of it, but enough. I told him I was a courier for the Czechs. I didn't tell him I tried to kill a Gestapo captain and ended up in a tribunal in front of Rudolf Hess, the deputy Fuhrer. I told him that I was forced to flee Austria after the Anschluss and that the Czechs sent my friends and me here as a favor. I didn't tell him that I was still working for Czech intelligence. That seemed not to matter.

"So you're still spying?" he asked.

"No," I said.

"So they set you up with a plush job as a bank president because they're swell people who were doing you a solid?" he asked.

"Yes," I said.

"I know that's bullshit and you know that's bullshit, but I like you, so I won't embarrass you by pressing for any more details. At least for a while."

I drank and thought for a second. The story really was pretty thin. Finally, I said, "Do you think Marc knows?"

"I'm sure if he doesn't know, he suspects. But he's more polite than I am."

We started talking about Hitler and Poland and what might be next. I had opinions. Herman had opinions. But as we kept drinking, and I kept working harder and harder to listen to what he was saying, it suddenly struck me that he was offering military details that were interlaced within the opinions. Finally, I stopped him and repeated back a statement he had just made about the thickness of the armor on some such model of a Panzer tank.

"Twenty millimeters on the sides, huh?" I said. "So now who's the fucking spy?"

"I'm not a spy. But I do continue to have, shall we say, sources of information within the German military establishment."

"That makes you a spy."

"Only if I covertly give the information to a foreign government, which I have not done. I am merely a humble reporter."

"Do you write this stuff?"

"A little. Enough so that serious people know I'm a serious journalist -- it helps sell the magazine, and my wife and I do need to eat. But I don't print enough to get us killed in our bed while we sleep."

"But have you been approached by anyone about getting more information?"

"Now who's being nosy?" he said.

I let it go, as we were both entering severe hangover territory and it wasn't even 9 p.m. For me, the decision was to leave now and have a chance for at least a somewhat productive day at the bank on Friday, or keep drinking and write off Friday as a sick day.

I decided to get up and leave -- because I did have things to do at the bank, and because I didn't trust myself anymore to keep the few secrets I had remaining from Herman. I stood up to reach for my coat from the rack next to the table, and he grabbed my arm.

"One more," he said.

"I can't."

"Then just listen. You might be interested. This is one I'm afraid to write -- partly because I don't have all of the facts nailed down, partly because I like living here."

He stopped and read what I assumed was the quizzical look on my face. I hoped that my quizzical face was appreciably different than my about-to-throw-up-in-the-gutter face. Apparently, it was.

"Just listen," he said. "I'm going to make a little speech here, so don't interrupt me."

I belched. Herman continued.

"We all know about the Swiss and their 'historical prerogative.' You know, their neutrality. They see it as some kind of divine fucking right or something, and, well, fine. They have their culture. They have their mountains to protect them. Fine. Even though there's a monster next door, fine.

"But what is neutral? What does that mean? They seem to think it means that you don't help either side and you keep doing business, at least a little bit of business, with both sides. Because they see that as their other divine fucking right -- keeping the cash register ringing, no matter what."

I was trying to follow what Herman was saying, but the fog had suddenly descended. He seemed to sense my predicament -- perhaps it was my mouth fixed wide open, or the permanent tilt of my head to the left -- and gave my arm a poke.

"I'm with you -- promise," I said.

Whatever. Herman talked faster.

"So the Swiss see it as their right to keep doing business with the Nazis," he said. "What does that mean? Well, Nestle sells chocolate to the Wehrmacht, so that the boys can have a little sweet before they lob a few more shells into Warsaw. Fine. It would be embarrassing if I wrote it, but only that. It would be a little more embarrassing if I wrote that Hitler was getting at least a few of his anti-aircraft guns from Oerlikon-Buhrle."

"A Swiss company? You sure about that?"

"Pretty sure. But that's not the real story. I can live with that. I think France and England could live with that. War brings out the greed in a lot of people, and it isn't that big of a deal -- I mean, if they didn't get it here, they'd just get the chocolate from someplace else."

I was more awake now. "So what are you talking about?" I said.

He leaned in and almost whispered.

"Gold," he said.

Again, my quizzical face, apparently.

"Look, you know Germany doesn't have sufficient resources," Herman said. "You know it first-hand -- you sold them that stuff to line their blast furnaces. They need iron, they need nickel, they need oil and food most of all -- you can't make war without them. Hitler needs money to pay for all of that. Most of the world won't deal with him. The neutral countries that will -- like, say, Portugal -- can't be seen as doing it. They can't take German gold, and they certainly can't take the gold the Nazis stole from Austria and Czechoslovakia.

"But you know what?" Herman said. "They can take Swiss gold."

Again, my face betrayed my ignorance.

"Don't you get it?" he said. "The Swiss are laundering the Nazis' gold for them -- maybe the national bank itself. And that is much bigger than some chocolate bars. And stopping it could be the difference between crushing this asshole or not."

11

I was pretty sure I wasn't stinking of alcohol when I arrived at the bank at 9:30 the next morning, but that was the only hint I wasn't offering of my consumption of the night before. I showered and did my best, but my face still appeared as if it had been spanked with a shovel, and there was no remedy but time.

I'm pretty sure Anders could tell. He grunted a greeting when he unlocked the door to let me in, which wasn't unusual, but it was the way he grunted. As for Marta, well, she was less opaque. Within seconds of me sitting down at my desk, she arrived carrying a tray that held a cup of coffee, a tall glass of water and a bottle of paracetamol. She didn't say anything, but she didn't need to. Her's was not a motherly concern. She pretty much dropped the tray on the desk in disgust, and I'm still not sure how nothing spilled. As it was, I nearly knocked over the water as I grabbed it with a shaky hand.

My diary was carried closed and under her armpit. She opened it and said, "You have Herr Stern at 10, and then lunch at Veltlinerkeller with Herr Cronstadt at 12:30." With that, Marta was gone. If disdain left a stain, we were going to need to have the carpets cleaned.

Cronstadt was from Kreditanstalt. He was offering me a sliver of the financing work on a municipal road improvement bond that was being floated by the city of Schlieren, just outside of Zurich. It wasn't a pimple on Kreditanstalt's ass, but it was projects such as this, doled out piecemeal to the smaller banks, that kept everyone in line. The deal would be done to Cronstadt's specifications, and I would be happy to be included in the grand Swiss money-lending ecosystem -- because a pimple on their ass was a big hill to me and the other small private banks. Kreditanstalt and Bankverein would use these deals, granting them as rewards for good behavior or withholding them to make a point. And if they did it just right, they would keep everyone financially sated, planets happily revolving around these dual suns, nothing to challenge the stable profitability of their world.

The deal was already done -- not that I really cared, other than that it was essential for me to seem that I cared if people were to believe I was a real banker. The lunch was just a reaffirmative formality. And by 12:30, and with the accustomed glass of wine at lunch -- OK, maybe two -- the day would likely be brighter. But first, there was Stern at 10. He was another one of Kerner's "nephews", here to make his first withdrawal, the first since Michael Landers was murdered. And I could feel the dread of this one in my head, my stomach, down to my bowels -- first what Herman Stressel told me the night before, now this.

I could say that the stuff that Herman told me upset me so much that I couldn't sleep, but that would be a lie. I somehow got back to my flat, passed out on the couch in my clothes, and slept okay. My memory was a little fuzzy, though. I remembered that he had told me about the Swiss somehow laundering Nazi gold, but I didn't remember how or exactly why. I think he mentioned the national bank, but I wasn't sure. My overall sense was that it was something very big, though, if he could prove it. It was also something I should tell Groucho, although that would be my first unmistakable step, and I just didn't want to get back into the game.

I kept trying to tell myself that, if I played it just right, I could maybe do this on my own terms. I could tell Groucho what I heard, but make up some shit about how it was all third-hand, and I didn't even know who I was talking to, and there was no way for me to contact the guy for more details or anything. What could he say to me at that point other than, "OK, thanks for the info, and if you hear anything else, let me know." So I would be in, and then I would be out, and there wouldn't be anything Groucho or his masters in London could do about it.

Over and over again in my head went variations on this strategy, and repetition seemed to make them more plausible. That made me feel a little better, that and the paracetamol and the coffee. I was approaching human status when Marta rang my phone to tell me that Herr Stern had arrived. I told her to walk him back, which she did, closing the door behind her, leaving behind another stare of disdain.

I think it was for the customer, though, another of the trust fund kids for whom she had no time. And he was a kid. I remembered wondering about his age the night I met them all and distributed the credentials that would allow them to make withdrawals if I wasn't around.

"No offense," I said after we settled into facing wing chairs in my office sitting area, away from the imposing desk. "But how old are you."

"Nineteen," Stern said, with all of the arrogance he could muster.

"No offense, I repeat, but that's bullshit."

"Almost nineteen," he said, the arrogance giving way just a bit, the eye contact disengaged for a second before reconnecting.

This was another reason I wanted no part of getting back in. I was more than twice this kid's age. Besides the physical stuff that he could do that I could no longer do, if it came to that -- run, climb, whatever -- there was something else. He was too young to know what he was risking. He probably had nothing, so he had nothing to lose.

The door of the office was closed, and the leather-padded walls were further protection against being overheard. Still, when we began to talk, I instinctively lowered my voice, just a bit, and Stern followed.

"What's your first name again?"

"Martin. Marty."

"Are you OK, Marty?"

"I'm a little shaken up -- we all are," he said.

"Do you have any theories about why Michael was shot?"

"That's the thing -- we don't. We have no idea. He wasn't into anything crazy, at least that we know of. And even if he was, it's almost like a gentleman's game here. Nobody gets arrested. Nobody gets deported. There's no fucking way anybody gets killed, but Michael did."

"What do you mean, a gentleman's game?"

"This doesn't go to my level or Michael's level," Marty said. "But the level above me, like Fritz Blum -- the spies all know each other. They all drink in the same place in Bern. I've been there -- German spies at one table, Czech spies at another table, French spies at another table, Swiss cops at another table. They don't talk to each other, not really, not much more than a hello, but they all nod to each other and acknowledge each other and buy each other drinks. It's not a big secret. It's not supposed to be dangerous. Like I said, just gentlemen shuffling paperwork in the paperwork capital of the world -- but then Michael ends up dead, and we have no idea why."

As it turned out, Marty had just finished up at the gymnasium. His parents wanted him to give university a try before taking over the family business, which was manufacturing nails in Winterthur. Or, as Marty said, "manufacturing fucking nails in fucking Winterthur," explaining that he convinced his parents to allow him to take a year off and live in Zurich. He found a job in a bookstore, where the ancient proprietor allowed him to live above the shop in a spare apartment. In exchange, he did all of the lifting and cleaning and watched the register while she napped after lunch. As it turned out, the bookstore was a place where the Czech spies passed messages. The proprietor was originally from Prague, and after he had figured out half of the story, she supplied him with the rest. He immediately wanted to join, and she was happy to have him.

"But why?" I said. "It's not your fight."

"Not yet," he said.

"The Swiss will never fight."

"The Swiss are fools if they think this doesn't affect them."

"All they care about is doing business."

"Well maybe that's the problem," Marty said.

The arrogance was back in his eyes. I walked over to the desk and made out his withdrawal slip. I went out to the small cash window, which was more of an artifice than anything -- we could have kept a cash box in Marta's bottom drawer just as easily -- and got the money. Marta eyed me up as I carried the pile back into my office.

I leaned over and told her, "Five thousand."

She shook her head. "Rich, wasteful fool."

"That's Herr Rich Wasteful Fool to you and me," I said.

She half-smiled.

After shuffling some paperwork for a while, the lunch with Cronstadt went as expected, and the two glasses of wine -- "Come, come, Herr Cronstadt, we must have a second glass to toast our agreement!" -- reestablished my equilibrium. I was actually feeling pretty good when I returned to the bank and was told by Marta that I had a last-minute appointment, a 4 p.m. at the office of Peter Ruchti, the police detective.

"Can you call him back and tell him I'm busy?"

"It wasn't a request," Marta said.

So. Coming so soon after Martin Stern's visit to my office, my nerves were naturally vibrating a bit. A shot of schnapps from the crystal decanter on my sideboard dulled them a bit. Then I sipped a second shot to maintain that level of anesthesia as I tried to figure out what Ruchti might know.

I kept coming back to the idea that he knew nothing. Michael Landers, he of the bullet in the eye, had been in my company precisely three times. Once was in Fritz Blum's home, when we were arranging the withdrawal credentials. His house was miles away from the center of the city, and no coincidence in the world would have had a witness place me there. For one thing, the meeting was at night.

A second time was an accidental meeting in a random bar, where we looked at each other and decided, what the hell, it's only one drink. There were only three people in the place, and we were two of them, so what were the odds anyone saw us? And it was over a mile away from the murder, so why would a cop go looking there to connect the two of us?

The third time was the most dangerous, the time I walked him into the bank on a Saturday afternoon to make a withdrawal. But thinking back on it, the day had been rainy, and we both were wearing hats and overcoats with our collars turned up -- and Lander was carrying an umbrella. Even if someone had occasioned to look out the window and see us, and even if they recognized me, there was no way they could have gotten a good look at Landers' face. No way.

The only other potential problem would have been if Ruchti had gotten a look at my diary. But he hadn't, and without being asked, Marta had covered over Landers' name with a relatively-believable accidental ink spill that blotted out several of the entries from that day. She even blotted out another afternoon, three months previous, to make the spill seem less unusual.

So what did Ruchti know?

His office was right along the Limmat River, in the police station at Bahnofquai 3. It was a building already famous for being the best-decorated police station in the world because of the murals that the artist Augusto Giacometti had painted in the lobby. I had never seen them, so at least I would experience a little culture before dealing with Ruchti's inquisitiveness.

As I waited for him to come down, I spent a few minutes with the murals. The locals call the place Blüemlihalle because of all of the flowers in the murals, but they weren't actually flowers but floral shapes, eight petals in a circle around a center.

There were flowers and crosses and a lot of orange and a lot of green, from floor to ceiling, forming roofs and arches and all kind of bordering around the main murals.

One featured a boy performing all manner of mathematical and geometry tasks, all angles and equations. In another, the theme was astronomy, with someone looking through a telescope at stars and a crescent moon. A third panel showed five stone masons building a wall, laying bricks, and troweling cement. One figure was of a man chipping away at a rock. And in the fourth mural, there were two carpenters. One of them was wielding a big saw. The first two murals were dated 1926. The last two, of the masons and the carpenters, were dated 1925.

Ruchti caught me in front of the carpenters. "Ah, Herr Kovacs. There you are, admiring a depiction of honest labor. Why would a banker be attracted to such a scene?"

This was the second crack about bankers that Ruchti had made. Yes, I was counting. I tried to keep things light as if that would matter.

"I'm surprised there is no mural of bankers," I said. "If this artwork is indeed a Swiss national treasure."

"Yes, how could a national treasure not contain a depiction of those in charge of the national treasure?"

"Perhaps because of the statutes prohibiting profanity?" I said.

Ruchti laughed. "Herr Kovacs, you are not like the typical Swiss banker. I find that intriguing. Perhaps you can tell me about your bank."

"Not much to tell. Small, wealthy clientele. Ties to Czechoslovakia. Some old Czech clients -- I think I can reveal that much without running afoul of the secrecy laws. But that is about it. You know as well as I do that I cannot say anything more. But there are several dozen banks in this city just like it."

He pointed past the reception desk and toward the front

doors. We began to walk along the river. If he had planned to arrest me, I figured he would have done it while we were inside. So, what? Ruchti said nothing as we strolled. I had matched his silence before, back in my office, and I could do it out there, too. Absent somebody who had seen Landers and me together, the only way I could get into trouble was if I dragged myself into it with an unthinking remark. So, silence, for one block, then a second.

Finally: "I always enjoyed this view," Ruchti said, pointing ahead, the Grossmunster on the other side of the Limmat, the lake ahead. "I like it better than some of the views from the Uetliberg. What do you think? Have you been up there?"

The Uetliberg. It was, on the one hand, a celebrated Zurich vantage point. It was, on the other hand, a hell of a coincidence for him to bring it up about two weeks after I had met Groucho there. Unless it wasn't a coincidence.

"Funny you should mention it -- I was up there recently," I said, riffing with a bit of the truth. "It was a cloudy day, though. I didn't get the full experience."

"But I'm sure you were enlightened nonetheless," Ruchti said. Then, again, silence.

Uetliberg. "Enlightened." If Ruchti wasn't delivering a message, then I wasn't nearly pissing myself, which I was. But it didn't make sense. He was a cop investigating a murder. It was hard to believe that he had access to the kind of manpower it would take to follow me around all day for weeks at a time. And for what reason? I really hadn't given him one. The business card in Landers' pocket wasn't enough to make that kind of commitment. I had explained it away, and it really was true -- I did give out about 50 of my cards every month. It wouldn't have been hard for Ruchti to find that out. All he had to do was ask another banker because we all did the same thing.

Maybe it was just my imagination.

We got to the lake, and then Ruchti turned us around and walked us back, retracing our steps along the riverbank. He said something about the weather. I said something back. We got to the police station, and he shook my hand. He said, "Okay, we'll be in touch." It was the same thing he had said in my office.

I watched Ruchti as he climbed the steps and re-entered the building. If his purpose had been to do anything other than mess with my head, I don't know what it was.

13

Manon and I settled into a relationship that I would describe as comfortably passionate. The passionate part was obvious enough -- we were spending about three nights together per week, right from the start. I was 40, and she was 30ish -- still not sure, exactly -- and there seemed little reason for pretense or the dating dance. She had a job, and I had a job, hers busier than mine but both requiring occasional overnight travel, and the thought of flowers and chocolates and such seemed silly. There was an attraction, and it was real, and I know that at least a couple of times a day, I found myself zoning out of a conversation or forgetting everything I had read on the previous page because I was thinking of Manon. I sensed that the feeling was mutual, and that was enough.

Some nights, she would just show up at Cafe Fessler when I was sitting at my stammtisch, going over a pile of bank paperwork after dinner. It was easy, natural. I would finish my work while she had a drink, chatting with whichever Fessler happened to be handy. Sometimes she brought a novel and sat with me and read while I plowed through the pile -- initial here, sign there, daydream for a second and feel the stirring below the table.

The Fesslers left us alone, for the most part, other than to say a quick hello. They would have this look on their face that unnerved me, just a bit. It was a shade on the beatific side, not a typical look between friends, and I even asked Henry about it at one point.

"Look, we're just happy for you," he said. I knew that was it, but I hated what it left unsaid. That is, that my life before had been such an abject pile of shit that Manon was somehow rescuing me from misery.

But here's the thing: I wasn't miserable. I enjoyed my own company, for the most part. I had been on a dry spell, and that was true enough. And I was finding it hard to meet new people, also true. But I was content. I was not miserable. I had dated more in Vienna and had a few somewhat serious girlfriends along the way, but Henry and his father had many times seen me very happily alone for significant stretches of time. I was not some kind of social basket case. Henry was always the one who seemed to need a girlfriend, and who fell the hardest when the relationship ended -- usually right after they found out what daddy did for a living. But I was never like that. My life was not an abject pile of shit.

This night, it was Liesl who made the quick visit. She looked at me and offered up the smile. Manon looked at Liesl and giggled as she walked away.

"What was that about?" I said.

"Nothing."

"Come on."

"She's just happy to know that I'm getting it on a regular basis."

"No way. Women don't think like that."

She stopped, shook her head. "For future reference, what's German for 'men are complete idiots'?"

I had been thinking about Johanna, the girlfriend I had in Vienna at the time of the Anschluss. She was the daughter of a baron and baroness whose star (and bank account) were fading, and likely to fade even quicker under the Germans. But she wouldn't leave when I left, for a lot of reasons -- and mostly because I didn't even ask her to leave in the end. We wanted different things, and she could never let go of the notion that she was tied to her family, and her family was tied to Austria, and that was that. But part of it was that I had kept the spying part of my life from her, and when I finally told her, she laughed in my face, laughed as if it were impossible to see the traveling magnesite salesman acting for any kind of noble, higher cause.

That her opinion stung went without saying. Her disdain then, the beatific smiles now -- how exactly did people see me? My Uncle Otto had taught me many things, but one of them -- "Cards to the vest, son, cards to the vest in life and in love" -- had stuck with me, maybe too much. I always figured, if you didn't let people in, they would just see what you showed them. But more and more, it was dawning on me that a blank canvas was just an invitation for other people to fill it in however they wanted.

I didn't want that with Manon. I didn't know where we were headed, but I didn't want that. So I wanted to tell her something about the spying part of my life, but I didn't want to endanger her or scare her. Because there was little doubt I was going to get in deeper. As soon as I heard about the Nazi gold, I knew. I couldn't just walk away from that kind of knowledge. I didn't know what to do with it, and I didn't even know if it was entirely true, but it was the kind of thing that could affect Germany's ability to fight in a very big way, and I had to pursue it. I just felt it inside, that I needed to get involved, regardless of the risk. And fuck Johanna.

But what to tell Manon? I couldn't tell her what happened in Vienna. And while I might be able to tell her soon about being the banker for the Czech spy network in Switzerland -- the Fesslers all knew, so what was one more? -- but it still seemed awfully soon for that. I settled on telling her the gold story but without the details of who told me or how or when. I said it was a guy from another bank who got drunk and told me he heard it third-hand. And that there was no proof.

Manon was simultaneously fascinated and enraged.

"The goddamn Swiss," is how she began, followed by a recitation of every lousy thing she could say about the country and its people, ending up with, of all things, "and that includes the fucking fondue."

"But I don't know what to do now?"

"You need to embarrass them," she said.

"But how?"

"You need to get the story published. Nobody here would ever do it, but you have that friend in Paris, right?" she said. I had thought about Leon. This is the kind of story he would kill to write. He had worked on a scandalous tabloid in Vienna, and he had worked on a serious broadsheet, and his heart was with the serious. To expose the Swiss banking system for making a deal with the Nazi devil would be his highest honor.

"But I don't even know if it's true," I said.

"Then you have to find out. Get your banker friend drunk again and go from there. You need to do this. Publicizing this is the only way to get these assholes to do the right thing."

There might be some other ways after I had spoken again to Groucho. But none of that came up as we made what turned out to be an extra-quick walk back to my flat.

14

_____

Arriving at the bank the next day, trying to figure out how I was going to contact Groucho, the answer came in the morning post. It was a picture postcard. On one side was a photo of the Fraumunster, the church that stares across the Limmat at its big brother, the Grossmunster. It was a photo of the outside of the church, marred by a red X that was drawn on the bottom right, in the foreground. It was just a random, stray mark, you would assume, except that on these kinds of postcards, there was no such thing as a random, stray mark.

On the other side were my name and the bank's address, along with this message:

It was great seeing you! Zurich has so many wonderful sites! One day, we saw 7 of them and, let me tell you, we were exhausted -- slept till nearly 11 the next morning. Heading home soon. Thanks again for the hospitality!

G

It was easy enough to figure out -- Groucho wanted to meet on the 7th at 11 a.m. at the spot marked by the X. The 7th was the next day. As it turned out, the X marked the spot of the Fraumunster Kreuzberg, the cloister. Behind an iron gate, open to tourists and worshippers and lovers of murals painted of nuns and angels, it was a courtyard in the center with the murals along the sides, tucked into covered walkways supported by marble pillars. Some of the walkways were darker than others, depending upon the time of day and the angle of the sun. I understood why Groucho picked the place. There were plenty of places to hide in the midst of a public place. From what I could see, there were six people in the cloister.

I stood in the center of the courtyard and scanned the scene, my face painted with as much religious fervor as I could muster, turning slowly, trying to spot Groucho, my left arm embracing my body, my chin cupped in my right hand. I sneaked a look at my wristwatch. It was 11:05, but I didn't see him. Then I heard a cough. It came from the side to my right, an area wholly darkened by shade and a spot I couldn't see because of one of the pillars. I walked over and found Groucho pretending to admire a painting of two nuns cowering behind a deer, their faces framed between antlers that the artist bathed in a kind of ethereal light.

"A fan, are you?" I said.

"It's art, I guess," he said.

"It's holy art, sir. In some circles, your skepticism would be heard as heresy. Your soul would be damned."

"My soul was damned a long time ago."

"Finally, something we agree on," I said.

I asked him what he had been doing during his stay in Zurich, and he really didn't answer, other than to say that he wasn't in Zurich the entire time. I tried to draw him out a little more, but he seemed uninterested in chitchat and eager to get to the point. I preempted him, though, and surprised him by saying, "I changed my mind. I'm in."

"Well, fuck me," Groucho said.

"Shhh," I said, and then pointed at the nuns on the wall.

He laughed. "I have to admit that I'm surprised -- no, shocked. I hesitate to ask why you changed your mind because I don't want to jinx it, but why did you change your mind?"

I told him the story about the Nazi gold. I had learned in my time working with Groucho that he was interested pretty much only in the provable and less in theory, which he dismissed as "intellectual embroidery" and with gruff interruptions that demanded a return to the facts. But while this was a story light on facts and heavy on theory, Groucho was mesmerized. His only interruption was a single "holy shit," half-whispered, followed by an encouragement for me to continue talking.

When I was finished, we stood there in silence -- Groucho and I, the two nuns and the deer. We had been there for five minutes, but no one in the cloister had interrupted us. Finally, Groucho spoke. He actually took an exaggerated deep breath before he started, as if steeling himself.

"Look, this is huge -- you can see that," he said. "We need to find out if it's true, that's the first thing. But you know, that might be the easy part."

"What do you mean?"

"I don't have to tell you that we work for smart people who sometimes have no instincts. I don't have to tell you that we might have stopped Hitler before he took Austria with a little show of Czech muscle. We might have stopped him before Munich if the French had a set of balls. It's obvious to you, and it's obvious to me what this gold laundering means, but part of me thinks our bosses won't see it the same way."

"How is that possible?" I was incredulous. Because while Groucho was right about the rest of it, as he had said up on Uetliberg, things were different now. This was much bigger. If he was right, France was next. They had to see what this meant.

"Look, I hope you're right," he said. "But I can just as easily see Benes sitting at the end of our big conference table telling me that, in the bigger picture, we must realize that upsetting a sovereign, neutral government that permits us to run our espionage operations from its soil and blah, blah, blah."

Then, more silence. Two 5-year-old kids ran by us, giggling and pointing at the deer. Their mother, or a harried facsimile of one, rushed past us in pursuit.

"But let's not worry about that yet," Groucho said. "First things first: we need to prove that it's true, that it's really happening. Do you have any ideas how?"

I really didn't. Then again, I really hadn't made up in my mind that I was going to get back into the spying business until the day before. Groucho began thinking aloud, about having me become a part of Fritz Blum's network.

"No," I said. "I'm a free agent here, or I'm out. I work for you and report directly to you. You can tell Blum I'm in the game, but I don't work for him. That's non-negotiable. Besides, it doesn't make any sense. I'm going to be fishing in a different stream than his boys."

"Well, then you're going to need a radio," Groucho said. "And you're going to need some training. There's a little more involved in this than just being a courier."

"How hard could it be? They fucking let you do it," I said.

My bravado was beyond false. I think Groucho knew that, too. He looked at his watch, and we arranged for another meeting -- this one, in his hotel room. Before he left, I wanted to tell him about the meeting at police headquarters with Ruchti, the one I found so unsettling.

"What's the cop's name?" Groucho asked.

"Ruchti."

"Peter Ruchti?"

"Yeah, you've heard of him?"

"You might say that," Groucho said. "Peter Ruchti is an officer in the Swiss intelligence corps, which is really about two guys whose idea of covert communications is using a couple of tin cans and some string."

"No," I said. "He's just a cop, a homicide detective. He's investigating the murder."

"No, he's a spy," Groucho said. "And seeing as how he used his correct name, my guess is that he wants you to know."

PART II

15

A fortress on Talstrasse, the Baur au Lac was Zurich's grandest hotel, where the swells had the swellest of times and paid handsomely for the privilege. The key selling point was in the name: the view of Lake Zurich. In my mind, though, it came up a little short in that department because the hotel was not on the lake itself but about a block back. And while it was true that the view was uninterrupted by any buildings, there was a small park and about six lanes of traffic between the hotel and the lake, traffic that you could hear with the windows open. It was not some perfect idyll within the city. Of course, that was the opinion of someone who had never stayed there and likely never would. I couldn't afford to be a regular customer, but that did not mean I couldn't afford to be critical.

Still, I was sitting in the lobby bar, having a drink, and surveying the swells. My tiny table was in the corner, my view of part of the lobby obscured by some sort of potted palm. This was an amateur mistake, but seeing as how I was an amateur on my first real spying mission, oh well. Better to miss part of the room than to get the waiter to change my seat, which would just have drawn attention to my presence.

I had been there for about 20 minutes, and my second Manhattan had materialized, and it was all very normal, other than the tightness of my sphincter. It was a busy room, and while the typical table had two people seated, there were plenty of singles -- having a drink before dinner, waiting for a companion, just reading the afternoon paper and unwinding amid the marble and the tapestries. In some cases, spying involved physical danger and derring-do. In my case, it involved drinking and observing people. So, as it turned out, I had really been a spy for my whole adult life.

The plan had been to stay for a third drink, but no more. Again, that would have likely drawn some attention -- from the waiter, if no one else. I wasn't sure exactly what I was hoping to see -- Groucho had said I should start doing this every night, here and at a couple of other hotels, just a drink or two. Between that and my typical roster of client lunches, I would see more than I imagined, he said, as long as I kept my eyes open. And so it was, near the bottom of my second Manhattan, when Klaus Berner arrived in the bar with a man who I recognized but did not know.

Berner was a vice president in charge of something-or-other at the Swiss national bank. They had a lot of vice presidents, and I had met most of them at one time or another. Precisely what they did was another question. Then again, precisely what I did in my day job was also open to debate, if anyone cared to think about it. And while I didn't know the name of Berner's companion, I did know the face. I knew it because it was one of the 50 or so men whose photographs Groucho had given me to study.

He had made me up a packet of portraits after our talk at the Fraumunster. Apparently, one of his tasks while in Zurich was assembling this Nazi rogues gallery, and now he was picking and choosing photos for me from a much more extensive collection. It filled an entire briefcase, and not a small one. I didn't bother asking him how he had gotten them, although they looked quite official, like the kinds of photos that big companies, or big governments, kept in their personnel files.

He appeared to have two copies of every photo. Included were the head of Germany's legation in Zurich, and a few other people who worked there who were known to be spies. I handed one of the snapshots back to Groucho.

"I already know this asshole," I said, explaining how I had come to be acquainted with Ernst Meissner, the smarmy census taker, and his story about offering business contacts and socializing opportunities.

"You know that's bullshit, right?" Groucho said. "The truth is, the Nazis have organized the true believers and made sure, if they aren't already, that they're armed and ready. You know, just in case the time comes when the Wehrmacht decides to cross the border and learn to yodel."

"We kind of figured that."

"Yeah, and you know what else? The Swiss have kind of figured that, too. I'm pretty sure it keeps your pal Ruchti up at night."

Berner and his companion sat at a table on the other side of the lobby. I'm pretty sure he didn't see me. I knew I had seen the face of his friend, and that it was in my collection of photos -- photos that, coincidentally, were in a file folder in the briefcase that was currently nuzzling against my right calf.

Did I dare? I scanned the room. There would be nothing unusual at all about a lone traveler grabbing a file folder from his briefcase for a quick peek. I was seated against the wall -- at least I had gotten that part right -- so no one could see over my shoulder. The big plant to my right -- which really could stand to be watered a bit more regularly, given the price of the Manhattan -- would shield me from that direction. So why not?

With the file folder as close to my chest as I could manage while still opening it, I riffled through the photos. About halfway through, I found my man. Now I needed to see that name written on the back, except I did not dare remove it entirely from the folder. So, instead, I kept my finger on the photo inside and flipped over the entire folder and then read what was on the back:

Walter Sparberger

Deputy Minister of Finance

On the one hand, there were probably a dozen reasons why the German deputy minister of finance would be meeting with a vice president of the Swiss national bank. On the other hand, if there really was a gold laundering operation underway, who better to coordinate it than a pair of functionaries who were pretty high up in their respective organizations, but not so high as to dirty the hands of the truly important people.

I was thinking all of this, and looking down one more time into the file folder, when a voice startled me.

"Herr Kovacs, a pleasure to see you."

It was Berner and Sparberger, standing at my table, standing above me and looking down at me and my file folder.

I flinched and yanked my hand out of the file and placed it on my lap. Berner said, "I apologize. I have startled you. Working after hours?"

He introduced me to Sparberger, offering his name and title. No secrets, then. I explained that I was just checking a contract for an error that, as it turns out, was not an error after all.

"Alone?" Berner asked.

"Stood up, it appears," I said, shrugging. The two of them

offered weak smiles. I said, "I haven't given up yet, though -- not until I finish this drink, anyway."

"Well, good luck," Berner said. He and Sparberger headed into the restaurant for dinner.

16

I stopped at my flat to change my clothes, then headed to Cafe Fessler. Manon was overnight in some godforsaken place at some godforsaken farm show. Or as she said, "Cutest goat contest, followed by judging the butter sculptures, followed by a half-hour of scraping the shit off of my shoes."

The weather had turned cold and wet, which kept most of the fossils at home for the night. The last one left the cafe at about 10:15, at which point Gregory locked up and turned off the outside lights. I had already told him that we had a job this evening, and he motioned into the back room and then up the staircase that led to his flat.

It was a massive space -- small kitchen and eating area, large living room and three bedrooms besides. Henry and Liesl had the same setup, two floors above. The level in-between could have been another apartment but was instead used as a storage space for tables and chairs and fixtures and such. This way, it gave them all a little more privacy.

Only two of Gregory's bedrooms were furnished. The third was used for storage, a maze of half-filled boxes and mismatched furniture pieces. Only now, in the far corner, hidden behind the warren of shit, were a wooden folding chair and a small round table, upon which sat the radio that Gregory would use to transmit Alex's report of the meeting between Berner and Sparberger.

"Let me turn it on," Gregory said. "It's going to take a little while to warm up."

He flicked the switch, and the dial lit up, and I wondered for the tenth time exactly what I had done by allowing Gregory to get involved in all of this. Slowly, you could hear the tubes inside the radio begin to hum. Gregory actually put his hand on the radio, to feel the temperature rise. He did it lovingly if that was possible.

It had started when Groucho insisted on the radio. He said, "If you're insisting on being a free agent, as you call it, then you will need it to communicate. The mails aren't quick enough except for the most routine messages."

He gave me a handbook on Morse code, as well as a copy of the King James Bible, all 1,279 pages of it. The system we used would be simple enough. If we were sending a message on August 20th, we would go to page 821 of the bible -- always add one page. Then we would substitute letters on the page for numbers. If we wanted to transmit the letter T, we would count the number of letters on the page until we reached the first T, and that number would be sent. It was easy to execute and pretty much uncrackable. Even if someone found the book and figured out the date part, the extra page would likely confound them forever.

"Okay, let me start on the message," Gregory said. I handed it over. It was simple enough: "Brenner met tonight with Sparberger." But seeing as how this would be our first real transmission -- we had performed one test -- we were both nervous.

Groucho had said that the radio would be shipped to me by regular mail, but he said that he would not risk it being sent directly to my flat or to the bank. "Ruchti knows you're up to something, which means the Nazis in the legation might at least suspect," he said. "We just can't take the chance. We need a third party."

My only third party was the Fesslers. So they had it shipped there. When it arrived, I would think of some explanation. And as it turned out, when it did arrive, Henry didn't even think twice. He signed for it and, when I came in for dinner, he said, "You had a package delivered here this morning. It's in the back. I'll get it for you in a few minutes." First, though, he was going upstairs to drop off his Manhattan and a glass of Riesling for Liesl. Then, by the bar, I heard Gregory tell him, "Don't bother, I'll get it for him." And then, a few minutes after that, Gregory brought me the package, about the size of a shoebox. It was apparent that he had opened it and rewrapped it.

"So, explain," Gregory said. He sat down, and the look on his face was one part excitement and one part disdain.

There seemed little point in lying. It's not as if I could argue that I was joining a shortwave radio club as a hobby. Gregory, Henry, and Liesl already knew about what I had done in Vienna, and the deal I had to make with Czech intelligence to get all of us to Zurich, and Leon to Paris. They knew I was running the bank as part of the arrangement. They had probably assumed that I was more involved than I was before somebody put a bullet in Michael Landers' head. So, well, what the hell. I told Gregory everything. The story about the Nazi gold really set him off.

"Those goddamned--"

"What ones? The Germans or the Swiss?" I said.

"All of them. But especially the goddamned Swiss. You have to stop them. And you have to let me help."

"Wait, wait, wait. No. This can't happen."

"You just told me you're a free agent. So you're free to recruit some assistance. I'm your assistance."

"No, damn it. No. Absolutely not. N-O. There's no way I can let you get involved in this."

"I'm already involved in this." Gregory pointed to the box on the table.

"No you're not, not really," I said. I think I spent the next five minutes babbling myriad variations of the phrase "no fucking way." All I could think about was Henry, and how much he loved the life where his father was just a normal father, not the guy who ran a protection racket, and how he would kill me if he found out.

"Just listen to me," Gregory said. I had pretty much talked myself out, and he waited until I was done. "If it wasn't safe to mail the radio to your flat, then it's just as unsafe for you to transmit from your flat. We both know that the technology exists to detect the transmissions, which means the Germans likely have that capability here. For all we know, that's why the guy got shot through the head, because they caught him transmitting."

"We don't know that," I said. I was weakening.

"Alex, you have to let me do this. It will help you, and you know it even if you won't admit it, but I really need this. I need it for me. I'm dying of boredom here. I miss the game. I miss the action. And if I can't ever have that back, I can have this. And I can do something for my country, for Austria. Alex, I need this. It might be my last chance."

Twenty years earlier, Gregory had hired me for a summer job at the restaurant -- Henry's dad, our friendly neighborhood mobster. Now he was begging me, half pathetic but half defiant. So I agreed. He learned the Morse code in a couple of days. The practice transmission went off perfectly. And now, on our first real night, after I checked over the message, Gregory sent it with a steady, even cadence. He kept the Morse code cheat sheet at his side, but it he referred to it, I didn't notice.

After sending, we waited in silence for an acknowledgment from London. The letter G would mean that Groucho received and understood the message. The letter R would mean that they needed a repeat. Silence for more than five minutes would mean they never received the message.

Two minutes, three minutes, then:

Dash, dash, dot.

The letter G.

Gregory and I hugged as if we had just bombed Berchtesgaden. He flipped off the radio and offered me a drink, but I declined. Turning to leave, I looked at him and nodded, and we both laughed as we repeated the one rule that both of us had agreed upon as inviolate:

"Henry can't know."

Manon went home to Lyon for Christmas and New Year's. I asked her if she was going to tell her family about me. Her reply was a laugh. Not a giggle, not a smiling titter, but a brief explosion of a guffaw. Imagine your best friend's drunken belly-laugh when he recalls the story of the time when you drank beer for the first time, and he literally dropped you in a heap just inside the vestibule of your building. Now cut that in half. That was Manon's reaction.

"Darling," she said. She must have seen the hurt on my face and was backtracking. "We are not children anymore. I do not practice writing 'Manon Kovacs' on the inside of my school copybooks. I do not gossip about you with my friends -- although Liesl does pry a few details out of me every once in a while, but that's more about her knowing you than anything else. Because I don't act like a schoolgirl doesn't mean I don't love you. Because I very much love you."

In all, it was a decent salvage on her part. But I would close my eyes and hear that laugh for weeks afterward.

The newspapers, all through that time, were full of talk of the "sitzkrieg" or the "phony war." The Poles didn't think it was so phony, of course. They had lasted about five weeks, give or take, before the Germans pushing from the west and the Russians pushing from the east strangled the breath out of a proud army that actually fought nobly, given everything. It was such a shame. When you talked to somebody about Poland, if one of you didn't use the term "poor bastards" to describe them, it was an upset. They had done nothing wrong. There was no good reason why they should be the volleyball of Central Europe, batted around strategically sometimes and simply smashed at other times. Their only offense was an accident of geography. Poor, poor bastards.

But since then, nothing. The Christmas markets in Zurich were their usual charming selves, full of kitsch and crap and smiling families from the hinterlands, making a day of it. Christmas in my flat was typical -- no tree, no lights, no kitsch, no crap. Liesl tried to embarrass me into decorating, but I refused to be embarrassed. Christmas was for children. Period.

Still, I bought a bracelet for Manon and received a necktie from her to go along with her belly-laugh. It seemed about right. I also bought small gifts for Henry, Liesl, and Gregory, because on Christmas Eve, the cafe would close at 2 p.m. and there would be a family celebration, and if they weren't my family -- along with Leon in Paris -- then I didn't have a family. My father and brother in Brno weren't speaking to me anymore after I chose a life of spying over a life of selling magnesite. But the truth was, they were jealous, seeing as how the Nazis had forced them to sell them the mine for about an 85 percent discount to what it was worth and to continue running it on a pittance of a salary. The root of their jealousy was that when they bought out my share in 1938 -- after I fought them just to give me a share -- they had not had such foresight and had only fucked me by about 50 percent.

The last time I had heard from my father, it had been a telephone call to the bank where he asked me to give some of the money back. It was a long call, in three acts. In the first, he said a rebate from me was the "sporting" thing to do. In the second, he said it was the "gentlemanly" thing to do. And then, in the third and final act, the man who had always treated both his brother Otto and me as some peculiar species of irresponsible wastrels, insisted that I owed it, "as a matter of family honor." That's when I hung up.

So, Merry Christmas. My spying activities had pretty much shut down for the holiday season, not because spies are particular fans of nativity scenes, except as places for a discreet brush pass of information or a quick conversation, but because the people I was spying on -- bankers, German ministers and the like -- all had families outside of their day jobs, and this was a family time. I was pretty much left with the newspapers, which speculated reasonably often about what might be next, but subtly. When it happened -- when Adolf's legions finally arrived -- it wouldn't be subtle, but for now, the talk was of unspecified "consultations in Berlin," and feature stories about the state-of-the-art technology contained within the Maginot Line, and friendly reaffirmations of Belgian neutrality, and the catch-all "awaiting events." Everybody was awaiting events.

Gregory opened a bottle of champagne on Christmas Eve, and we sat around and told the old Vienna stories. Gregory got misty when he brought up his wife, who died of breast cancer in 1930. I got misty when I told my Christmas story about Uncle Otto, the one from soon after the war when he bought me a new suit and handed me a train ticket and a list of hotel reservations, officially giving me my first three clients, saying, "God, you were born to do this. Sometimes I think you really are my kid."

And then Henry and Liesl locked arms and announced she was pregnant. Gregory wept for about five minutes and then sat stunned as if clobbered by an especially mighty right hand. As best as the doctor could figure, she was due in late May.

Walking home, picturing in my head the whole way just how happy Henry and Liesl and Gregory were, I wondered if I was close to that. Or was I kidding myself? Was a life with Manon just some invention of my imagination, one that she never considered a possibility? And if she did think it as a real possibility, would I be able to commit when the moment arrived? Or was I always destined to be Otto's nephew, continually holding life at arm's length?

Questions. And then, beneath my front door, someone had stuffed a flyer. It read, "Unite Against Nazi Aggression!" It was advertising a rally for the following Sunday, New Year's Eve, at the end of Bahnhofstrasse, right in front of Lake Zurich. The sponsors of the rally were not identified, which seemed odd, and I wondered if it was a request for a meeting from Groucho or another of the Czech spies. But I looked outside and saw the same flyer sticking out of from under a half-dozen doors. I snatched one and compared it to mine, just to make sure.

As it turned out, they were identical. It was just a flyer. Next week, I knew, there would be another one, not for a pro-Hitler rally -- that would just be crass -- but for "a celebration of German culture and heritage" or some such thing. In a neutral country, divided by German influence in the north and east and French influence in the south and west, this tugging in both directions was a near-constant.

I grabbed the bottle of schnapps from the sideboard. And by the time I was finished comparing the two flyers, and wondering about what morsel of news the morning papers might bring, and considering when it was time to start trolling the hotel bars again, I wasn't thinking about Manon or babies or what might be anymore.

18

January 4th was the first Thursday of 1940. Cafe Tessinerplatz was even more crowded than it was for the typical Thursday promotion. It was filled with men, almost exclusively, men who likely had seen enough of their families recently. Or, as Albert the waiter said as he seated me, "You can overdo it with the kith and kin, am I right, Herr Alex?"

Marc Wegens, my army friend, was nowhere to be seen, though. I was two Manhattans deep, and he was still absent, which was unusual but not unheard of. Even during a phony war, as a major in a phony army, Marc likely was dealing with a lot of last-minute re-figuring of, well, everything an army figures. It was such a strange outfit, the Swiss military. They didn't have a general except when things started to get hot, and the legislature picked a guy to deal with the heat. The legislature just did that, and the papers said the guy's name was Guisan, and they called up a couple of hundred thousand people from the reserves. The whole thing sounded like a logistical nightmare. Hence, I figured, no Marc.

I was about to call it a night when Herman Stressel, the German magazine editor, walked in with another man I had not met before. He caught my eye, and the two of them sat at my table.

"Vlad Brodsky," the man said. He stuck out his hand and began talking before Herman had time to make the introductions. "And you are Alex Kovacs, who might or might not be doing a little undercover work for the Czechs. Am I right?"

I looked at Herman. "Motherf--"

"Calm yourself, my friend Alex," Brodsky said. He put his hand on my arm, as familiar as if we had known each other since kindergarten. "You must not blame Herman. I wheedled it out of him. I can be very persuasive."

"He can help you," Herman said. He sat, half-smiled, half-shrugged. "I promise you, he can help."

I didn't know what to say. They ordered drinks from Albert, and we sat in silence until they arrived. I don't know if it was the alcohol, but the rage I felt at the instant of hearing that Herman had blabbed to Brodsky ebbed almost instantly. Soon, I was calculating how this might help me, waiting for one of them to say something -- which Herman finally did.

"The reason I could tell Vlad was because, well, Vlad is in the same business," he said.

"Sort of," Vlad said.

"Let me put it this way," Herman said. "Vlad is in a couple of businesses. Do you understand what I am saying?"

I had no earthly idea what he was saying, which I told him, substituting the word "fucking" for the word "earthly." Vlad snorted his approval.

"You are so careful, my dear Herman," he said. "It is the German in you, always walking on the eggshells -- that is the expression, yes? Hitler has you spooked. You're in a free, neutral country but you act as if the Gestapo is listening over your shoulder."

"For all I know, they are," Herman said, pointing at Albert.

"I don't think so," I said.

"You know nothing," Herman said. "You are so naive."

"Listen -- I once tried to kill a Gestapo officer in Cologne. I had spent time stripped naked in a cell of a Gestapo prison. I'm not fucking naive."

"Now this is interesting," Brodsky said, rubbing his hands together in delight. "You will tell me that story another time. But in the here and now, let me spell out what our friend Herman has been attempting to explain in his riddles. When he says that I am in a couple of businesses, what he means is that, under my cover as a journalist -- I'm a correspondent for a newspaper in Helsinki -- I am working as an intelligence officer for some important people in Moscow."

I looked at Herman, my eyes as serious as I could make them. "But, in case you haven't been reading the papers, that makes you Herr Hitler's partner at the bridge table," I said. "Are you doing his bidding."

"This is where my businesses get interesting," Brodsky said. "I have sources here and there, in Germany and elsewhere, including our friend here," he said, waving at Herman. "When I get a piece of information, I send it in one of three directions. If it is bullshit analysis or gossip, I send it to Helsinki to put in the newspaper. If it is military information that I believe will benefit the Soviet Union for the day when Hitler turns on us, as we all know he will -- even Comrade Stalin does, I believe -- I send it to Moscow. But for information that I believe might benefit the French or the British or the Belgians or the Dutch, my inclination is to send it in their direction."

"Those are his businesses," Herman said.

"And this is where you come in," Brodsky said. "I have begun to receive information that I would like to send westward, and I would like to do it through you."

With that, Brodsky began to tell his story. From a source just outside the German high command -- "but he's very close, and not a damn janitor, although they can be quite lucrative sources" -- Brodsky had obtained the bare bones of the Wehrmacht's western invasion plans. Their name was "Case Yellow."

"Terrible name," I said.

"Terrible people," Herman said.

"Shhhh," Brodsky said. He went on to explain that he knew only two things: that the plan involved the invasion of Holland and Belgium first, and that it was likely to occur before the end of January.

"Sounds like the last time," I said. "Why do they think it's going to work this time after what happened the last time?"

"Come now, you read the papers," Herman said. "You've heard Hitler's speeches. You know why they think they lost, right? It wasn't because of a bad plan or any military failure. It was because of the Communists hiding in the government. It was because of the Jews most of all. German territory was intact, the army was entirely in France, and it got stabbed in the back, right when it was on the verge of victory."

"With the country starving and millions of men already killed and wounded," I said. "That the Jews' fault, too."

"Of course it is," Herman said. "Where have you been?"

"But it's more than that," Brodsky said. "If you look at the map, there really aren't a lot of ways in, especially if the Maginot Line is all that it's cracked up to be. If the Germans come in a little stronger and a little faster this time, they could do it. They came damn close at the beginning last time. They were this close to taking Paris."

We debated back and forth about our understanding of the Battle of the Marne, and the soldiers ferried to the front in taxi-cabs to join the fight, and how much was truth and how much was propaganda. In the end, though, I needed to get the message to London, and quickly.

"So we can work together?" Brodsky said.

I nodded.

"And if you come across any crumbs that might benefit me?"

I nodded again.

We agreed on a signaling method if either of us needed a meeting. On the path around the perimeter of Lake Zurich, used by families taking a stroll on pleasant days and solitary men smoking cigarettes and walking their dogs in the evening, there was a marble fountain with some fish and other assorted designs displayed as part of a tiny-tiled mosaic. At the top of the fountain, it said "MCMIX."

"If either of us needs a meeting," Brodsky said, "we will just leave a mark with yellow chalk on the side of the fountain's basin. You'll need to check it at least every other day, and definitely on Thursday." He then said the meeting place would be at the Barley House, a bar on Escher-Wyssplatz.

"Way out there?" I said.

"It's right on the tram line -- the stop is right out front. And nobody will ever think anything of it. It's full of people pretty much all day -- the brewery down the street is running three shifts these days."

That settled, we decided to have one more. I had so many thoughts running through my head that I almost forgot. I looked at Herman, and it was as if we remembered at the same time.

"The gold," I said.

"I know, I know," Herman said. "I do have a little something -- not much, but maybe it can get you started. I still don't have any details about the mechanics of the transaction. I can't even prove it's happening, not definitively. But there is somebody at the national bank -- Herr Jan Tanner. Somebody who I trust told me that if this is happening, he is the person making it happen."

"Spell the name," I said, and Herman complied, and I repeated it back.

19

The next night, Gregory and I sent the information that Brodsky had given me to London. It was the longest message we had sent and by far the most important. We still weren't exactly sure what risks we were running, although the picture of Michael Landers with his eye shot out was never far from my consciousness when Gregory was tapping away on his radio key. But whatever the risks, this was worth it. As he finished up, Gregory looked at me and said, with a kind of solemn excitement, if that was possible, "If this were to make a difference, I would be proud to die right now. Maybe for the first time in my life."

"You don't mean that," I said.

"I think I do. I was proud of my marriage. I am proud of Henry. But I have never been proud of anything I ever worked on. I made money. I did it within the rules of my profession. I wasn't a thief. The punishments I inflicted, or had inflicted on others, were always within the understood boundaries. But I never fought in a war for my country. I never did much charity work, other than within the context of the business."

"That isn't true. I rememb--"

"It is true," Gregory said. He was disconnecting the Morse key, placing it in the drawer of the table along with the copy of the Bible, not so much to conceal them as to keep things tidy, even amid the stacks of crates and crap in the spare bedroom of his flat. We were still waiting for the acknowledgment from Groucho, though. If it didn't come, Gregory would just have to pull out everything from the drawer and start again.

"My life was about money and power but mostly money," he said. "What could I tell God when he asked for my accomplishments? That I never stole from people, even as others did? That I never had anyone beaten up just to make an example of them? Alex, there has to be more than that."

We sat for a few seconds in silence. I didn't know what to say, even as I knew what Gregory was feeling. The more I thought about it, the more I recognized the parallels in our lives. I wasn't a mobster, but until Groucho had recruited me in 1937, my life had been strictly about money and comfort and avoiding personal entanglements.

"I think you understand what I'm saying," Gregory said. He stared me down, locking eyes until I nodded. The moment was broken by the acknowledgment code from London, dash-dash-dot, the letter G.

"You sent the whole thing?" I said.

"Of course."

"The last part, too, about how we are awaiting further instructions?"

"Yes, yes, all of it," he said. "This was pretty big news. They might need a few minutes to digest it."

We had a drink and distracted ourselves with talk about the baby. But it was a temporary thing -- I barely slept, seeing every hour on my bedside clock, worrying about the impending German invasion and how the French and British would react to our message, wondering how they might use me from here. The truth was, I was excited.

I remembered something Leon told me, about the first time he covered a murder for *Der Bild* in Vienna. He said, "So it's this horrible fucking scene, the guy's head was half hacked off of his body. The cop let me have a peek, and any normal human being would have thrown up on the spot. But I started taking notes from the scene: the cut of the dead guy's hair, the color of his jacket, the blood dripping over the curbstone in a tiny stream and falling into the gutter. Recording the details was like an instinct for me. That's when I knew for sure that I was in the right business."

And this night, and what I was feeling every time I woke up and looked at the clock, that's when I knew.

But there really wasn't anything I could do until Groucho sent some instructions. Gregory would turn on the radio every night at midnight for five minutes, in case there was a message. There had not been one in the weeks since we had started, but he listened every night.

In the meantime, I had Herr Jan Tanner to investigate. In a bookcase behind where Anders spent his day, we had copies of the yearly directories published by the national bank. The next morning, I went and grabbed the 1939 edition -- the heft of the book, with its brown leather cover, buckled my wrist for a second, until I adjusted. I felt Anders staring through my back as I reached up to take it. I could make small talk with anybody, but I had given up trying with that guy, and I usually just saw his blank expression for what it was -- blank. Lately, though, and especially since the murder, his look had seemed more menacing. Or maybe it was just my imagination, which admittedly had undergone a few recent jolts.

The book told me that Tanner's official title was director of currency and physical assets. I assumed that physical assets were gold bars and bullion and coins. He had held the position since 1935. His main offices were in the bank's building in Bern, but the book also listed another office in Zurich. I guessed that he had to spend at least a third of his time here or they wouldn't have bothered to give him the second office. So that is where I would concentrate.

As I considered, Marta barged through the door with my diary open before her. "We need to do this," she said, accusing me of ducking her attempts at organizing my schedule for weeks. The truth was, I had only been ducking her for days.

She sat in the chair next to my desk -- Marta was the only one who ever sat in it -- and, from a separate notepad, began firing off questions and answers. A dozen lunches, dinners, coffees, cocktails, and conferences were decided upon, with Marta doing most of the deciding. She wrote the appointments in the diary in ink -- always in ink, despite the inevitable changes that would occur.

Her handiwork complete, she paged through. She got to the last week in January and stopped. This was suddenly having the potential to be a pretty big week in my life, in all of our lives, after what Brodsky had said, but that wasn't why she stopped. Instead, it was because of a longstanding appointment that had been winking at me for weeks, ever since it was first entered.

"Liechtenstein," is what it said, simply.

In Liechtenstein -- which wasn't 100 miles from Zurich but still a hump, whether by train or by car -- Count Miroslav Novak lived in exile. A member of the Czech nobility -- not major but not a bit player, either -- the count was, as we liked to say in the refined confines of the banking industry, totally fucking loaded. And, out of some sense of nostalgia, or patriotism, or something, he was interested in storing some of that load within the secure walls of Bohemia Suisse. But he wanted to meet me first, and he wasn't dragging his ass to Zurich for the privilege.

Marta dropped the diary on my desk and started thumping on the "Liechtenstein" entry with her forefinger.

"You have to decide now," she said.

"Okay, okay."

"Car or train?" she said.

"Car."

"So you drive on Wednesday. I'll call and set up the meeting for lunch on Thursday. I'll let the Count pick the place. Do you want one night in the hotel or two?"

"Two."

"Which hotel?"

"There's more than one?"

"Fine, I'll pick one," she said, standing up, clutching the open diary to her breast as she left the office. She whistled a few notes of an unfamiliar tune. Marta was never happier than when that damn book was in order.

20

I didn't know what Tanner looked like, and I didn't know what days he would be working out of his Zurich office -- so staking out the bar at the Baur au Lac seemed a waste of time, assuming he stayed over, and stayed there, and didn't just commute from Bern every once in a while. The only certainty was that there had to be a secretary who assisted him in the Zurich office when he was there, and who ran things when he wasn't. So she would be my target.

Tanner's Zurich office was in the Altermatt Building, on Barengasse, a healthy goal kick from the edge of the Paradeplatz, a comfortable distance from which to bless or frown upon the latest maneuver of the Paradeplatz twins, Kreditanstalt and Bankverein. No one thought that the national bank did much frowning when it came to those two, but it was at least a possibility.

My play consisted of two separate maneuvers. The first was reconnaissance, and simple enough. I needed to see the secretary first. The easiest way I could think of was to look at the building directory in the lobby and find Tanner's office. It was on the second floor, 209. Then I looked at the directory and spotted Lindner Investments, which was in 309. And then I went up to Tanner's office and let myself in.

"Can I help you?" said the woman seated at the desk in the entrance area.

"Yes, can I speak to Carl Lindner, please?"

"I'm sorry, you're in the wrong office."

"This isn't Lindner Investments?" I looked as helpless as I could. This was something I was good at, and the woman smiled a bless-your-pathetic-little-heart smile. She told me to wait right there while she grabbed the building directory. It was in a cabinet behind her desk. As she stood, and then bent down to reach for it, I was doubly rewarded -- mostly obviously by the view of the skirt that climbed the back of her thighs as she reached down for the book, less obviously by the sight of her left hand as she reached. No ring.

This could not be more perfect: single, late 20's, attractive besides. Homely might have been better, to be honest, but this would work. This would work fine.

"Here it is," she said, thumbing through the book. "Ah, that's your mistake. You're in 209. Lindner Investments is in 309. Right on top of us."

"Are they noisy?" I said. I was whispering, one conspirator to another. "Are they fat? Are their footsteps heavy? Are they dancers?"

She giggled.

"Thank you so much, Miss ..."

"Buhl," she said. And then, after a half-beat. "Sophie."

As I turned to leave, I noticed on the wall behind me a series of vanity photos, undoubtedly of her boss along with various dignitaries who I didn't recognize. But it was easy enough, by process of elimination, to identify Jan Tanner -- he was the only guy in every picture: shaking hands, toasting something-or-other, turning over a shovel full of dirt at a construction ground-breaking. It would be an easy face to remember, mostly because of the ears. They stuck out like the wings on a strutting rooster.

Mission accomplished. Three days later, when I staked out the building and managed to run into her accidentally on the street, Sophie Buhl accepted my assertion that fate must be bringing us together and agreed to meet me for a drink the following night.

For my cover, I adopted my previous life as a traveling salesman for a magnesite mine, peddling the stuff that lines blast furnaces for fun a profit. I didn't push her for many details of her work life, but by the second drink, she had volunteered that her boss was in town only three or four days a month and that most of the time, she answered the phone, took messages, and accepted document packages from bankers which she then assessed for future action. The routine stuff was filed away. The semi-important files were sorted and stacked for action the next time Tanner was in town. The urgent material was couriered to Bern.

By the third drink, which was a glass of wine over dinner, Sophie was telling me that Tanner was "nice enough," but that "whenever he smiled, it looked like it hurt his face." She giggled that same giggle when she said it. She also reached for my hand. Suddenly, we were headed in a direction that I knew was possible from the moment that I gamed out the strategy, but tried not to think about.

It all came down to one question: Would I?

One of the advantages of living a life without many serious girlfriends was that there had been relatively few periods of my adulthood when an impromptu fling would be considered cheating. But, well, here I was. Despite the guffaw and my doubts about the long-term with Manon, I was most definitely in a relationship in the here and now. But if it came to that -- if the lovely Sophie were so inclined -- would it be considered cheating if I slept with her, or would it be considered just a part of the job?

The first time I noodled over it, I actually laughed out loud in the back of a taxi, startling the driver. Just a part of the job? It sounded like an excuse three buddies at a bar would concoct after one of them admitted to something that involved three Martinis and a chance meeting with an old teenage girlfriend on a business trip. But in my case, I really thought it was the truth. If I didn't have the information I needed, and if it was essential to continue the relationship with Sophie to get it, and if she was eager, how could I not? I didn't have to press her, and I wouldn't, but if she was inviting, I could lose everything if I turned her down. She would think it was odd, mostly because it would be odd. There was no way around it if that's where we were headed.

So how could I not? Rationalizations aside, this was about the Swiss laundering Nazi gold, a practice that could assist Germany's war effort in a way unlike any other. Other than Stalin agreeing to guard Hitler's east-facing backside, there was nothing that could bolster the German war machine like the Swiss agreeing to oil the Nazis' financial gears. This had to be nailed down, and then the Swiss had to be pressured to stop -- on the governmental level, by popular disdain because of press reports, or somehow.

This was about stopping fucking Hitler, I kept telling myself, even as I closed my eyes and re-ran the film of the skirt inching up Sophie's thighs.

A few minutes after she held my hand in the restaurant, all doubts were erased. Just after the waiter cleared away our entrees, I suddenly felt Sophie's foot, sans shoe, probing between my legs. I flinched, startled. She laughed.

"Jumpy?" she said.

"Let's call it pleasantly surprised," I said.

There was no question how this was going to play out. My

only hope was that she would tell me she had a roommate, at which point I would tell her I had a cousin staying with me for the week and ask for a rain check. She would buy that as an excuse, and that would buy my prematurely guilty conscience some time. But, no. As we got out of the cab and I leaned over to kiss her goodnight, she grabbed my hand and pulled me over the threshold and up the stairs and inside.

I thought about Manon. To be completely honest, it was for about two seconds.

An hour or so later, I was buttoning my shirt and suddenly having a hard time making conversation, which never happened to me. Sophie had no problem, though. She was a bit drunker than I was, and she talked about maybe getting together the following week, that she might be able to take off all day Wednesday, that her boss had a big two-day meeting in Bern with "some big Nazi" on Wednesday and Thursday. She giggled again when she said "big Nazi." She said the meeting had been on the books for weeks and would never be canceled. I made some excuse about sales appointments in Strasbourg and promised to call her and find another day for our next date after I checked out my diary.

I had been successful. I had gotten the lead on Tanner and the big Nazi and the two-day meeting in Bern that I needed. I was not a shithead. That was the mantra that got me to sleep.

21

I called Manon around lunchtime the next day. I was still bipolar on the subject of my business task of the previous evening, justifying it half the time, crippled by guilt the other half. But I knew that talking to her would wrench me back toward normalcy and that doing it over the phone would be the most effective way to disguise the shame that must have been painted on my face.

She picked up on the first ring. I started telling her a story about a tram accident I had seen on Quaibrucke that morning -- an out-of-control Daimler hit the tram so hard that it tipped it over on its side -- but she was beyond uninterested. She didn't even pretend to be listening.

"Is this a bad time? You sound distracted," I said.

"What does that mean?"

"I don't know. Are you mad about something?"

"No," she said. "Should I be?"

There is no way she could know. I had purposely chosen a restaurant outside of the center of the city and away from the old town where I lived, and where Cafe Fessler was. Those are the only two parts of Zurich that Manon knew, and it isn't as if she had a long roster of local friends who might have spotted me having dinner with Sophie. Now that I thought about it, I had not met any of her friends, other than Liesl. So there was no way unless Manon saw me herself -- and that really was beyond unlikely.

"What's the matter with you?" I said, redirecting her inquiry.

"Nothing. Just tired."

"Do you still have that rug manufacturers thing in Geneva? When is it? Tomorrow? You should just cancel. Fucking rugs."

"I can't cancel," she said. "This is what I do. Smile pretty and admire the carpets and point out the fine French craftsmanship."

"Do you think it makes a difference? Do you really think it sells more rugs."

"I don't know," Manon said. She paused. I could hear her sigh through the receiver. "Not that you can quantify specifically. It's more about public, I don't--"

She stopped again. "I don't know," she said. "I don't know about anything anymore."

I asked her if she wanted to come over to my place that night, and she said no. I asked her if she wanted me to go over to her place, and she said no. I was going to ask if she wanted to meet for a drink after work, but I reconsidered. She really was in a foul mood. A little distance might not be a bad thing. Besides, I needed a decent night's sleep before my trip to Bern.

I walked home the long way, taking a detour on the path around the lake. It was a miserable evening, the wind icy off the water. I came to the MCMIX fountain and looked discretely for a yellow chalk mark. There was none, only a poodle wearing a red sweater, lifting its leg.

22

The trains from Zurich to Bern ran hourly, greasing the wheels of Swiss commerce between the banking center and the national capital. It was an easy trip, the cars populated at whatever time of day mostly by men in dark gray business suits, their faces buried either in newspapers or manila folders stuffed with papers of two sorts: columns of numbers or legal contracts. It was not a place for frivolity, for children laughing and running up the aisle. Most of the train cars were stone silent, other than the clatter of the wheels and the conductor calling for tickets. If you listened carefully, you could hear the man across the aisle calculating the compound interest in his head.

Even as it was the national capital, Bern was a small town compared to Zurich. The walk from the train station was only a few blocks, passing through a mundane shopping district. Then, along the bank of the Aare River, you first come to a park. In it, there was a statue celebrating the postal union, with figures representing the continents handing over letters from one to the next. Such a Swiss thing, celebrating the delivery of the mail. I kept searching for the statue of the man who invented the green eyeshade. Some sculptor was really missing out on the next Swiss masterpiece.

Then came, in quick succession, a government building, the parliament building, and -- God bless Switzerland -- a big square with three banks on it. One of them was the national bank, and it was the closest one to the parliament building, just across a narrow street. It was almost near enough to touch, which was just about perfect. Somewhere inside was undoubtedly where Jan Tanner did his business.

And then, after the government block, came the Bellevue Palace, the hotel of hotels in Bern. In other words, you could ride in on the train and, after a short gambol, be bought and paid for, or buy and pay for someone else, and then rest your head after a full day of nefarious commerce in luxury. It was all so convenient.

I checked in at the front desk and attempted not to faint at the rates -- not that it was my money, but still. A single room with a bath was 20 francs per night. A suite was 40 francs. If you brought your man with you, or your chauffeur -- you know, if you had a man or a chauffeur --- it was 13 francs more, and he would live in a triple with someone else's men or chauffeurs. I wondered if the big Nazi was bringing a man.

It was 3 p.m. on Wednesday. I could only guess, but Tanner and the Nazi were likely having the first of their two days' worth of meetings, after which they would probably meet up here for drinks and dinner if the Nazi were like every other high-level traveling businessman in the capital. If he wasn't, I was screwed, but I tried not to think about that.

The lobby was imposing, expensive looking without being ornate. The floors were creamy marble topped by oriental rugs. The lobby bar had three stools, and the rest of the space was filled by an array of leather chairs, couches and low tables of varying shapes, all beneath a stained glass dome ceiling. The design above was mostly plain gold and blue stained glass panels around the perimeter. What drew your eye at the top of the dome was a set of large spiral designs.

At 3 p.m., three tables of women were having tea. It was too early for my lurking to begin. I checked in, unpacked, and returned at five. There was one table of tea drinkers, and one man had grabbed a leather club chair and what appeared to be a wholly satisfying Martini, given the relaxed sigh that he let out after the first sip. Again, I grabbed a chair of my own, my back to a wall. If I didn't sigh after the first sip of my Manhattan, I should have.

The evening trade was as expected, men in suits meeting other men in suits. I was looking for one particular man in a suit, the only one likely to be sporting elephant's ears. It actually made the stakeout pretty easy, even though the space was pretty busy. And while it wasn't possible to tell a typical Nazi without his party card, I still played the "is he/isn't he" game with every sausage-necked suit I spotted, just for fun. The game distracted me just enough that I never saw Peter Ruchti until he was already sitting in the other chair that shared my little table.

"Looking for anyone in particular, Herr Kovacs?" he asked, almost in a sing-song.

"And what brings you here, detective? Did somebody get poisoned by the pate?" It was lame, but the best comeback I had.

"Alex, I don't have the energy to play this game tonight," he said.

"What game?" I said, stalling.

"You have no idea what you have gotten yourself into," he said. And then we were both silent for what seemed a long while, but that was probably only about 15 seconds. I was calculating exactly how much truth I should tell, how much I should acknowledge, and I'm sure some of that showed. Ruchti just looked tired. Finally, he said something.

"Okay, let's pretend that I am a mere homicide detective and you are a humble private banker. Let's go with that for now -- I mean, what the hell? My guess is that you have never been to the Bellevue Palace before. Well, I have. So let me offer up an assessment of the premises.

"Over to our right," he said, pointing openly. "Over there, behind the bar, is La Terrasse restaurant. If you were to go inside, all the way in, you would see the tables with a view overlooking the river. It is quite nice, but I don't think it would be for you."

"Okay, I'll play along. Why would it not be for me?" I said.

"Good, good, I'm glad you're playing. The reason it would not be for you is that on most nights, and this is definitely one of them, La Terrasse is exclusively an eatery for espionage practitioners of the German persuasion, along with their friends from Japan, Italy, and Russia."

I made a face. He smiled back.

"This is quite so," Ruchti said. "It has never been more true. But there are other places to eat in the hotel, and they are patronized by espionage practitioners of different heritages. The French, say. And the British. An American or two has been known to stop in for a bite. And the Chinese. Yes, the Chinese -- they are frequent customers, mostly because it seems they are worried about the Japanese. In the Salon Royal or the Salon du Palais -- yes, they are all more than welcome."

He was pointing now toward his left. The different restaurants weren't 100 feet apart.

"You're kidding, right?" I said. Martin Stern had mentioned some of this to me, but it still sounded bizarre. "What you are describing is some kind of stage play, and a bad one at that."

"But it gets better," Ruchti said. And then, after a sweep of the arm that took in the entire lobby, he said, "After dinner, this is the place where they all might mingle if they so choose. The

Germans might be at one table, the British and French at another, the Czechs -- your countrymen -- at another, and the Chinese at another still. There might be a short bit of conversation between the groups, there might not -- you never knew. A newspaperman or two might be leaning up against the bar because this evening quadrille is well-known and respected throughout the journalism profession, a fertile fount of gossip and even the occasional fact, one never attributed to anything but 'sources' in the next day's paper.

"And usually," he said, "often right at this very table, is a representative of Swiss law enforcement, whose job it is to keep track of all of the players from the various nationalities and to be seen keeping track by those players. That is the most important task -- being seen. The Swiss authorities want them to know they are being watched, because the last thing we want is for one of those players to end up lying in a gush of his own blood on Rennweg, with a bullet through his eye. Such things make the government ministers nervous."

"And the bankers," I said.

"Same thing."

With that, his lesson for the day must have been completed. Ruchti stood to leave, groaning the groan of a man 20 years his senior.

"Enjoy yourself," he said. "But it's too early for me. I'll be two blocks over, back toward the station, at Brunckhorst's. I can't afford to drink here all night. You must have a better expense account than the police."

23

I checked my watch -- five had become six, and six had become six-thirty, and only I knew that Ruchti had left me balls-naked in this crowded lobby bar. Since he made his exit, I had spent half of the time convincing myself that only he knew my secret. The other half of the time, I plotted my escape and wondered if I should go get my suitcase or just leave it behind when I fled.

I didn't feel ready to play the game. I didn't feel ready to accept it as a game. I understood the adrenaline jolt might be similar to executing a goal-saving slide tackle -- I had felt it before, so I got that -- but a game? No. And with rules and courtesies and bows and polite little laughs out of a bad English drawing room comedy? Fuck no.

Still, as I eyed up dinner groups as they left the bar -- some to La Terrasse, some to the Salon du Palais -- I made mental notes and came to harsh, reflexive judgments. It was only natural. Although, it was probably a bit overboard when I watched two 70-year-old ladies shuffling themselves into La Terrasse and muttered to myself, "Goddamn Nazi bitches." I mean, they were probably just two local grandmothers having a night out.

I had ordered a third Manhattan and theatrically looked at my watch and mumbled something to the waiter about, "Meetings always running late," as if I needed an excuse for ordering a third drink. But the truth was, I was getting a little worried about my plan. What if the Nazi wasn't staying here? What if Tanner took the guy to his house for a home-cooked meal? I really didn't have a Plan B, other than maybe to sit outside the entrance to the national bank in the morning and see if big ears walked into the building with a companion. Then again, seeing as how I had no idea what the Nazi's name was, and given that my memory for faces was, frankly, shit, I'm not exactly sure what that would accomplish. Then again, I wasn't exactly sure what sitting in this bar was accomplishing, either -- until, that is, the table next to mine came empty, and two men sat down, one of them with a pair of ears that could block out the sun.

I was sitting at a 45-degree angle from the table, with my back mostly facing it, so I didn't have to worry about making eye contact or anything. My biggest concern was appearing to lean over too far in an attempt to overhear what they were saying. Because the truth was, I couldn't hear anything. Or didn't I mention the lobby piano that was currently being played by a gentleman in white tie and tails? It was hardly intrusive but precisely loud enough to camouflage whatever you were saying from a table about 5 feet away. Which, I guess, was at least part of the point.

Part of me wanted to walk over to the piano and give the guy a couple of francs with a request to take a break. But I decided to just stay put. I was nervous -- about Ruchti, about being a little bit drunk, about being so close to their table -- and the last thing I wanted to do was draw attention to myself. I figured the thing to do was sit, and maybe catch a snatch of the conversation if I got lucky. If I had to, I could possibly ask the waiter what the Nazi's name was after they had left, pretending I recognized him from somewhere, maybe an old school chum from Wiesbaden or some such thing. We were probably about the same age.

I did need at least to make an attempt at memorizing his face. So I did manage, at one point, to lean over and tie my shoe and take a peek. As it turned out, memorizing it would be easy, because the big Nazi looked very much like my old neighbor from Vienna -- that is, if Rudolf Kreizburg was about 10 years younger, and sported some kind of mole on his neck that was about an inch in diameter and must have been a bitch to shave around every morning. They were quite the freak show, mole and big ears. If I were properly introduced to them, I don't know what I would have stared at first.

So I sat there, sipping the Manhattan, waiting them out. They ordered a second drink, and I ordered a fourth, along with my bill. They were going to have to eat soon. And, as it turned out, the piano player did take a break just as they were drinking up. I did get to hear a little bit.

"...it's a couple of hours," Tanner said,

"My driver or yours?" the big Nazi said.

"Mine. But maybe it would make sense for yours to follow in your car. That way, you'll be starting that much closer to home."

"We'll be done then?"

"Yes, I'm pretty sure," Tanner said. "I just want you to see how it works. You can inspect the procedures and suggest any changes you think necessary, although I'm confident you will be satisfied. If we need to speak further about anything, there is an office we can use there. Then you can be on your way."

Then they swallowed their last swallows and stood up. The Nazi motioned toward the waiter, mimicking signing his signature with his index finger on the palm of his hand. The waiter rushed over with the bill and a breathless "Herr Steiner," and

Herr Mole Steiner signed the bill, and he and Big Ears Tanner made their way to La Terrasse. Of course. Goddamn Nazi bitches.

After they had left, I asked the waiter, "Is that Ernst Steiner? I went to school with an Ernst Steiner, and I haven't seen him in 20 years, and he looked a little like him. But, you know, 20 years and four Manhattans..."

The waiter smiled that you-are-a-smudge-of-shit-on-my-shoe smile that they all must perfect before being accepted for employment.

"Matthias Steiner," he said.

"Perhaps he is Ernst's brother," I said.

24

I had a name and a face. I had the fact that they were going to drive someplace for a meeting the next day. I had that the someplace was closer to Germany than Bern was. I also had four Manhattans in my system and had long since abandoned the idea of eating a proper dinner. So I decided to go up to my room and call down to the kitchen for a sandwich.

The obvious thing to do was try to follow them to wherever they were going, although I really had no idea what I might see when I arrived. After all, a private meeting here would likely be followed by a private meeting at the next place. It isn't as if they had plans to advertise what they were doing, even if both sides probably were able to justify it to themselves -- the Germans, obviously, and the Swiss because, well, they were Swiss.

The truth was, even if I learned nothing more, I had learned a few things -- and the name of Matthias Steiner most of all. When I got back to Zurich, Gregory could send it along in our next message to London, and it would add to the picture. As Groucho once told me, "This business tends to be less about the snapshots and more about the tableau." This would be another little piece, like filling in a jigsaw puzzle.

The sandwich -- cold, rare roast beef, sliced thinly and piled on brown bread, horseradish on the side, accompanied by a pickle and a beer -- filled my stomach as my mind churned. I was less drunk and determined to see at least the outside of the place where Tanner and Steiner were meeting the next day. Of course, I had no idea how early they were leaving, which meant I would not be getting much sleep.

But following them would mean having to hire a car at the last minute. I needed to go down to the front desk and speak to someone there, even if it was almost 11. The desk clerk said the concierge was off for the night, but that he would be able to get a few phone numbers for car hire businesses if I didn't mind making the arrangements myself. I said that was fine, and he walked over to the concierge's desk and began rifling the drawers, searching for the numbers.

Leaning on the front desk, I picked up a brochure advertising tours and tastings at a nearby winery. I thought it might be a fun trip for Manon and me -- a night or two here at the Bellevue, along with some wine and whatnot. I thought, maybe in the spring, if we weren't at war. There was always that caveat now: if we weren't at war. Then I immediately remembered that we still had not received instructions from Groucho about our next move. Well, maybe Gregory had in the last day.

I looked over, and the desk clerk was still foraging. Then I saw behind him, the lobby bar. It was well after dinner, well past the let's-have-one-more crowd. Bern was buttoned-up early -- all of Switzerland was -- and this was likely the scene that Ruchti had described. Two guys were leaning against the bar -- maybe the newspapermen that he had mentioned. And, not surprisingly, there was Ruchti himself, his back to me, at the same table that he and I had shared a few hours earlier. A couple of other tables, mostly of twos and threes, were likely populated by the spies that Ruchti had said would be mingling there, seeing and being seen on their comfortable turf. There was even a table of Chinese, as he had said.

And then I saw, and it took a second for it to register. Sometimes, when you see somebody out of their normal context, it can take you a bit of time to put a name to a face. That wasn't the problem here. The issue, in this case, was the inverse, or the converse, or the reverse -- I never could keep those straight. But sometimes, when you see a familiar face in an unfamiliar setting, it can take you a second not to recognize the face, but to recognize that the context is all wrong.

Eventually, though, it hits you. And it hit me, my sudden happiness and surprise turning to something much darker, when I saw Manon, laughing it up in the bar with two men in dark suits, men who were not rug manufacturers at a trade show in Geneva.

25

"The construction will be first-rate, as good as the working people of Zurich have ever experienced," Mark Grosvenor said. A Brit who somehow landed here in the mid-'30s, he owned a construction company. He was a decent guy with a lot of personality, more fun to have a beer with than to do business with, to be honest. His latest project was an apartment block on Schweighofstrasse, out in a working neighborhood. He was hoping that Bohemia Suisse would provide a piece of the financing.

"Toilet and tub in every unit goes without saying. Kitchens with new appliances -- gas stoves and electric iceboxes."

We were having lunch at Veltlinerkeller. I had the knockwurst with sauerkraut and a pilsner. It was my favorite meal in Zurich, I think mostly because of the mustard that came with the knockwurst. There was just something about it -- a tang, a spice, something. I once asked the thousand-year-old owner if he could let me take some home with me, or at least identify the special ingredient, and he looked at me as if I had asked to sleep with his daughter.

My favorite meal and I couldn't taste it. Two days after seeing Manon with the spies of Bern, I was still pretty much in a fog.

"Nice hardwood floors," Grosvenor was saying. "Not the cheap stuff that warps on the first humid summer afternoon. Quality wood, and owners who pre-pay before construction begins will have their choice of finishes."

I did my best to nod occasionally. After a professional lifetime of acting like I was listening when I really wasn't, I rarely got caught. Of course, I had seldom been in a position where the woman I thought I loved was actually hiding this huge secret -- that she was a spy, and that our relationship might very well have been built upon her spying on me.

"Pre-construction or after, we'll paint for the new owners, pretty much whatever color they want," Grosvenor said. "We'll have faux marble wainscoting in the common areas. And for customers willing to pay 10 percent extra, the men will be able to receive a free weekly blowjob from a woman who lives in the basement."

I heard it, but not soon enough. My reaction was apparently too slow.

"Am I boring you, mate?" Grosvenor said. "What's the matter. For the whole lunch, you've been even less focused than usual, which is saying something."

I made up something about coming down with a cold. By the end of the lunch, we shook hands on a deal for me to provide 25 percent of the financing. I had already read the prospectus and a copy of the plans, and it was a decent opportunity for the bank. Walking over, I told myself that I wouldn't go more than 20 percent. But then I just didn't care.

After seeing Manon in the lobby bar, I never hired the car, never followed Tanner and Steiner to wherever they were going. Instead, I checked out of the Bellevue Palace on the spot and told the kid behind the desk to ship my bag. He told me it would be a few minutes before he could make up my bill, and I just dropped some francs on the counter and told him to ship the bill with the luggage. And then I wandered out of the hotel and in the direction of the train station, buying a small bottle from the next bar along the way. I was pretty sure -- no, I was confident, given the configuration of the lobby -- that Manon had not seen me.

The next morning, I was beyond useless. Because the more I thought about it, the more I became convinced that the whole relationship had been a sham, that I was not Manon's lover but her target. Thinking back on it, the entire thing had been just a little too coincidental. Seeing her at the bank retirement reception had been one thing, but her suddenly befriending Liesl on the same day strained credibility for anyone doing their thinking with their big head. Which I wasn't.

Concluding that I was the target was one thing. I almost got used to the idea after about 24 hours. The other issue: who was she working for? I assumed it was France. I prayed to God that it was France -- although, as with the prayer I said on the day Michael Landers was murdered, I wasn't sure exactly how effective a prayer would be that included the phrase, "Just please don't let her be working for the fucking Nazis."

The damn diary on Marta's desk had another meeting for me after the lunch with Grosvenor -- a drink at five with Thomas Koerner, president of Bank du Lac, another private joint like Bohemia Suisse, a place that was about as big and as influential. That is to say, not very.

Koerner was on a kick to have the small, private banks join together into an association that would give us more leverage in our dealings with the big two, Kreditanstalt and Bankverein. That this was a surreptitious aspiration went without saying. He never met with more than one other private banker at a time, so as not to offer even the slightest hint of a conspiracy. Because the truth was that, if they found out, the big two would castrate Koerner in the middle of the Paradeplatz and sell tickets -- and we all would buy one. We might buy two, just to demonstrate our fealty to the current structure.

"But aren't you tired of sucking at the hind tit?" Koerner always said, before his first drink was empty. This time, he said it before the first drink even arrived. His idea actually had a small bit of merit, provided the association was large enough. The problem was, we were dealing with bankers here -- and let's just say that bankers are significantly more loyal to the columns of figures in their ledgers than they are to the truth. There was no way to trust that the association would hold together -- and as it collapsed, there would be carnage. It just wasn't worth the risk.

Which is what I always told Koerner. Except for this time, I didn't have the energy. I just let him talk, which he much enjoyed.

"The older directors at Kreditanstalt will never go for it, but I know two of the younger vice presidents, and they know the world is changing, and..."

I zoned out and kept thinking about Manon. I had accepted that she was a spy and that I was probably her target. But the smallest part of me wondered. It all went back to her guffaw when I asked if she was going to tell her family about me. Oddly, even counter-intuitively, that very hurtful laugh was my main hope. I figured that if I was her target, and she was desperate to keep me close and interested, that she never would have laughed at that question. She would not have risked it. She would have invented some plan to tell them at Christmas dinner or something, layering loving detail upon loving detail.

So that's where I was, clinging to a hurtful moment as my greatest hope. After extricating myself from Koerner, I returned home and called Manon, because that is what I would typically do after she returned home from a trip. My hand shook as I dialed the number and my voice cracked as I said hello. Manon sounded a lot better than she had before she left. I could hear the life in her voice immediately. I wondered if she could hear the hollowness in mine.

I asked her how the trade show in Geneva had gone. She said it had been fine, and told a story about two of the rug manufacturers -- one portly, one with a hairpiece, "a rug man with a rug" -- competing with each other to bed one of the display models hired for the show. It was a funny story. A week earlier, I would have laughed.

26

My booth at Cafe Fessler. Another meal that I did not taste -- fried perch with little round potatoes and green beans, a dish that Gregory actually thought the kitchen did well. "I could have served this one in Vienna with a straight face," he said. But, again, I couldn't enjoy it. I couldn't enjoy anything.

The paperwork made for a big pile after the dishes were cleared -- everything signed in three places, one copy for the customer, one for the files, one for the regulators. Except some of the transactions were entirely secret and unregulated, which meant a second copy in a second set of files. I once asked why. The answer I received was so unsatisfactory that I never asked again, instead just whistling quietly whenever I saw the quarterly line item for paper supplies that the bank purchased.

Manon came in at about 8, got a drink and chatted with Liesl, who was showing now. She came down to the cafe for a glass of milk most nights now, and maybe for a beer once a week. This was a beer night. Manon had ignored me after a quick kiss when she arrived, dropping her coat at the booth. That was fine. I didn't want our confrontation to happen here.

At about 8:30, I gathered up my file folders and shoveled them back into my briefcase. I put on my coat and carried Manon's over to her, managing a minute or two of banter with Liesl about how nervous Henry was about impending fatherhood.

"We were over at one of my co-worker's house on Sunday, and they have a newborn, and Henry was afraid to hold her," Liesl said. "He was afraid he would drop her. He wouldn't take her until he was sitting on the floor so the distance wouldn't be so great if he went oops."

"Wood floor?"

"Yeah," she said. "At least we have carpet upstairs."

"Maybe you can leave pillows out everywhere."

Manon and I decided to go to her place. We didn't exactly alternate -- it was based more on who had the earliest appointment the next day -- and she had a breakfast meeting. I had gone over in my head how I wanted to do this, but couldn't settle on a particularly artful approach. Unless something hit me at the last second, I was just going to blurt it out.

It was only about a five-minute walk from the cafe, and we were able to pass the time in a comfortable silence. We got inside and took off our coats, and she walked toward the kitchen, asking over her shoulder, "Do you want a whiskey?" I would normally say yes, and she would carry the two drinks into the bedroom, where I would usually be undressing. Normally. Usually.

"No, I want to talk to you for a second," I said.

She must have sensed my tone. I don't know if it was hurt, or mad, or severe, or just different. She stopped and walked back toward me.

"Something wrong?" she said.

Nothing had come to me, so I just blurted.

"Bellevue Plaza, lobby bar," I said.

I was watching her intently for a reaction. There was just the hint of one, just a millisecond of something, but then it was gone.

"Is it nice? I bet it's nice. We should go sometime," she said.

She was playing the only card she had. She undoubtedly was hoping it was just a coincidence that I had brought it up. The smile on her face betrayed nothing other than the excitement for a little potential trip, maybe for a dirty weekend in Bern.

"You were just there. Wednesday night," I said.

"You saw?"

I nodded. And with that, I finally received an honest reaction, the look of being caught. Or at least I thought it was honest until she opened her mouth.

"I don't know what to say," she said. "I am so ashamed. I could insult your intelligence, but I won't. I wasn't in Geneva with the rug manufacturers. I was in Bern with a friend. Another man."

I said nothing. Into the silence, Manon kept talking.

"I know this must hurt you," she said. "We have become close, and I do love you. But in my defense, we never said our relationship was exclusive. And this was an old friend, someone I knew before you."

So that was her play -- to pretend it was an affair, and maybe to ask for my forgiveness. I will give her this, that she was very good. I might even have believed it, had I not known. Part of me wanted to wait her out, to listen more, to hear how she might embroider the story, to see just how well this devious mind could operate under pressure. But I couldn't. I blurted, again.

"That's all a lie," I said. I was almost whispering, looking down at my hands. "You're a spy."

Now Manon was speechless. She knew that I knew, and that was that. There was no more fiction for her to spout. There was no worthy denial. But I was the one who ended the silence this time, asking the question that had been foremost in my mind since I saw her in the bar.

"Thank you for not denying it," I said, as a kind of preamble. Her eyes were welling up. It was the only card she had left, but it completely set me off. The tears in her eyes, manufactured female bullshit, turned my hurt into rage.

"Fuck you with the tears," I said. "Is that in the manual, learning how to cry on command? Is that what they teach you when your job is to target a man and lead him around by the dick?"

"It's not that simple," Manon said. Now she was the one who was almost whispering, even as I got louder.

"But that was it, right?" I said. "I was your target. You wanted to find out what the banker from Bohemia Suisse was really up to. So you lifted your skirt and reported back to Paris what I was doing, who I was meeting, like that. Did you go through my briefcase after I fell asleep? Of course, you did."

"It only started out that way," she said.

"Fucking bitch," I said. It almost under my breath, except we were only about three feet apart. Her anger flashed.

"Well, it's not like you haven't kept any secrets from me," Manon said. "I mean, you're a goddamn spy, too."

"And that had nothing to do with you. That had nothing to do with our relationship. My feelings for you were real. By not telling you, I was protecting you. My love."

I spat those last two words. She just looked at me.

"Yeah, well what about Jan Tanner's secretary?" she said.

It surprised me that Manon knew about Tanner. Then again, I don't know why it should have.

"What about Jan Tanner's secretary?" I said. "It was just business."

"Fucking her was just business? You had to fuck her? There was no other way? Come on."

I thought about denying it. Then I thought, the hell with it.

"Yes, fucking her was just business, just a way to get information. How can you even ask me such a question? You were fucking me for business. You were fucking me to get information. For all I know, you're fucking half of the association of bankers for business."

Things degenerated from there if that was possible. I called her some really vile names. The worst thing she said about me was that I was "naive." A couple of times, she attempted to say that her current feelings for me were real, however they started, but I cut her off every time.

"I don't believe anything you say. How could I?"

She reached out to touch my hand. I jumped up and away from her as if it were radioactive. I grabbed my coat.

"Fuck this, I'm done," I said. When I slammed the door of her flat, it didn't feel as good as I had hoped.

27

Cold, wet, snow, Zurich. Only this year seemed worse. People didn't need what I had just gone through to be depressed in Zurich in January. All they needed to do was open their front doors and begin the morning trudge to the office.

I drank through the weekend of my confrontation with Manon. The phone rang a few times in my flat, but I didn't pick it up. I didn't know if it was her and I didn't care. As far as I was concerned, the slam of that door was the final punctuation on our relationship. There was nothing more to be said, no need for any kind of follow-up. If she started showing up at Fessler's, I would find somewhere else to eat and drink. It's not as if the town wasn't full of half-empty restaurants selling mediocre food.

By Monday, I was in reasonable emotional shape, better than I had been since the night in Bern. The bank was a decent distraction, especially given that January was our informal audit month when Marta and I tore apart every record from the previous year and checked them against our ledgers. We set up at our big conference table, which was about the only time we used it all year, and ordered in lunch for two or three days, however long it took to go through everything. By the end, we had fixed any discrepancies and could know with some certainty that our books were in order.

It felt good to dive into the minutiae of the business. After the audit, it was back to my never-ending series of bullshit sales calls and lunches and drinks and whatnot, with less time spent in the office and a couple of nights of paperwork at Fessler's. It was there, one night, when Gregory sat down. I had just walked in and sat at my booth, and he brought me my Manhattan without asking. He had one, too.

"I didn't think you drank those," I said.

"I don't."

"But..."

"I don't but, I have to be honest, I've been drinking more since we started," and then, with a flick of his eyes, indicated the stairs up to his flat, and the radio. "But I don't get drunk, not on beer or wine, not anymore. So I'm trying these. I'm so excited, just thinking about it, that I need to take the edge off."

We each gulped a mouthful, me trying to warm up a bit from my walk over to the cafe, Gregory trying to settle himself.

"Are you sure you're OK with this?" I said. "I can work out the radio a different way if--"

"Don't even think it," he said. "I told you how alive I felt with this, and it's all true. I'm just not used to feeling this alive if that makes any sense. Just the edge -- I just need to take the edge off."

He gulped again.

"You should be careful." I pointed at the mostly empty glass. "You never know when you're going to have to use that magic finger. Can't have you slurring in Morse code."

"Don't worry -- but I have something to tell you. London messaged last night. First time, right at midnight. I wrote down the message, but then I didn't want to leave it laying around, so I burned it. But it said, and this is exact because I memorized it,

'Source says G plans postponed indefinitely by weather. Await further updates.' That was it."

"Why didn't you tell me immediately?"

"We never worked out a procedure."

"You could have called last night. You could have come by the bank this morning."

"Are you sure that's safe?" Gregory said. He was right. I had no idea. For all I knew, Manon was somehow still watching me. Or somebody else. Or that my phone had been tapped. And the last thing we needed was for someone to think Gregory was something more than my old friend from Vienna.

"You're right, you're right," I said. "You did the right thing. We need a system."

As it turned out, I walked by the cafe every morning on the way to the bank. This would be easy, a variation on the yellow-chalk-on-the-fountain scheme I had with Brodsky.

"Take some chalk," I said, pointing at the menu slate that they changed every day with the specials. "Make a mark near the bottom of the black pole that holds the cafe sign out front if you have a message that I should know about. Unless you just want to grab me walking by in the morning."

Gregory thought for a second. "No," he said. "Henry would wonder what I'm doing up and in the cafe so early. He really doesn't like having me underfoot in the morning. And the truth is, I spend enough time down here as it is."

"Okay, now we need a place for you to leave the message."

"How about this?" he said. "The last thing I do every night is check the trash out back. The bins are in a wooden enclosure -- you've seen it, right?"

I nodded.

"Okay," he said. "Where the fence post on the left joins the two sides of the enclosure -- I'll just jam a folded piece of paper with the message into the space between the post and the side.

I'm sure it'll fit, and nobody will ever see it. And Henry won't suspect me being down there -- I check the trash every night. And you would have to be pretty unlucky to get caught back there by Henry. He's never out there early, never before the deliveries start. That's about 10 o'clock."

This would work. It was actually kind of exciting, just working out the details. There also was a feeling of relaxation, just a little bit, because the German invasion plans had been put on hold by the shitty winter. Maybe there was still time to head it off, although I had no idea how that might be accomplished.

Between thinking about that, and my paperwork, and my Manhattans, I was actually having a pretty good night, until Liesl came down to the cafe with a look on her face that was part concern and part disappointment. She obviously knew that Manon and I had split up and didn't even need to say it. I had no idea what Manon had told her. My only certainty was that it wasn't the truth.

"What happened?" she said.

"Ask her," I said.

That was the entire conversation. I picked up my stuff and left.

28

The trip to Liechtenstein, which had been like a stone in my shoe for weeks, suddenly seemed a relief. The weather was still crap, snow piled everywhere, but the sun fortuitously appeared as I got behind the wheel and, as it turned out, I made pretty good time. There are a couple of ways into Liechtenstein from the Swiss side, and I chose the route that took me over the Alte Rheinbrucke, a narrow, covered wooden bridge that was rickety enough that I was second-guessing my decision about halfway over.

That was technically the border, halfway over the bridge in the middle of the Rhine. But the way the customs niceties worked out, you received a passport stamp and a hearty wave from a guard on the Swiss side, drove through the wooden cavern, and received another stamp and wave from a guard on the Liechtenstein side. It all seemed a farce. Both guards were probably in their 60s, and the last time either of them actually left their semi-warm shelters and opened a car trunk or a piece of luggage was likely the previous October.

As it turned out, there were three small hotels in the center of what passed for a town. Their actual names were irrelevant. If they had been called by their level of luxury, they would be called The Kind of Shitty, The Shitty, and The Unalterably Shitty. At least Marta got me into The Kind of Shitty, and I was early enough to be able to grab a late lunch.

Two things about the dining room were notable, neither of those things being the food, which was standard, overcooked, and vaguely institutional. In other words, the mutton I ordered was cooked extra-long, as if they were attempting to make absolutely sure that the poor animal was dead. The two notable things were the thin film of grease on the water glass -- who needs water, anyway? -- and the three German officers who were eating at three separate tables, equidistant in the large dining room, so far apart from each other that it didn't seem possible that it was an accident. There was never a nod between them, never a sign of recognition, not a wave, not a look, not a salute, nothing -- not even when the one sitting in the back was forced to walk within about five feet of another one as he headed for the exit.

Liechtenstein was about 15 miles long and, in many places, only two or three miles wide. On one side of the two or three miles was Switzerland, and on the other side was Austria, which was now part of the German Reich. It would not be unusual at all for Wehrmacht officers to be stationed in Austria, near the border -- and the truth is, they probably didn't have a lot to do if they were posted to this hinterland, and they did need to eat lunch.

But a general and two colonels, in the same hotel dining room, where the food really was like the entire establishment, kind of shitty, didn't make a lot of sense to me. The fact that they were alone, without any subordinates for companionship, and that they didn't acknowledge each other in any way, just made it weirder.

Most waiters would object to a question about the whole

scene because waiters were trained to be unhelpful assholes above all else. But the guy who was working in the dining room that afternoon, fitting in perfectly with the surroundings, was a little light on the customary protocol. In other words, he couldn't seem to muster the energy to be an asshole. So I took a shot.

"Can I ask you something?" I said. He did not reply, but he did not turn away. I figured was in.

"Those officers, eating all alone, not seeming to know each other or even look at each other -- what's that all about?"

"Same every day," the waiter said. Again, he did not turn away, so a follow-up question seemed, if not welcome, at least a possibility.

"But why? It's not like the food here is--"

"It's not the food," he said.

"Then what?"

The waiter did not answer, other than to gesture to the right, toward the front windows of the dining room, with a flick of his head. As he walked away, I looked out the window. The colonel who had just left was walking across the square and then into one of the two banks that stared each other down, dominating the space.

Of course. You pop over for lunch and then, before heading back, you take a piece of your latest pay packet and deposit it into a bank in Liechtenstein -- you know, just in case the whole Thousand Year Reich thing doesn't work out as it's painted in the brochures. It's a little insurance, and nobody's the wiser -- and you're just over the border if you need to get the money in a hurry, and two miles from Switzerland after that. No wonder they couldn't look each other in the eye.

My meeting with Count Novak was for lunch the next day, at his home. It wasn't gigantic, but it was just fine, thanks, a baby castle with a turret and a drawbridge over a stream, all gray fieldstone and surrounded by a couple of acres that ran into a vineyard. He gave me the quick tour until the sky started spitting.

"It's a pity about the weather because the views are unique," he said, pointing, "Liechtenstein that way and Austria that way."

The truth was, the property abutted the Austrian border, which frankly scared the hell out of me. Before driving over, I made the hotel concierge draw me a map of the route with the Austrian border highlighted in red ink. The last thing I needed was to wander into the Reich by accident and find my name on some list. Like, you know, the list of Czech spies who were put on trial in 1938 after attempting to kill a Gestapo officer.

Lunch with the count went well. He was, indeed, fucking loaded. The deposit he would be making at Bohemia Suisse was larger than I had hoped. By the time we were done, it was nearly 3 p.m., and the weather had deteriorated. Part of me wanted to drive home anyway, but between the snow/sleet and the fading daylight, I decided to act like a grownup for once and spend another night in The Kind of Shitty.

Lunch had been big enough and late enough that I didn't need to subject myself to another night in the hotel dining room. After a short nap, I decided to settle in at the lobby bar and consume the day's remaining calories there. The Manhattans were well-made, and the glasses were, in an upset, clean. There was nobody to talk to -- the bartender was making drinks for the dining room, too, and doing a lot of running -- but that was fine with me. I did not have a university degree, but I owned a doctorate in amusing myself at hotel bars. Besides, it was going to be an early night followed by an early wake-up and the long drive.

That was the plan, as my third drink arrived. I couldn't imagine anything would change it, until an older gentleman in a military uniform sat down at the stool next to mine and said, "Alex, it's been too long."

I did a double-take, like out of a bad comedy. It was Fritz Ritter. His day job was as a general with the Abwehr, the German army's intelligence section. In his spare time, he was the highest-placed agent that the Czech intelligence service possessed.

29

The last time I had seen Ritter, it was early on the day of the Anschluss, when the Germans came over the border into Austria and were greeted with cheers and flowers placed into their rifle barrels by what was at least a significant minority of the Austrian citizenry. I liked to tell myself that it was not a majority, and I tended to believe it. Most days, anyway.

Ritter had sneaked me into Austria from Germany, through back farm roads, as the Wehrmacht massed along the border. He had broken me out of a Nazi jail only hours before I was to be sent to Dachau, and had me masquerade as one of his aides as we drove out of the prison, and for that, I should have been grateful. But he also had used me as a dupe to save himself, and put my life at risk, and so I really was not grateful. When he left me, down the street from the train station in Salzburg, I didn't say anything as I walked away. I didn't know what to say or how I felt, not completely. Nearly two years later, I still wasn't sure.

"Alex," Ritter said. He attempted to lock eyes, but my gaze quickly fell. He repeated my name, and his voice cracked a little.

"I always attempted to protect you," he said.

"You put me in jeopardy."

"I always had it under control."

"So you say."

"I did. I never would have put you in mortal risk. Your uncle meant too much to me. You have to believe that. It's important to me that you believe it."

Ritter and my Uncle Otto had met in the 1920s and were occasional running buddies, aging bachelors who traveled a lot for work. When the Gestapo got too close to Ritter's secret, that he was spying for the Czechs, Otto got caught and killed after a completely accidental meeting with Ritter. Then Ritter used me to help frame the Gestapo captain who was his pursuer.

"How can you say I wasn't jeopardy?" I said. "Remember that tribunal? Remember Rudolf Hess acting as the judge? That squirrelly fuck could have had me shot on the spot."

"We had it covered, I promise you," Ritter said. "We knew he was going to rule in our favor."

"So you say."

That was the best comeback I had: so you say. Most of me actually believed him. And the more I got into the spy business, the more I came to recognize that some risks can be justified in the cause of the greater good -- and that saving an intelligence asset who happened to be an Abwehr general probably qualified as the greater good.

We sat in silence for a few seconds. "Let's have a drink," I said, waving over at the harried bartender, who was just back from the dining room with a tray full of empty glasses. It was as close as I was going to come to saying "I believe you," or "I forgive you," and Ritter accepted it as such. His smile was his acknowledgment that the message had been received. When the drinks had been delivered, we carried them over to an empty table, away from the bartender. We had our pick of the round, marble tabletops and cherry cane chairs. We were the only people in the place, still.

"So, are you still--"

"I am," Ritter said. "And I hear that you are, how shall I say, more involved. That is why I'm here tonight."

"So it isn't an accident?"

"It is not," he said. "And I have to be back to Innsbruck in," and he looked at his watch, "shit, about two hours. My adjutant thinks I have stepped out for a romantic liaison. But we have a meeting tonight before continuing on an inspection tour in the morning. So this needs to be quick."

"What needs to be quick?"

"I have a message for you to get to London."

And with that -- after shushing my interruption with a "just listen" -- Ritter began to tell a story about a recent meeting in Berlin, and a change in plans. About how Hitler had always hated the plan to invade France through Holland and Belgium. How he had always wanted something new, something different, and how the general staff had insisted that there was no other practical route.

"But then, this one officer, Manstein, a Lieutenant General, he came up with something," Ritter said. "His bosses told him to shitcan it, that it would never work. But Manstein somehow got the plan in front of Hitler, and he loved it. And so they refined it some, but then they adopted it."

"And what is it?"

"They not going through Belgium or Holland anymore," he said. "They're going through the Ardennes."

I knew about as much geography as the average guy -- probably more, given how much I had traveled over the years. But I had never been to the Ardennes. I could find it on a map, but I had never seen it. I heard it was pretty in the summer, with narrow, winding roads through thick forests, but that's really all I knew. I guess the questions were evident on my face.

"Look," Ritter said. He grabbed a cocktail napkin and a pen from his pocket and began sketching.

"Holland and Belgium up here -- nice and flat and easy to traverse," he said. "And the Maginot Line down here. The French think it's impregnable, and the Germans likely agree. It had better be, all the money they spent on it.

"And the Ardennes is here," he said, circling the area between the top of the Maginot Line and the border with Belgium."

"But isn't it all mountains and shit?"

"It is all mountains and shit, as you say," Ritter said. "No one ever seriously considered it as a possibility. I mean, how do you get the tanks and the big lorries through on those little, windy roads? They'd have to go so slow if they could fit at all. They'd be easy picking for the French air force, you would think. At least that's always been the theory. But this Manstein has convinced Hitler, and the general staff has gone along with it."

"You think it's mad?"

"I don't know what to think," Ritter said. "I'm no tactician. Then again, I'm not sure Hitler is, either. But I guess we'll all find out. The point is, you have to get this to London. It's urgent. I think it's the most important thing I've ever passed along -- and I got them the Polish invasion date. Of course, they didn't believe me."

"What?"

"Long story, not your problem. You just need to send this as soon as you get home. Tomorrow, right?"

"How much do they need? Manstein, all of that?"

"No, just the basics: that the planned point of invasion is no longer Holland and Belgium, that it's the Ardennes instead. You can fill in the colorful details the next time you have an in-person meeting."

"Do you know when?" I asked. "Is there an invasion date?"

Ritter said that there was no date, but he believed it wouldn't be until at least spring. "I'm pretty sure they've moved back the date on the original plan at least five times because of the weather, and now I think they've just given up. But I don't have a date."

Five minutes later, Ritter was back on the road, headed for Innsbruck. Before he left, though, I asked his opinion about the Nazi gold and the importance of nailing down the details. He was surprised and fascinated, but ultimately skeptical. He said, "I'm just not sure the Swiss can be embarrassed into stopping doing anything that makes them money. They consider it their God-given right."

"I still have to try," I said.

"You wouldn't be you if you didn't," he said. "When I first thought of Otto's nephew as a spy, I thought it must have been some kind of mistake. Getting so involved? Risking so much for such idealistic reasons? I loved Otto, but that wasn't him. I never thought I would see it in you. But it's there. Goddamnit, it's there."

I hugged Ritter when he stood up to leave. And he looked at me and said, "Just send my message. It's more important than stopping Nazi gold. It's stopping Nazi steel."

PART III

30

I met up with Henry and Gregory at the cafe, and we walked the few blocks down the cobbles of Oberdorfstrasse to Bellevueplatz, where a few of the tram lines came together. The cold was just this side of bitter. The sun was out, though, somehow. It might have been the first time all week.

We took the tram out to Hardturm, a stadium out away from the center of the city. It left you about a mile from Letzigrund, the FC Zurich home ground, where the game was being played. We could have taken a different tram and gone right there, but that would have missed the whole point of the exercise, in Gregory's mind.

"This is the best part of the whole thing, much better than the game," he said. We were safe and warm on the tram, and he unbuttoned his coat and reached deep into an interior pocket and pulled out three steel mini-flasks, one for each of us, and handed them around. His smile was pure contentment, like a kid -- a kid, that is, who was taking his first pull of schnapps at 11:30 a.m.

"You're lucky the weather turned a little nicer, old man," Henry said. "Because you know how delicate Alex is."

"Yes, Alex, our little flower," Gregory said. "But look at that sun." He turned his face toward the window and basked.

The reason we were taking this tram was that it would leave us right across the street from the Grasshoppers' stadium. This is where FC Zurich fans would gather and walk through the streets, maybe 1,000 of them, and we were FC Zurich fans because Gregory had become an FC Zurich fan in the two years when he lived here by himself. Many would spit on Hardturm as they walked by. Several would stop and piss on the wall. That Gregory would join the pissers went without saying. As he buttoned up and rejoined Henry and me, he shouted, "Saving that up for the fucking Grasshoppers since I woke up." A couple of 20-year-olds cheered and clapped him on the back.

The walk was about a mile, give or take. There was singing led by the leaders. There was always a jackass or two with some firecrackers, just to make sure everyone knew they were there, and the smell of gunpowder filled the air. As we walked in a great amorphous pack, Henry got to talking with a couple of the pyrotechnic conspirators who apparently knew of a couple of extra-large steel trash cans in a pen next to one of the buildings up ahead. Henry followed them. He shouted over to us, "Back in a sec. Just studying the native culture." His departure gave Gregory and I a minute to ourselves.

"Anything?" I asked him.

"Silence," he said.

"How long has it been?"

"Eight days, nine, I don't know."

The information from Fritz Ritter was the most important we had sent, and it wasn't even close. My hand shook, just a bit, as I wrote the message, and then edited to make it shorter, then edited it again. Gregory, too, seemed just a bit hesitant on the Morse key.

This is what I finally settled on: "Highest source says G invasion plan changed. Now targets Ardennes, not H and B. No date yet. Please advise."

I hoped that "highest source," a term I had never used, would indicate it was Ritter. There was no way we were sending his name, no matter how secret the code. I didn't even tell Gregory who it came from, other than that the source was of the highest caliber, and unimpeachable.

"Why can't you tell me?" he said.

"Come on, I'm protecting you -- and the source."

"Nobody's going to torture me unless it's for the shit that comes out of my kitchen."

"This isn't a game, Gregory."

"Hell, I know that. But..."

I think he knew there were risks, but he always tried to dismiss them. Sometimes, he needed reminding, which is why, I assumed, his voice trailed off.

We received the dash-dash-dot reply almost immediately, the single letter G. So we knew they had received it. But, as before, Groucho and his bosses in London were offering no replies, no further instructions. Part of me thought that this might just be how it worked. But if this were a real intelligence operation, wouldn't there be subsequent leads to follow or other sources of information to target? Why wouldn't I be involved? Or was I just a conduit?

Standing there within a football mob, both of us wondering, there came a great, percussive boom that startled both of us -- not shit-yourself startled, more like heart-skips-a-beat startled. Henry reappeared seconds later.

"My ears are ringing," Henry said. He was shouting. "Like, really ringing." He oddly seemed as happy as Gregory had been on the tram.

We continued walking. There were several amateur artists carrying thick pieces of chalk who would affix the letters FCZ on many available wall spaces, much to the consternation of the apartment superintendents along the route. One dumped a bucket of water on one of the calligraphers, which would make for an uncomfortable rest of the afternoon for the gentleman in question. Then again, this presumed he could still feel anything. Given the number of empty beer bottles that stood like sentries on the curbstones, one could only wonder. All of this was watched by a small squadron of police who formed human barricades at several intersections, not to confront anyone or stop any of the vandalism, just to make sure the mob was funneled in the proper direction.

Grasshoppers were the posh team, and FC Zurich was the working-class team, which made Gregory's an easy choice when he arrived in 1936. It's funny. Back in Vienna, he left the Hutteldorf neighborhood -- real working men, real people -- when he had the opportunity to bring his "business" inside the Ringstrasse and to claim that upper-class territory for himself. He liked what that said about him and his family. But at the same time, he never gave up his tickets to the SK Rapid games in the old neighborhood. Henry talked about growing into adulthood in the rowdy standing terrace of the Pfarrwiese, Rapid's home ground. He marked the first time his father allowed him to stand with the men as his father's first acknowledgment that was an adult. "He taught me to shoot a pistol two years before that, but it wasn't until the terrace at Pfarrwiese," Henry would say, and actually get a little misty.

So FC Zurich it would be. As we walked, Gregory was inhaling beer out of a bottle that one of his new best friends had provided -- his people, his team. And he was a true and rabid fan, even though the side was terrible, relegated to the second division, with no chance at all in the game coming up against the Grasshoppers.

When we first arrived in Zurich -- Henry, Liesl and I -- the football team was the only thing that really got Gregory going, got him engaged. But there was something else now, as only I knew.

"Hey," Gregory said. He was leaning in and whispering into my left ear, not that it would seem to matter, given that Henry was still digging into his ears, one at a time, as if he were mining wax. The ringing obviously had not stopped.

"Hey," he said, again. "I was thinking, maybe we should send another message to London, just to remind them we're still here."

"Sounds a little needy," I said. "A girl would never respect that if you tried it."

"Like you're such an expert at relationships," Gregory said. He obviously knew that Manon and I were kaput, and so did Henry, but I refused to talk about it, and they gave up asking after a couple of days.

"Okay," I said. "Let me think. Some of it does seem kind of needy. But there's also at least a little danger of being discovered every time we transmit. It doesn't make sense to send needless messages."

"Needy and needless. Your vocabulary is quite limited today."

"Fuck you, old man." I put my left arm around Gregory and my right arm around Henry, and we walked in the midst of the throng, singing the club song. At this point, I even knew the second verse.

Once inside Letzigrund, Gregory's wisdom played out before us. The final score was Grasshoppers 3, FC Zurich 0, and the game probably wasn't that close. The walk over from Hardturm had easily been the best part of the afternoon.

31

L iesl was due in about two months, and she had begun to waddle more than walk. The library wasn't a half-mile from the cafe, but she said she stopped at least twice to rest when she walked to and from work. Henry offered to drive her, but she said the exercise was good for the baby. Still, for all of the talk of the glow of motherhood, Liesl looked like hell.

We had gotten through our last couple of conversations without her bringing up Manon. But let's just say that the third time was not the charm. I didn't have any bank paperwork with me -- this was just going to be dinner and out for me -- and when she sat down with a glass of milk and a piece of chocolate cake to join me, we talked mostly about the baby and how Henry seemed less hapless and more assured about fatherhood.

We both loved him, and we expressed our love by lovingly shit-talking him behind his back. And so, when Liesl said, "At least he's stopped practicing the drive to the hospital and timing it down to the second," my natural reply was, "He was probably shaking so much from the nerves that he dropped the stopwatch."

We were doing fine, and the dishes had been cleared, and I was getting ready to make my excuses.

"Don't go," Liesl said. She looked at her watch. It was just past 8 p.m.

"Early night for me." I reached for my coat on the rack next to the booth.

"I wish you would stay."

"Why is that?"

"Because Manon might be stopping in." She just blurted it out, seeing no other way to get me to stop. She apparently had not thought this through.

"Might be?" My voice had risen several decibels. One of the fossils looked in our direction, just for a second.

"Calm down," she said. It was more a hiss than a statement.

"Why can't you leave this alone? Why can't you leave me alone?" I shucked my arms into the sleeves of my coat and began buttoning.

"Because I care about both of you, and whatever happened can't be all that bad. You have to be able to fix it."

"Have you ever considered that it might be that bad? Have you ever thought for one damn second that I don't want to fix it?" And with that, I kept walking, away from the pregnant matchmaker and out into the Zurich night.

It was still early, and it was Thursday, and I remembered that I had not checked the MCMIX fountain since Monday. It was in the wrong direction from my flat, but it was only about 10 minutes away, and I had energy and anger to burn. It must have been 20 degrees, maybe lower, and the wind cut. I hated scarves but had taken to wearing one in the previous few weeks. On this night, I was more than glad -- scarf, collar up, hat secure, head ducked into the wind, eyes slightly tearing up. It was from the cold, I knew, not any thoughts about Manon. I really was done. It was only natural that I would still get upset at Liesl's meddling, but I really was done. I did wonder, though, why Manon had agreed to come to the cafe. Perhaps Liesl had assured her that I was out of town or something.

The moon was full, the light shimmering off of the lake. It was cold enough that the path around the lake was empty, the typical nightly dog-walker undoubtedly setting for a quick smoke for himself and a quick piss for Sparky in the alley behind his flat. And standing there at the fountain, standing quite alone, I saw two yellow chalk marks. I didn't know if two meant something different than one, because Brodsky and I hadn't worked that out. My first thought was that the extra mark signified some elevated level of urgency, but I didn't really know. Whatever it meant, I figured, it wasn't even 8:30, and maybe it was urgent. Bellevueplatz, where a handful of tram lines came together, was only a couple of hundred yards away. I would be at the bar, the Barley House, in 15 or 20 minutes.

32

The tram ran north and west of the old town and ended up on Limmatstrasse, parallel to the river and about a block away. This was working-class Zurich, and there was no more honest work -- God's work, some would say -- than working in a brewery. In this case, it was the Lowenbrau brewery, a red brick fortress which we passed on the right just before reaching my stop, Escher-Wyssplatz. Lowenbrau was more than drinkable, much more than the Feldschlösschen piss that was sold seemingly everywhere in the city. Lowenbrau also was superior to Hurlimann, another local, a semi-piss on the official Alex Kovacs rating scale.

The Barley House was, as Brodsky had said, right outside of the tram stop. I got off the train and looked to see if anyone was following. No one was -- I was the only departing passenger, just as I had been the only person getting on the tram at Bellevueplatz. So far, so good.

The bar was, as Brodsky had said, jammed with men wearing blue coveralls with a little Lowenbrau crest on the breast. The second shift was likely on its lunch break. If I had to guess, the brewery staggered the break times, as there was a group of workers leaving and heading back to the brewery just as another group was arriving, several of them shoveling down the last of their sandwiches at the door. A two-minute walk in each direction left 26 minutes available for the purposes of hydration, and the Barley House was quite available.

Inside, a layer of smoke about a foot thick was clearly visible along the ceiling, even in the dim light. The walls were once white, probably, but were by then covered with the brownish stain of a million cigarettes. The floor was sticky. But the time from order to mug-in-hand was perhaps 30 seconds, which made up for the amenities. So armed, my search for Brodsky began, and I wended my way through and around the knots of brewery workers, most of whom were standing. The search, too, took about 30 seconds, as Brodsky and I were two black swans in a heaving sea of blue coveralls. He was sitting at a small table off by himself, the last one before the toilets.

"Quaint, isn't it?" he said. I could barely hear him.

"It's a shithole and a goldmine, a rare combination." I had leaned over and was nearly shouting in his ear. The notion that anyone could possibly overhear our conversation was out of the question. Brodsky had chosen well.

"The owner is a friend, and you're right -- they print money. They're only closed two hours a day, between 2 a.m. and 4 a.m., when they hose down the floor, and open all of the windows, and try to clear the fug. He is just a neighborhood guy, but he actually owns a chalet near St. Moritz. But he never can get away."

"He must have to burn his clothes every night," I said. Then I theatrically sniffed the air. Picturing the owner of this place, sitting by the fire at a ski resort, sharing a fondue pot with the Duke and Duchess of Something-or-Other, was too absurd to consider. I actually chuckled out loud.

"What's so funny?" Brodsky said.

"I don't know. Life."

He scolded me for not checking the fountain for chalk marks. The reason there were two marks, he said, was because he left one on Monday and a second one on Wednesday.

"I've been drinking here four straight nights now," he said. "My liver isn't made for this. Or my lungs."

"So what's so urgent?"

"Only the fate of the free fucking world."

"So the non-Soviet part?"

"Let's agree to argue about dialectical materialism another time," he said. "At a quieter place, with proper drinks. And maybe a fire. Now just listen."

Brodsky leaned in closer and began telling a story that, as it turned out, I already knew. It was the same story Fritz Ritter had told me in the bar in Liechtenstein -- well, pretty much the same story. The critical point was the same -- that the German attack would come through the Ardennes, and not until at least April because of the weather. The reason he offered was different, though.

"There was a little plane crash," he said. "Two guys in a tiny plane, the one guy carrying the German invasion plans. He was supposed to be dropped off in Cologne or something, but the plane veered off-course and crashed in Belgium. Apparently, the guy tried to burn the plans before the Belgians caught him, and he thinks he succeeded. But the Germans don't believe him.

"He was carrying the original plan, to get to France through Holland and Belgium. So Hitler demanded something different."

Brodsky's was a more exciting tale, but the end result was identical to Ritter's, and that was the important thing. Without tipping off my source, I then leaned in and told Brodsky what Ritter had told me. He sat silently for a second. He looked kind of hurt.

"What?" I said.

"Why didn't you tell me before now?"

The truth was, I had never thought about telling him because, well, I had never thought about it. Ritter was our guy, and he was too valuable to risk by sharing the info too widely, even though I wasn't sure exactly how it would be a risk.

"I thought the deal was, I would share information that directly affected the Soviet Union," I said.

"And this doesn't?"

"No, not directly. Hitler can't try to screw you guys until after he's done with France and England. It's not like that's going to happen tomorrow. I wasn't given a solid date for the invasion, either, not that it would matter much to Stalin. Well, not unless he was planning to fuck Hitler while he was busy in France."

"Ah, the pre-emptive fuck," Brodsky said. "It isn't a bad theory but, no, that isn't it. I just thought you would share it."

"I couldn't risk the source," I said.

We were quiet again, and in the silence was an agreement to disagree. The important thing was that we each had a second source for the German invasion plan -- and given Brodsky's background, and Ritter's connections, and the differing rationales in the two accounts, it seemed unlikely that the information originated with the same person. This was not a second parroting of the same information. No, this was confirmation.

"I have to get out of here -- like I said, my liver," Brodsky said. "You have one more and then go." Which is what I did. I don't know what it said about me, but I felt more excited than depressed that I was now in possession of a re-affirmation that Hitler was about to try to overrun France.

Luckily, the tram arrived within about five minutes, which meant I could still feel the tip of my nose when I got on, barely. I walked home and chose a route past Fessler's. It was nearly 10:30, and the door was locked. But a few lights were on, and I knocked softly on the glass.

Gregory was just finishing up, an apron tied around his waist, a white towel tossed over his shoulder. He unlocked the door, and let me in, and immediately commented on how bad I smelled. He made me take off my coat and hang it out the back door of the cafe before allowing me up the stairs to his apartment. There, we sent the new information to London. The reply arrived almost immediately. Dash, dash, dot.

33

The postcard was waiting for me at work about a week later. On the one hand, I was thrilled that Groucho had finally acknowledged the information we had sent and was ready to involve me in whatever was coming next. On the other hand, the picture on the postcard was of cold-assed Uetliberg, again. Wednesday at 2:30.

And so, as instructed, I took the train out to the mountain. Seeing as how Ruchti knew about our last meeting, and likely knew about this meeting, I didn't even bother much with the counter-surveillance rigamarole that I had begun to develop, like taking the tram one stop too far and walking back to the station. Besides, there wasn't another soul in my train car. On a Wednesday afternoon, in the first week in March, after a miserable winter that had yet to bless us with its final belch -- 34 degrees and light rain were on the day's menu -- who would even think about an outing to Uetliberg?

And so, I clambered up the iced-over path to the top, thankful that the gravel embedded in the ice somehow saved me from a pratfall. I considered the fact that I never once landed on my ass to be one of the great athletic feats of my life, second only to the time in 1914 when, at school, I won a head-to-head race against Bruno Sensenbrenner, a 100-yard dash organized by the faculty, thus gifting those in my grade having last names beginning with A-to-M a week off from physical education class. I was a hero for the rest of the term. Students I barely knew were suddenly clapping me on the back in the school hallway. If only they could see me now, lurching from one patch of gravel to the next. Back then was mere speed. This was pure athletic grace.

At the summit, it wasn't hard to find Groucho, mostly because there wasn't another person up there, not even the hot chocolate man. The first thing I said to him was, "Will you please get some different fucking postcards before you leave town this time?"

He responded by offering me a pull from his flask. I reached into my pocket and showed him my own, and we toasted the low cloud that hugged the mountaintop like a sweater. The drizzle had stopped but, looking out, you really couldn't see shit.

"So?' I said, and Groucho began. His bottom line was that the British and the French didn't believe the German invasion would come through the Ardennes. I exploded with a "you've got to be fucking kidding me," and he told me to calm down and repeat everything I knew, which I did. It took me a few minutes to get through the story from Ritter about Hitler being unimpressed with the original plan, and Manstein supplying the new one, and then the story from Brodsky about the plane crash and the original plans falling into the possession of the Belgians. Groucho took it all in, nodding a few times in seeming recognition, surprised by other details and making me repeat them. Then he took a long pull from the flash, a few drops dribbling out of the side of his mouth. He wiped it with his sleeve.

"Okay," he said. "The Manstein bit is new to us -- and that's from Ritter, yes?" I nodded.

"This is what we have," Groucho said. "We believe the plane

crash is the key element here. From the information that we have gathered, the plane crashed, and the officer tried to set fire to the plans before being captured. He was in some farm field, and a farmer even helped him with some matches, but they were captured before too much was burned up. Then they took them to a jail and left them alone with the plans for a few minutes, then the officer burned the shit out of his hands on a hot stove, trying to shovel the plans into the fire inside. They caught him, and the plans were pretty scorched, but they rescued enough of them to get the gist -- that they were coming through Holland and Belgium, very much like 1914."

"But your best source, a fucking Abwehr general, says it isn't true anymore," I said. "And my Russian confirms it. Why won't they believe it?"

"Because they don't think it's possible."

"Who exactly is they?"

"The French and British general staffs," Groucho said. "The truth is, they don't tend to agree on shit, but they agree on this."

"But why?" I was shouting at this point.

"They just don't see the Ardennes as a possibility. They say, 'The terrain is prohibitive.' If you look at a map, it's hard to argue."

I had looked at a map, but I also had looked Ritter in the eye. I couldn't believe they were dismissing his intelligence.

"This is what they think happened," Groucho said. "They see the Holland and Belgium route as the only one that makes sense militarily, given the obstacle of the Maginot Line. When the plane crashed, and we got the plans, it just confirmed what is sound military thinking. We tried to let it leak that the officer managed to burn up the plans and that we didn't really get much information. It's hard to know what the Germans believe about that. But the French and British see this Ardennes plan as misinformation from the Germans, to throw us off from the only plan that makes sense."

At which point, I completely exploded on Groucho.

"He's your best fucking agent," I said.

"Well, yes."

"And now I have confirmation from the Russian."

Groucho nodded.

"What am I not getting here? He's as good a source as you've ever had. He's been right about so many things. He's been right about fucking everything. He was right about Poland -- and you ignored him then."

"How do you know that?" Groucho said.

"How do you think?"

I stood there, cocooned in cloud on the top of Uetliberg, seething. I had agreed to do this, to run this risk, and now my information was being ignored. I mean, what was the point?

"Look," Groucho said. "I shouldn't tell you this, but we are a little concerned about Ritter?"

"Concerned how?"

"Not what you're thinking, not that he's turned on us. But we're worried that the Germans might have discovered that he has been working for us and are using him to send us false information."

"But why?"

"Because the Ardennes just doesn't make any sense -- how many times can I tell you? The people in charge of knowing about such things just don't believe it's possible to move a mechanized army into France on those windy roads through the woods. They consider the whole idea 'foolish.' That's what one of the Frogs supposedly called it. 'Foolish.'"

I was thinking about quitting on the spot -- the spying, the bank, all of it. I had enough money, and I had two passports, Czech and Swiss. I could go anywhere, as far away from this whole thing as I wanted to go. The truth was, I could steal a lot more from the bank than was in my account and be over the border before anyone knew. What were they going to do -- sue me?

"I don't know if I've ever told you this," Groucho said, "but it's dangerous to get too attached to any agent, even someone like Ritter. You need to know that. And besides, why are you defending him so strongly? I thought you believed he fucked you."

I had thought about this. I had thought about this a lot -- how Ritter had set me up in order to neutralize the Gestapo captain who suspected him of being a Czech agent, set me up and then rescued me. I had thought about it and come to terms with it. When I answered Groucho, I wasn't yelling anymore.

"I don't think he fucked me," I said. "But he did use me. But the more I have thought about it, I believe he used me for the right reasons. And I think he did intend to protect me if it went wrong. And in the end, he did protect me. In a rotten fucking business, that isn't a terrible set of facts."

We parted without a handshake or a plan to meet again. Groucho left first. I stared off into the gauze, emptying my flask. Then it was down the path for me, the descent even harder than the climb. About halfway down, I fell. The gravel tore through my pants and my drawers and ripped the skin of my ass. I felt through the hole in the cloth and then looked at my fingers. I was bleeding.

34

T he next night was First Thursday. Marc Wegens had become a regular no-show, which further led me to believe that Hitler was going to be in the neighborhood sooner rather than later and that Marc was running around under orders, from unit to unit, attempting to maximize the abilities of Switzerland's pop-gun army in any way he could. I wouldn't have minded talking to him about the Swiss theory of the case -- whether they really thought Hitler might invade their mountain-protected, enchanted land of chocolate and hard currency -- but he might have seen that as a bit intrusive, seeing as how Herman kind of believed that Marc knew I was a spy.

Whatever, he wasn't there. But Herman and Brodsky were, and getting shitfaced seemed to be on all three of our schedules for the evening. Dark did not begin to describe my mood, after what Groucho had told me. And after I told Herman and Brodsky that nobody believed what we had been told, it was a suitably morose threesome.

"So let me get this straight," Herman said. "You have information about the Ardennes being the invasion point from an excellent source with an impeccable history. And Brodsky has information from a source of his that confirms what your source told you. And they still don't believe it?"

"That's about the size of it," I said.

"Are they idiots? I mean, truly mentally deficient?"

"That's not it." Brodsky had been quiet, and he was still quiet, barely audible above the cheery background music, some big band I didn't recognize, lots of happy clarinets.

"They're not idiots," he said. "They're just so married to what they know that they can't accept that they might be wrong, that the thing they believed in for so long might not be true after all."

"But there's evidence," Herman said. "There's more than one piece of evidence. They each confirm the other."

Brodsky shook his head. "It's the curse of old men. They stop listening at some point. They stop learning. It's like they never opened a book after 1918. If it made sense then, it makes sense now. If it was smart then, it's still smart now."

"But it didn't fucking work the first time," I said. "Why do they think the Germans will try it the same way again?"

"It almost worked," Herman said. "Close enough to give it another go."

"But the sources? The information?"

"You're not listening -- the book is closed. The old men will not open it. How old is Gamelin? Sixty-what?"

"Sixty-seven -- I read it in the paper the other day," I said. "The story was all about the wisdom of the French high command, and listed all of his postings through the years."

"Sixty-seven, there you go," Brodsky said. "He probably made up his mind about things somewhere along the Somme, and he will never change."

"And the evidence be damned," Herman said.

"Experience becomes blinding," Brodsky said. "The three most dangerous words in any language, especially for a soldier, are 'I remember when...'"

In an effort to join Gamelin in his blindness, we rotated through rounds of each of our cocktails, first my Manhattans, then Herman's rye and ginger ales, and then Brodsky's vodka shots. The waiter just brought the bottle, and we emptied it by the end of the night.

Somewhere along the way, we began to debate whether or not it made sense for either Herman or Brodsky to publish what we knew about the German invasion, Herman in his magazine or Brodsky in the Finnish newspaper. We were talking more than thinking at that point, given our alcohol consumption, but even drunk, it seemed like a bad idea. Making the Ardennes possibility public would not be alerting any decision-makers to information that they didn't already possess -- the French and British already knew, and so did the Germans, obviously. All the publication would be doing was drawing attention to Herman and/or Brodsky, attention that would only make their further attempts at unearthing information more difficult.

As Herman said, "The last thing I need is even more Nazis up my ass. They look at me warily now, and keep half an eye on me -- I know all the Zurich legation guys at this point. They don't even try to hide it when they're watching me. But it's only half an eye. I don't need both eyes."

"I get that," I said. "And it's easy for me to say, seeing as how I'm not at risk if you publish. But if they're going to ignore the information we all get, what's the point? Don't we need to find a way to make a difference here?"

"You're kidding yourself, by the way," Brodsky said. "About not being at risk on this one. Let's say the Germans are playing your source, even a little bit. If his information gets published, you will be a link in the chain. You don't think they'll find out, but you don't know. The Gestapo is pretty good at finding things out. For all we know, they're outside in a big black Daimler right now, waiting for us to leave so they can make a report to whoever about the strange coincidence of the three of us being here together, all of us already on their radar."

I knew well about the Gestapo. I knew Brodsky was right. There was no such thing as not being at risk, not for me, not anymore. Not unless I bailed out and headed to Argentina, which had been on my mind all day after reading an article about it in the travel section of Neue Zürcher Zeitung.

"So we do nothing?" I said.

"We just keep doing what we're doing," Brodsky said. "And we hope that it matters in the end."

On the way back from a trip to the toilet, I bumped into a slender brunette, maybe 30 years old. I literally knocked her off of her shoes, and she grabbed me to keep from falling. My profuse apologies were likely adorable, as she invited me to join her and her two friends at a table on the other side of the cafe. My charm somehow supplanted my intoxication, apparently, as the two friends grabbed their coats and said their goodbyes soon after. I was too drunk to catch the signals that my girl, Angela was her name, had sent to her friends to hasten their exit. Maybe they were telepathic.

All I knew was that, as soon as the friends were out, I was in. It was about 1:30 a.m. when I got myself buttoned up and began the cold walk home from Angela's flat.

35

The next morning, I called Sophie Buhl from the office. Since the night we had spent together, we had missed each other a couple of times, partly because I felt so bad about Manon, partly because I had become sidetracked away from the Nazi gold business while collecting the Ardennes invasion information from Fritz Ritter, and then being ignored. But I didn't feel bad about Manon anymore, and the Nazi gold was all I had at the moment as far as a promising avenue of information-gathering.

When she said, "Come on over to the office at 2:30, I think I can find a towel to protect the couch in my boss's office," I was already 80 percent out of my hangover and confident of the rest of the distance. I did think about Manon, but just for a second. By 3:00, my second sex act with a second woman in a 15-hour period was complete. Walking back to the Bohemia Suisse, I decided to place a call to Paris to tell Leon, just so I could get it on record with someone who would appreciate the accomplishment. Predictably, he started by calling me an "amateur," and ended by saying, "My little boy, you're all grown up." It was good catching up, and I asked him what his newspaper and the rest were saying about war.

"They're not writing it, but we're fucked," Leon said.

"We? You've only been there a year."

"I was born to be a Frog," he said. "It's, I don't know, freer than Vienna. I can't imagine how much looser it is than tight-assed Zurich. I don't know how you stand it there. Although, twice in 15 hours --"

"What did you mean by fucked, though?"

"They love their army," he said. "But if you talk to people on the street, just in the bars and cafes, half of the rich people are kind of rooting for the Nazis -- they won't lift a finger against Hitler. As for the rest, I'd say half of them would rather the country go to the Communists -- and they're never going to fight anybody. So, fucked."

I did that math in my head after we hung up. Half of the country in a reasonable state of mind, a quarter Fascist, a quarter Communist. Even if the numbers were a little bit off, it didn't add up to French success under normal circumstances, and it especially didn't add up to success if the thinking of the military leadership was cemented in 1918.

I had placed the call without Marta's assistance, which annoyed her. A few minutes after the call, she marched into the office with the diary pressed to her bosom. Her style of walking always told me what I was in for, and there really were only two possibilities. A whistling sashay meant I had screwed up some-thing and she was there to fix it. Marching meant annoyed. Those were my two choices, and this was marching.

"How was your call?" she said.

"Fine, thanks." I was offering no details, and she couldn't leave the office without having regained the upper hand in our relationship, so she put down the diary and began paging for something-or-other that I had messed up. I stopped her.

"Tomorrow, that thing with Greitzinger, you're going to have to reschedule it."

"It's not a thing. It's the closing of that Bierman deal. You remember -- big building, nice profit for the bank."

"It's not that big, and the profit isn't that nice," I said. We were providing something like 1/64th of the financing of a seven-story office building a couple of blocks off of Bahnhof-strasse.

"There are attorneys involved. They'll be quite angry."

"They'll get over it. We can do it next week. You pick the time."

"Why do you have to cancel?"

"Meeting in Bern," I said.

"A new client?"

"A big new client," I said. She was pulling out her pen and preparing to write a new entry in the diary.

"Very big? Name of?"

"Sorry, that's confidential," I said.

"Confidential? This isn't Bankverein, for God's sake. It's you and me. I see everything. What does confidential even mean?"

"It means that this is a private bank, and that it's my job to find the clients, and that this client is seeking the utmost discretion as he considers our services, and that until he's ready to sign the papers and back up an armored car full of his money, it's confidential."

There was nothing Marta could say in reply.

"Confidential means just me and him." I was enjoying this thoroughly.

She stood up, snatched the diary off of my desk, and marched out. I almost never got the pleasure of seeing the reverse-march, which meant that she was still pissed and had not, in fact, regained the upper hand. It was a glorious sight. I stared at her walking out as if she possessed a backside worth staring at, which she did not. At least, you couldn't tell, given the gray flannel tents that Marta favored for office wear.

I shouted, "Don't worry, I'll make the train reservation myself," and received not so much as a growl in reply. What a day.

Then I thought about Sophie's backside -- you're not responsible for where your mind goes, you know. And then I wondered about what I would find the next night in Bern, where Sophie had told me that her boss and the big Nazi were meeting again.

36

It was just past 5 p.m. when Marta marched in again, this time wearing her overcoat and hat. She carried a stack of mail, the afternoon post. She usually had it on my desk by 3, and I couldn't resist.

"Was the postman late today?" I said.

She dropped the pile on my desk, literally dropped it from about a foot. The letters scattered but didn't spill off of the side. But the one on top did flip over. It was sealed with a circle of red wax that had been melted on the flap, which was beyond formal and archaic. The last time I had received a letter sealed with wax, it was back in Vienna, an invitation to a fancy wedding where the reception was held in the old Royal Apartments.

Marta snatched up the envelope as if her real purpose was straightening the stack. She handed it to me and said, "Well, aren't we special. 'Personal and confidential.' Well, well."

That's what it said on the front, in the bottom right corner, 'Personal and confidential.' But that wasn't what got the majority of my attention. Neither was it the decidedly feminine writing, nor the faint whiff of perfume that hung in the air. There was no doubt that the wax, and the writing, and especially the smell, were what grabbed Marta's attention.

The first thing that stood out for me was the postmark. It was severely smudged, but it looked like Liechtenstein. I don't know if Marta saw that or not -- you really could barely read it. I wasn't 100 percent sure where it was from, to be truthful. But what I really couldn't stop staring at was the return address, preprinted on the envelope. The letter had been written on hotel stationery. The hotel was the Torbrau in Munich.

Marta stood over me as I held the letter and considered. There was no way I was going to open it in her presence, though, a fact that she realized after about 10 seconds of me just staring at the envelope. For the second time, I was treated to the reverse-march.

"Have a wonderful night," I called out, as sweetly as I could. She did not reply, never even breaking stride.

The Torbrau in Munich. I had never stayed there. I had never seen it, I was pretty sure. I had only heard it mentioned one time. It was when Fritz Ritter was telling me the story of the time he and my Uncle Otto first met.

It was in the 1920s, and both were middle-aged bachelors who happened to travel a lot for work, and who happened to find themselves one night sitting on adjacent bar stools at the Torbrau. One drink led to another, and the two of them decided to venture out into the night in search of whatever. In this case, whatever arrived in the personages of a pair of sisters. Back in the flat shared by said sisters, before anything really interesting happened, Ritter and my uncle and the girls found themselves on their knees, half-dressed, peeking out of the windows and observing the start of what would later come to be called the Beer Hall Putsch, the failed coup that nonetheless led to Adolf Hitler becoming a household name in Germany.

So, there was no question who the letter was from, handwriting and perfume aside. Ritter had made that obvious, if only to me, which was the point, after all. I looked at it, held it, tapped its side on my desk blotter. At the front door, though, Anders was still at his post, bouncing on the balls of his feet, apparently waiting for me to leave. I walked out and sent him home, telling him I had some paperwork. He offered to stay. I insisted, and then I locked the door behind him.

The letter, in the same feminine hand as the envelope -- I wonder who Ritter got to write it? -- was a mundane, it-was-wonderful-seeing-you-again kind of note. It was benign, dull even. It began with "Dearest Alex," and the signature was "Fondly, Clarice." It could have been written by an old maiden aunt.

I left the letter on my desk and walked out to the lobby to jiggle the front door again. It was still locked. Returning to my office, I pulled down the window shades. In my bottom right drawer, there was a candle and some matches. Groucho had taught me what he called the "half-assed, quick-quick" version of revealing secret writing on a letter. As he said, "It wouldn't fool a professional, but 90 percent of the time, you don't have to. We have invisible inks that we use, and constantly update, that can only be revealed by a special reagent. We change them every month, probably. But this is quick-and-dirty."

"Ninety percent, huh?" I said.

"The other 10 percent of the time, they slit your throat," he said. "Kidding. Kidding. If the letter is mailed in Germany, you have to be more careful -- because the Gestapo reads everything they can. Outside, though, police and intelligence officers in other countries don't have the manpower or the urgency that the Krauts do. So this is good enough."

What you did was light the candle and run the flame back and forth over the underside of the letter, close enough to scorch the paper but not to set the thing on fire. And if there were secret writing between the regular lines of the letter, it would be revealed if it had been written with water. I didn't believe it until Groucho showed me, but it did work. And there in my office, as I passed the letter back and forth over the flame, words began to appear between the lines of the existing letter.

The message:

Vogl is back with the Gestapo. He was in Poland with them during the invasion. He is now part of a unit that is likely headed west. We both need to be careful.

Suddenly, my wondrous day, with its two sexual encounters and two views of Marta reverse-marching out of my office, was over.

Vogl. Shit.

37

I decided to drive to Bern. The roads were good, and so was the weather, finally. The 75 miles would take maybe two hours, and that was if I took my time. I needed to clear my head and, for some reason, the open road helped more than the train. It would help to have the car, too, in case I had to follow Big Ears and The Mole who knows where. Or maybe, if nothing were happening, I would just commute, and sleep in my own bed, and maybe hide underneath the covers.

Vogl. Shit.

Werner Vogl was the Gestapo captain who I tried to kill in 1938. He was responsible for my Uncle Otto's death, even if he wasn't the one who pushed him off of the bridge and into the Rhine. He used Otto in an attempt to gain information on Ritter, information that Otto did not have. But Vogl didn't care -- he tortured Otto in the basement of the Gestapo's headquarters building in Cologne, and then either he or his people shoved Otto's bruised body into the river. Vogl did that, and I might have been next, had I not decided to kill him instead, an absurd notion that would have worked. But then Ritter interceded, using me as a pawn in an elaborate scheme to frame Vogl as a traitor to the Reich before Vogl could prove the same thing about him.

Ritter's plan worked, and Vogl was theoretically headed to Dachau, or worse. When I asked him if it wouldn't have been better just to let me kill him, Ritter said, "No, it wouldn't work. I mean, first off, we couldn't count on you following through -- and I was running out of time. We couldn't afford it if you chickened out. But more than that, killing Vogl wouldn't solve the problem -- it would just put it off. If he's dead, his replacement just picks up his old cases. But if he's disgraced, and found guilty of fabricating evidence against me to preserve his dirty secrets, the case is closed. Nobody's going near me now."

Except something happened between then and now. Mostly, a war happened -- and, well, time heals all disgraces when the bullets start flying. Vogl was a smart guy, and organized, and ruthless -- all of the things a good Gestapo man should be. He also had been right about Ritter, and his suspicions about me hadn't been far off. He probably did a little time in a camp somewhere -- but a nice camp, or the nice part of a bad camp. Or, if he had a patron, maybe he just got stripped of his command of the station in Cologne and sent to shuffle paper in the file room in Berlin for a few months. And once the shooting started, well, who knows what evil stood watch in Himmler's heart, and how Vogl might have been a useful instrument.

He should have just let me kill him -- which is easy enough for me to say now. I was ready to do it, in an alley behind a bar where Vogl played his weekly chess game. As the cops say in the movies, I had motive, means, and opportunity -- the means was going to be Otto's old knife, a cliche, but I didn't care. I had always been more of a thinker than a doer, and a bit of a physical coward besides, but I had worked out the details of the plan, and it was a sound plan, and I was literally seconds away from doing it when Ritter intervened. Now, a lot can happen in a few seconds, but I had whipped up a mental rage, a noise in my head, and I really didn't think I was going to back down. I was going to do it. I was. I might or might not have killed people during the war -- who knew, from hundreds of yards away? -- but this was going to be for real, and for Otto.

But it didn't happen, and now Vogl was on the loose. And suddenly the shittiest thought crossed my mind -- that I was hoping the Germans' western invasion would arrive soon because Vogl-in-battle would not have the opportunity to be Vogl-the-investigator. He wouldn't have the chance to settle up his old accounts.

That was pretty much all I thought about during the drive. I left at 12:30 and actually broke the ride in half, stopping for lunch at a half-timbered roadside inn -- sliced liverwurst, buttered pumpernickel, pickles, pilsner. It was kind of a dead time of day when I arrived in Bern, and I lucked into a parking spot on the street, almost right in front of the Bellevue Palace's front door. I walked around and window-shopped in town for a while, mostly to kill time but a little bit to see if I was being followed somehow. I stopped, reversed direction a couple of times, checked out the reflection in a few store windows, and nothing. If anybody gave a shit that I was in Bern, they were doing it from a very, very discreet distance.

Right about 5, I entered the hotel and headed for the front desk. I asked if Herr Steiner was a guest because I wanted to leave him a note. If the answer was yes, I had an old business card ready to hand over, with the words "Call me, G" written on the back -- so old that its original bearer, Gerhard Gruen, had since taken a heart attack and retired to the great depositary vault in the sky. But as it turned out, the big Nazi was not registered at the hotel.

I figured I would give it two hours in the lobby bar. I took the same table as the last time, ordered the same Manhattan, and settled in. The place was dead. I found myself staring up at the design on the glass dome above me, almost hypnotized by it. I barely noticed when Peter Ruchti joined me with the admonition, "Close your mouth, you look like a goddamned tourist."

I wondered if he had been following me. Fuck it, I just asked him.

"Don't flatter yourself," he said.

"So, just a coincidence?"

"You're the one who's in my bar, buddy. What coincidence?"

"Your bar? I thought you couldn't afford to drink here."

"I can't. That's why the banker with the salary out the ass is buying."

A minute later, two more Manhattans arrived -- Ruchti must have signaled the waiter while my eyes were aloft. We drank in silence for a good while. There was only one other table occupied, an older couple having a cocktail before dinner, in all likelihood. The music coming from the lobby piano was the only ambient noise until the words just started to burst from Ruchti.

"I don't know what you're playing at," he said.

I just looked at him.

"This isn't some fucking game."

I did my best to appear bored.

"Look -- you're up to something. You know it, I know it. I mean, come on -- you spend more time on Uetliberg than a champion yodeler. You get mysterious envelopes sealed in wax -- no, we didn't open it. You're not big enough for us to bother with, not yet. But we're not the only ones who have noticed."

At this, my face must have betrayed something.

"You're an amateur -- you know that, right?" Ruchti said. "We just had an amateur who ended up with a bullet through his eye, you might remember. When that happens, my boss gets up my ass. My entire job is to make sure nobody else ends up lying in a pool of blood on Rennweg. That's why they pay me the big money."

"The big money?" I said. "So you're buying the next round."

"You don't get it," he said. "How many times can I say this -- it isn't a game. Hitler's boys aren't kidding around. They don't want to make us uncomfortable here in the great neutral Switzerland, but they'll do what they deem necessary. And another thing. You might have sensed that I'm not a big fan of bankers."

"Yeah, I got that."

"Well, I can't prove this, but I sometimes believe that, shall we say, representatives of Swiss banking interests occasionally also drink in this bar, with me and the Germans and the French and the British and the Chinese and whoever else."

"What?" This had never dawned on me as a possibility.

"My job is to keep track of the players and do everything I can to make sure none of them ends up dead -- or at least not dead on Swiss soil. Because too many dead bodies could lead to diplomatic incidents with unexpected consequences. In case you haven't gotten it by now, the bankers here in Switzerland don't make money off of unexpected consequences. They're not looking for the big score. They make money by rote, by taking a tiny piece of a million transactions, by grubby certainty covered up by a starched collar. My boss has a saying: 'We don't care if the game is dirty as long as the playing field remains clean.'"

Ruchti got up to leave, and I suddenly needed to get out, too. I paid for the drinks and decided to drive home. He hadn't scared me, but Ruchti had widened my field of vision in a way that I hadn't expected. I needed to think some more. It was as if checkers had become chess.

I got in the car. After only about a second, I realized that I smelled Manon even before she said my name from the floor of the back seat.

38

If Ruchti had been following me, I never saw him. If Manon had been following me, I never saw her. I really must have been an amateur.

She got out of the back seat, opened the driver's side door and told me to move over.

"Or else?" I attempted to adopt as much of an assholish tone as I could, and I think I did pretty well.

"Just slide over," she said. Her tone was warmer.

There were a dozen things I thought about saying. Part of me was furious. A smaller part of me was intrigued. A much smaller part of me saw the quick half-smile on her face as I slid my ass over the leather bench of the front seat and melted. What the fuck?

Which is what I ended up saying. "What the fuck?"

"We're going for a drive," she said. "And I'm driving."

"Where?"

"Basel?"

"What's there?"

"You'll see."

"Why now?"

"Has to be now," she said.

"This is bullshit--"

"Alex, please shut up. I'm trying to make this up to you."

"That's not possible."

"Maybe, maybe not," Manon said. "But let me try."

She started the car, and we headed north. I slid as far to the right in the car seat as I could, leaning against the door. There were a good two feet between us.

It was past 6 p.m. and dark, but Manon drove confidently and without a map. I had made the drive before. It was a little more than 60 miles, and it was actually pretty nice in the summer. In the winter, though, the fog was persistent, and you usually couldn't see shit. At night, you really couldn't see shit. We went through St. Ursanne, a little medieval town that I remembered as being very charming, and then up past a couple of viewing points along the road where people routinely pulled over in the summer so they could gawk. But we just drove, the dark road interrupted by the occasional hamlet, mostly in silence.

What the hell was this all about? It was the question that kept circulating through my consciousness. I had been over Manon -- 90 percent over her. Well, maybe 75 percent. But I was getting there. The whole spying thing, when you think about it, is pretty damned dehumanizing. You're in the information-gathering business, and you use people to acquire the information, and then you dispose of the people because the information is paramount -- because the information is being gathered in service of The Cause, and The Cause is the most important thing of all, the reason you agreed to take the risks you're taking. The people are incidental.

I knew that, but I never understood it, not deep down, not until Manon, not until she used me the way she did. I had begun to rationalize it, that I was going to have to learn sometime, and that I would be a better spy because of it -- a crappier person but a better spy. And, well, with Hitler, with everything, you couldn't convince me that anything else could be the most important thing.

My mind raced. She broke the silence.

"How have you been?" she said.

"Splendid."

"No, really."

"Yes, really."

Then silence, again. Soon, we were in Basel. If Bern was sleepy, Basel was its drowsy twin, about the same size but close enough to the German and French borders that you could smell them both. If Bern was mostly about the government, Basel was mostly about the university, which made it marginally more interesting. The nightlife in the few blocks right around the school undoubtedly was a bit more robust, but as we drove through the streets, all was buttoned-up and closed down. It wasn't even 10 p.m.

Manon maneuvered the car easily, again as if she were more than familiar with the route. For a while, it was as if she was taking evasive action, circling one particular part of the city and then going the wrong way down a one-way street. It was only about 200 feet, little wider than an alley, but the direction was clearly marked.

"Are we being followed?" I said.

"Just being careful."

"So, no."

"I don't think so," she said.

Her tone was not entirely convincing. In a minute, though, she seemed satisfied enough that we parked in another alley. It was like we were in a tunnel, a dark tunnel. There were no overhead lights. We had a view of the back of some building. It looked like a loading dock of some kind, and it was well-lit. But it literally was the light at the end of the tunnel. She parked and turned off the car's lights, and we were likely invisible from either end of the 500-foot alley, about equidistant from the streets at either end.

"Now what?" I said.

"Now we wait," she said.

She sighed, leaned her head back, closed her eyes.

"If you fall asleep, what happens then?"

"I won't. But if I do, you'll know when it happens."

"When what happens?" I said.

She reached into her handbag and handed me a small leather case. Inside was a set of binoculars, as tiny as I had ever seen.

"Amuse yourself if you want," she said.

"These are something," I said. I turned them over in my right hand. They weren't much bigger than the palm. "Swiss precision?"

"Okay, they're good at binoculars. But that's all."

She closed her eyes again, this time with another of her half-smiles. I continued to lean against the door on my right. The distance between us was still about two feet, as big as I could make it.

Fiddling with the focus wheel between the eyepieces, I was quickly able to get a clear, sharp view of what was, indeed, a loading dock. I also was able to read the small sign on the wall to the right of the gate. From our lair in the alley, I was looking at the back of Basel's Swiss national bank building.

39

"There's movement," I said. It must have been an hour later. The night was still quiet, but an outer gate was being opened in the back of the bank, and an inner barrier was being lifted. Two guards carrying rifles watched the other two work out the mechanics. They all wore blue blazers and gray slacks.

I reached over, nudged Manon awake, and then resumed my distance. She barely stirred.

"Tell me what you see," she said, and I did.

"Tell me if you recognize anybody," she said, and I didn't.

If she opened her eyes, I didn't catch it. I followed up with a spare narration of what I was seeing. Gates open, the four blazers stood and chatted, apparently waiting for something. After about five minutes, it arrived -- an armored car, not enormous but big enough. It sat low to the ground, no doubt straining the shock absorbers. It just looked heavy more than anything. And from the front right fender, a small German flag sat limply on a short pole.

"Nazis in the house," Manon said. "Showtime."

She was awake now, but there was still an exhaustion about her. She seemed beaten somehow. She caught me looking at her and pointed toward the front windshield, and the bank beyond it.

"Keep looking," she said. "And you haven't seen anybody that you recognize yet?"

I had not. The armored car was just sitting there. Then, out of the passenger side door came a man in a business suit. I couldn't tell who it was until he turned and appeared as if he were looking directly at our car in the alley, and at me. It was Matthias Steiner, the big Nazi.

As if he were waiting for Steiner to show himself first, a door of the bank opened, and the blue blazers were joined by a suit of their own. It was Jan Tanner, a.k.a. Big Ears.

"Fuck," I said. "Is this what I think it is?"

"It is," Manon said. "This is how it works. This is how the fucking Swiss are going to win Hitler the war."

It was nothing special, just a mechanical process, but I was transfixed. Back-when, I had unloaded delivery trucks as part of a summer job I had at Gregory's restaurant in Vienna, and there was nothing particularly exciting about it -- produce in the kitchen, liquor in the storage room behind the bar, and hurry the hell up, will you? But this was gold, and this was the banality of evil, and I had to watch.

Steiner handed Tanner some paperwork, keeping one sheet. In turn, after peeling off a sheet for himself, Tanner gave the rest of the paper to one of the blazers. And then the process began, just a simple transfer of small, obviously heavy boxes that two blazers wrestled onto a wheeled dolly that they struggled to push up a small ramp and then into the bank.

I didn't know how much gold was in each box, and I didn't bother counting the boxes, but there were several dozen. Tanner and Steiner counted, though. Steiner used a pencil to make tick marks on his copy of the paperwork. The whole thing didn't take 15 minutes and, when the last of the gold was inside, Tanner and Steiner each signed the paperwork -- first Steiner's copy, then Tanner's copy, then the blazer's copy.

After watching all of this in silence, I turned to look at Manon. The exhaustion I had sensed earlier had turned into something else. I caught her just as she was wiping away a tear.

"Goddamn it," she said, reaching into her purse and beginning to rifle through it. I reached into my pocket and started to hand her my clean handkerchief, but she looked at it as if it were covered in fresh snot.

"No," she said. "No, damn it." Inside the purse, she found the sheet of paper she had been looking for and handed it to me.

It was written on the national bank's letterhead, addressed to Steiner, signed by Tanner. It contained the terms of the transaction.

"How'd you get this?" I said.

"I didn't have to sleep with anybody if that's what you're asking," she said. "Let's just say that Herr Tanner isn't always very careful with his trash."

It was all right there, the figures in neat columns.

To unload: 0.03 pro mille

To place on deposit: 0.015 pro mille

To dispatch: 0.9 pro mille

"They get paid coming and going," Manon said. "They get paid to accept it, to hold onto it, and to ship it. Bastards don't miss a fucking trick."

The tears had given way to anger now.

"Goddamn it." She knew better than to yell, and so her whisper seemed unusually harsh, bitter.

"You know how this works, right?" she said.

"I have some idea."

"Well, here it is, exactly -- well, we think. The Swiss take the gold in here. You see how they're all still standing there? They're waiting for a briefcase to be brought out from inside. It's full of Swiss francs in large denominations -- you might not have seen it, but Steiner's guy went inside at the start to count it. It'll be a pretty big bag, enough to hold a couple of million francs."

"This seems kind of, I don't know, small-time?" I said. "Shouldn't this be handled by wire transfers or something?"

"Nope. It's just this. They show up with a truck full of gold, and they leave with a bag full of money."

"Okay, then what?"

"Here's how it works," she said. "Let's say Germany needs to buy wolfram from Portugal."

"What the hell is wolfram?"

"An industrial metal. They use it in armaments. Portugal is lousy with it. And because they're officially neutral, they'll sell it to anybody. But here's their problem: the gold. Nazi gold is no good to them because other countries won't take it for the stuff the Portuguese need to buy. Nazi gold, Austrian gold, Czech gold, and any other gold the Germans manage to steal from Poland or wherever -- Portugal doesn't want any of it."

"Isn't gold just gold? How does anybody even know where it's from?"

"The bars are marked. Stamped, with a mark from the country of origin and maybe some kind of serial number."

"So?"

"So," Manon said. She pointed at the bank. "That's where these assholes come in. They take the Nazi gold that nobody else will touch, and they give the Nazis Swiss francs in return. You've heard the phrase 'good as gold,' right? Well, that's the Swiss franc. So the Germans buy their wolfram, or whatever, from Portugal, and they pay them from the suitcase full of Swiss francs. And then the Portuguese turn right around and come to the Swiss national bank and trade in their Swiss francs for gold. And guess what?"

I just stared at her.

"That gold they brought in tonight? That Nazi gold? Based on what we've heard -- and I admit, the information is a little shaky -- the Swiss are going to melt it down and re-form it into new gold bars, with nice Swiss stamps and serial numbers on it. Or they're just going to use the same ones they have, because if you get it from Switzerland, whatever it is, it has the international seal of approval. And they're going to give those gold bars to the Portuguese in exchange for those same francs that they stuffed into that suitcase tonight. It's a neat trick."

"And the Swiss take a cut of every transaction along the way," I said.

"They always get their fucking cut," Manon said. "It should be their national slogan. It ought to be written on the back of their money."

She was crying again.

"And nobody fucking cares," she said. "My bosses? They couldn't be bothered. The French government knows this is happening and won't do anything about it. No strong arm, no formal diplomatic protest, nothing. It's like we're afraid of them. I get that we share a border and that we want to maybe be on good enough terms that they'll let us take a shortcut through Swiss territory on the way to Germany if we need to--"

"But this is bigger than that," I said. "This is about Hitler's very ability to make war. Can't they see that?"

"They can't see shit."

The tears were flowing freely. Her chest was heaving, just a bit, and she was having trouble catching her breath. I had never seen Manon like this, even during our breakup fight.

I leaned over, touched her face, and wiped away a tear. She looked at me, and I looked at her, and neither of us said anything. We ripped off each other's clothes and somehow maneuvered around the steering wheel. Once, then again, and then we fell asleep entwined, covered as best we could by our coats and clothing. Hours later, the rising sun woke us as it shone through the front windshield. It lit the alley.

40

W e eventually did talk, Manon and I, but really not that much. I had accepted the start of our relationship for what it was and compartmentalized that part of it. The rest, I truly believed, was real. Beyond that, there really wasn't a lot to say.

The night in the car bonded us in a new way, and not just the sex. We shared, well, not only a profession but a growing disgust with the people who ran that part of our lives. They sent us out, at significant risk, and would not listen or act on the information we brought them. They couldn't see the big picture or what was truly important. They clung to their old ways, and they cared most about preserving their patch of turf. Manon and I were on the road to disillusionment, but at least we were on it together again.

For one thing, it got Liesl off of my back. Given her size, in the ninth month of her pregnancy, this was no small burden. She was so happy when we showed up together a couple of days later at the cafe, as were Gregory and Henry, and they stuck around the booth for too long. Eventually, though, they left us. We did have something to talk about.

Or, as Manon said, once we were alone, "So exactly how much are we going to tell each other?"

"I've thought about it a little bit," I said. I had different levels of secrets, as I assume she did. For instance, there was the question of Gregory's involvement. Could I tell her? Would Gregory view it as a betrayal if he found out that she knew? That might have been the trickiest one, but there were plenty of landmines along the way. Should I tell her about Brodsky and where I met him, or about Herman and First Thursdays? Or should I just pass along the information I gathered and remain secretive about, as they said in the trade, my sources and methods?

"Here's what I've come to," I said. "If I'm out on bank business, I'll tell you that. If I'm on other business, I'll tell you that, too. And I'll share whatever information I get, anything I think might be of any value to you and to France. But contacts? Sources? The where and the when? I just don't think that's the way to go."

The relief on Manon's face was plain.

"Thank God," she said. "I've been thinking the same thing. No more lies about rug manufacturers in Geneva, or wherever the hell that was supposed to be. Oh, and remember that story about the rug manufacturer with the rug? It was true, just a couple of years old.

"But giving up sources, I just don't think that's smart, and I'm glad you don't, either. I mean, we promise them discretion as part of the bargain, even if it's unspoken. They probably figure we're going to tell our superiors -- but even then, I have one guy who absolutely refused to deal with me unless I offered him total anonymity, even from my boss."

"And to add another intelligence service, none of these people signed up for that," I said.

"And God forbid something happened to one of my guys

after I revealed his identity to you -- it could just create issues between us that we couldn't survive."

"I'm glad we see it the same," I said. "But I am concerned about one thing. The very nature of some of the information I get, and that maybe you get, could naturally point the finger at the source. And the more people who know, the more potential fingers."

"You're right," she said. "But I think that's always a risk. We just play that one by ear, case-to-case. The more important the information, the more risks we assume."

"All right, I guess this is a plan," I said. "Maybe not perfect but close enough for spies in love."

"When they make the movie about us, that's the title."

"I was leaning more toward 'Sex Beneath the Gear Shift.'"

"That can be the adult version," she said.

"Well, since we now have an arrangement, I have something to tell you."

"Let me use the ladies' and pick us up one more drink." Which is what she did.

The day before, I had met up with Herman at Honold, the tea room on Rennweg. It wasn't an accident -- he said he had waited for me outside of the bank, hoping that I was in the mood for a second fruhstuck. He joined me in the line. Honold was a monument to the Swiss style of full employment. In the front of the restaurant, you had to pick your food from a glass case -- sandwiches and pastries and such -- where one of the two women working there reached under the glass to fill your plate. Then you paid your money to a third woman, sitting behind a cash register. Then you walked to the back of the tea room and sat down at an empty table, where a different waiter took your drink order. Then you paid him, for the second time. And if he refilled your coffee, you paid a third time. Whatever. The salami on white bread with pickle and tomato was an excellent second fruhstuck.

"So, to what do I owe the pleasure?"

"I heard something," Herman said.

"What kind of something?"

"Interesting something. Bad something."

"From one of your old friends across the border?"

Herman nodded. His news was a stunner. His source said that Hitler had decided to come west, but northwest -- he was going to invade Denmark and Norway on April 9th.

"Excuse me," I said, grabbing a newspaper off of a neighboring chair. The woman at that table waved at me weakly. I just wanted to see the date. It was Monday, April 1st.

"I guess I see what this couldn't wait till Thursday," I said, which was First Thursday at Cafe Tessinerplatz.

"That would have been cutting it close."

"But Denmark and Norway? Does that make any sense to you?"

"It does," Herman said. "They're constantly worried about supplies and materials in the high command. Hell, you know that -- what was that shit your family mined and sold them for their blast furnaces?"

"Magnesite," I said. It hadn't even been two years, but it seemed like a lifetime ago.

"Well, think about iron ore," he said. "Think about nickel. Stuff like that, stuff that Germany doesn't have, or doesn't have enough of. Well, a place like Norway is full of natural resources. You take them first, you guarantee your supplies for the armaments factories. Krupp's happy, Hitler's happy, and France and Britain will still get it in the end."

And when she came back with the drinks, that is what I told Manon -- not about Herman or Honold or my second fruhstuck, but about Denmark and Norway and April 9th. And, after she let out a low whistle, I offered her the rationale that Herman had provided, about nickel and iron ore and whatever. Then, another low whistle, followed by a look at her watch.

"Your place?" I said.

"Can't. Now I have this to deal with, and also a ceramics show tomorrow afternoon in Lausanne."

I looked at her skeptically. I would come to call it my rug manufacturers' look.

"Hey, I still have a day job, too. As do you."

"All right, I'll walk you," I said. It was only a couple of blocks. I shouted at Gregory as we got to the door. "I'll be back in 10 minutes for one more. I need you to explain to me how they haven't shot that goalkeeper of yours yet. What's his name? They should call him the Holey Ghost -- H-O-L-E-Y."

"Alex, you are too harsh," he said. "You did not see the game. I did. Only four of the goals were really his fault."

"Okay, you're right. Maybe they should give him a raise instead."

Thus armed, two of the fossils would still be badgering Gregory when I returned. I had the one drink, and then another as I helped him tidy up after closing. Then we went upstairs and sent the message about Denmark and Norway to London.

41

The yellow chalk mark on the MCMIX fountain was being peed on by a spaniel-ish mutt when I happened upon it. The lower half was likely washed away, deepening the color of the puddle at the base. I would be sure to tell Brodsky to recalibrate his aim the next time. Maybe we would even laugh about it, which would be novel. Laughs were growing shorter and shorter in supply, at least when it was the two of us getting together.

As it turned out, when I got off of the tram and tripped into the Barley House, all was as before. Hitler's army was on the move, and the Nazi gold was undergoing a fresh laundering in Basel, but the Lowenbrau brewery was still running three shifts, and the Barley House remained a dark, loud, smoky, blue convention. It might even have been more crowded than the last time.

After getting my beer -- again, the longest part of the process was the time it took me to reach into my pocket for some money -- I walked toward the same table in the back corner, shouldering through the blue coveralls. But there was a surprise this time -- Brodsky had already been joined by another man, as conspicuous and he and I were, black coats amid the blue. It was Herman.

"It isn't First Thursday," I said. "The people at Cafe Tessinerplatz are going to be furious if they find out we've been cheating on them."

"I think we're safe," Herman said. "Cafes are like wives. A little part of them expects to be cheated on."

"Something you're not telling us, Herman?"

"Past life," he said. For some reason, I began wondering if he was sending a little something home to the former Frau Stressler, and how that might be possible, given that running a specialty magazine that didn't sell shit would seem to make for some pretty tight budgeting for the current Frau Stressler as it was. But that was his problem, and I just didn't have time for it. I also didn't care.

We started talking about Norway and Denmark. The information from Herman's source had been spot on. Both the countries and the dates were exactly correct. The Wehrmacht went in on April 9th. In the days afterward, the newspapers were full of color and details about the great Nazi war machine. Unfortunately, it appeared that most of them were true.

"Although," Brodsky said, at one point. "It's hard to measure exactly how big and bad the Wehrmacht is when Denmark rolls over in six hours."

"They didn't even buy them dinner," I said.

"Just fucked," Herman said. "Fucked, fucked, and fucked again."

"At least Norway fought a little bit," Brodsky said.

"And the government and the king got away -- can't have too many kings," I said.

"And that jackass," Herman said. "What's his name?"

"Quisling," I said.

"Right, Quisling," Brodsky said. "Talk about following which way the wind is blowing. But look, I didn't get your here to re-hash everything that's been in the newspapers."

"Well, maybe we should talk about how nobody is listening to the information we're bringing them. I mean, shit -- that information was dead-on, but there was no reaction that I could see. They just let Hitler walk in. I mean, are they even fucking listening?"

Spying was, by its very nature, a solitary existence. But I was fortunate, in that I could share at least part of what I was doing, and what I was feeling, with not only Manon but also Herman and Brodsky. They were living the same life, to varying degrees. They dealt with the same frustrations. And while I sometimes wondered if there was always a tension between field agents and the people who ran them, just as in any employee-boss relation-ship, the disconnection between the information being gathered and the decisions being made, or not made, was profound.

"Am I wrong, or does this seem really fucked up to you?" I said, looking first at Brodsky, then at Herman. "I mean, nobody's fucking listening."

We all sat and drank. Herman stood up and got us three more. The fug along the ceiling seemed particularly thick. Metaphors were everywhere if you looked hard enough.

"This is going to make you feel even worse," Brodsky said. "But here's why I called you both. I have new information on the Ardennes invasion. It's a pretty good source, and it's in two pieces. Yes, he also has heard that the focal point of the invasion will be the Ardennes, and not Belgium and Holland. And I didn't lead him at all -- it all came from him."

"Great," I said. "Three confirmations now. But if they didn't listen to two, three won't matter."

"But I also have a date," Brodsky said.

I actually leaned forward to get closer to him. Herman dd, too.

"So?" I said.

"May 10th," Brodsky said.

"This is solid?" Herman said.

"Yeah, my guy says it's solid. He's in the Soviet high command. He says the Germans have consulted them as a courtesy."

May 10th. Three weeks.

So this was it. France and Britain had two weeks to get their shit together. They were either going to listen to information that could not be more solid, that came to three different spies -- a Russian, a German and a Czech -- from three different sources who had access to the German military. Hell, one of them, Ritter, was in the German military, and so was Herman's source, probably. Nothing in life is certain, and that was perhaps even truer when you were dealing with a homicidal lunatic like Hitler, but this was not ignorable anymore. They had to listen.

Once again, Gregory got one whiff of my overcoat and insisted that I hang it outside before entering his apartment. The message he sent was as short and unemotional as I could muster: "Russian confirmation of Ardennes invasion. Date set is May 10." The reply was swift, as always. Dash-dash-dot. G.

But as Gregory and I drank and talked, I got more and more worked up. I mean, this was it. There was no getting around it anymore. I had been forced to leave Austria and would have been forced to leave Czechoslovakia if I hadn't beaten the Wehrmacht to the border by a few months. Now Hitler was coming my way again, probably not here, not to Zurich, but who knew? Britain and France were going to stop him here, or he wasn't going to be stopped. It was that simple, and there had been no signs thus far that indicated they realized it.

I grabbed a pencil and scribbled out another message. Gregory read it.

"Really?" he said.

"Yes, really."

"This is a bad idea."

"Just send it."

"Alex--"

"Just fucking send it," I said. It came off harsher than I had intended. Gregory translated from the bible page and sent it in silence. The message read, "Are you even fucking listening?"

We sat and finished our drink. He was pissed, and I didn't have anything left to say. There was no reply from London, no dash-dash-dot confirmation, nothing. Gregory looked at his watch.

"Should I send it again?"

"No, fuck it," I said. It was time for me to get out of there. I needed to get over to Manon's flat, to wake her up and tell her the latest.

42

The stack of paperwork on my desk at Bohemia Suisse had begun to lean, ever so slightly. One more bulging file folder might just topple the whole mess, and there was no question who was going to be picking it up and reassembling the folders if it did. The end of the month was always like that, but even more lately, given my other preoccupations. Mostly it was just initialing and signing, but some of it was more in-depth. One afternoon a month, I carried the adding machine from the nook it usually occupied near Marta's desk and brought it into my office for a series of calculations that required a double-check. They were never wrong, and I don't know if Marta resented it more than she resented everything else I did, but it was mostly an exercise that forced me to pay attention to the key financial aspects of the bank. Besides, I kind of enjoyed the clicking noise the machine made when it came time to total a column of figures.

That's what I was doing when Marta came in.

"One of the nephews is here," she said.

"Does he have an appointment?"

She said that he didn't. I asked her if she could handle the withdrawal, attempting to minimize how curious I was that one of the spies was in the bank, one who had never been here before. I also knew that we were currently in a spot in our relationship that whenever I said "white," Marta would reply "black." So I wasn't surprised when she said he asked specifically for me.

"Give me 30 seconds," I said, getting up from the table where the adding machine was sitting, rolling down my sleeves, and slipping on my jacket. That was another thing I liked about the adding machine, the excuse it gave me to unencumber myself a little. I was just shooting my shirt cuffs out of the sleeves when Kensinger walked in. I didn't remember his first name. I had only met him one time, but he was memorable, a 20-something-year-old kid with mostly gray hair. He was carrying a brown leather satchel, almost like a schoolboy's, with two buckled straps in the front.

I walked around the desk and shook his hand, then walked the few additional steps and closed the office door. As I did, I caught Marta's look of disapproval, or maybe disappointment that she wouldn't be able to hear through the leather-padded door.

I pointed him to one of the two facing wing chairs and offered him coffee from the pot on my sideboard. It had been there a half-hour but was still hot enough. That would be it for the niceties, as it turned out. Kensinger was not much interested in small-talk.

"I'm here to take almost everything in the account. Do you have a problem with that?"

I was interested, certainly. But a problem? No.

"I have no control over the account," I said. "This is your decision. The bearers of the account have all of the power. The bank is just a repository."

"Good."

I sat, silent. Five seconds. Ten seconds. I put on my placid face, but the nervousness grew on his. At 15 seconds, he just began blurting.

"We need the money to go further underground."

Again, placid face.

"You have to understand," he said. "It's nothing specific, but the Germans are just strutting more. Have you noticed it? Do you deal with anybody at the legation? They're just -- they're such arrogant assholes anyway, but it's worse now. We can all sense it."

Silence. Maybe a small nod.

"We've been doing some digging," he said. "There might be 1,000 of them in Switzerland between the embassy in Bern and all of their legations. There's about six of them -- here, Geneva, Basel, St. Fucking Gallen, pretty much anywhere there's a dozen Swiss families."

"A thousand?" I said. "Seems high."

"Between the actual embassy employees, and the locals they've put on the payroll, we think it's 1,000, easy. And they're just starting to show up in the oddest places. I nearly bumped into one of their guys -- like physically bumped into him -- outside of a little Italian restaurant a couple of blocks away from where I grew up, and where my family still lives. Grimaldi's -- you ever heard of it? It's good, but it's no Orsini's, and it's about five miles from here, and there are 10 places just as good between here and there. There's no way somebody from the German legation would be in that neighborhood for no reason. It's got me spooked."

"I get that." Just keep him talking.

"Things like that have been happening to all of us. You try to convince yourself that life is full of coincidences, but there are just getting to be too many of them."

"So what does Blum think?" Blum was the controller, the one who dressed up as the old man to open the original account.

"He doesn't know what to think," Kensinger said. "Between you and me, he isn't that smart. And he's getting nothing from London. Like, no direction at all. So we've decided to act on behalf of self-preservation. We're going to take the money and use it to go deeper, go darker -- new safe houses, maybe a small base over the border in France. Hair dye for me, done professionally. Fuck it. The only thing I know for sure is I have to get this away from my family."

When Kensinger walked in, I wasn't 100 percent sure that he did not know of my further involvement. But the fact that he never asked me what I had heard, or what I knew, and that he was willing to crap on his boss in my presence, told me that he did not consider me to be a player. I was just a connected outsider in his mind, maybe a shoulder to cry on because of the connection, nothing more than that, which was a relief. Part of me wanted to tell him what I knew, about the Ardennes and May 10th, but it wasn't my place to tell him. Besides, given that it only took 15 seconds of silence to break him, I didn't think trusting him with any of my secrets made a lot of sense.

"Leave 5,000 francs and give me the rest," he said. I looked up the balance -- it was in the pile of paperwork on my desk -- and had him fill out a withdrawal ticket. He waited in my office while I took the satchel and handled the transaction myself. Marta was dying to get up from her desk and walk across the bank and look over my shoulder, but we still had enough of a boss-employee relationship that she stayed in her place. Besides, she would see the withdrawal ticket within minutes of Kensinger's departure, anyway. It was her job to keep the books.

As it turned out, it was precisely four minutes.

"Are you kidding me?" Marta said. She was waving the withdrawal slip.

"It's his money."

"And you just let him take it?"

"I tried to talk him out of it."

"Father to son?"

"I went more for big brother to little brother," I said. "But it's their money. I don't know how many times I can tell you. Their money, their rules."

"It's still wrong," she said. She was waving two things, actually -- the withdrawal slip and a telegram, which she remembered when she saw it. "Here. This came while you were doing such a bang-up job talking some sense into that spoiled brat."

Marta had put me back in my place. All was again right in her world. She hummed as she sashayed back to her desk.

Safely alone, I opened the envelope. The telegram said:

Fred arrival May 10. Please prepare welcome and menu including apple fritters.

"Fred" was France.

"May 10" was May 10.

"Fritters" was Fritz Ritter.

This was a confirmation of the invasion date that Brodsky had received from his Russian army contact. It was entirely unsolicited, and it seemed beyond unlikely that Ritter's source was the same officer in the Russian high command. So May 10th was it. There could be no doubt now. Gregory and I sent the news to London that night.

43

Sechselauten was Zurich's "Six O'clock Festival." It was always near the end of April, always on a Monday, but the date hopped around a little bit from year to year, for whatever reason. It might have been my favorite Zurich-y thing. It was a celebration of the arrival of spring, and its roots were in the 6 o'clock church bells being run to signal the end of the workday, back-when. In the winter, you worked until it got dark. But as summer approached, and the days got longer, that wasn't practical -- so when it became necessary, they rang the church bells at 6, and everybody got to go home. This was a celebration of those bells, and the chance for the workers to see daylight again. They had bonfires and pageants and shit, and the highlight was the burning of Bogg, this great stuffed dummy held high on a pole. They said he was supposed to represent Old Man Winter. I think he was really supposed to represent their bosses.

Whatever, it was an excuse to drink outdoors after work, down by the lake. Manon and I walked around and got lost in the crowds, drinks in hand, hand in hand, and I actually forgot about Hitler and the Ardennes and the Nazi gold and the rest of it, at least for a few minutes. We had 11 days before May 10th, 11 days for our bosses to get their heads out of their asses. There was still enough time to make a difference.

After witnessing Bogg's glorious demise -- I had forgotten how much little children could squeal at the sight of a big fire -- we decided to walk back to Fessler's, not for dinner but maybe just dessert. We weren't two blocks away from the festival when the real world began crowding our thoughts.

"Did I tell you the latest from my boss?" Manon said.

She had not. I did not know her boss's name. I knew he was a man, based upon her choice of pronouns -- as in the phrase, "he's such a fucking asshole" -- but that was it. I had no idea about his age, or what he looked like, or where his office was, or anything.

"I asked him about May 10th," she said. "And you know what he tells me? I can give it to you exactly, a direct quote. He says, 'May 10th is just a single date. The calendar is full of them. We must be prepared for all of them.' Jackass. He didn't say that. I said that. Fucking jackass."

"May 10th is just a date, one of many," I said. "The Ardennes is just a point on the map, one of many. Shit. When you prepare for everything, you prepare for nothing. We are so doomed."

"You hearing anything from your side?"

"Not a word," I said.

It was hard to know what might get their attention at this point. We had the Ardennes location from three different sources and the May 10th date from two. Short of a personal letter with the invasion plans, signed by Adolf himself, I don't know what else we could give them, or what else would make the French and British generals move.

They had completely ignored the Denmark and Norway

information. I mean, if they warned either country, it sure didn't show up in the military defense efforts. But this was different. This was France. This was the whole goddamned game. How could they not see? I mean, how could they ignore it? Did they really just sit around and drink sherry and talk about Verdun all night?

"Christ," I yelled. We had been walking in silence for about a block, and it must have seemed to Manon to have come out of nowhere.

"I'm sor--"

"Forget it," she said. "I do it in the office all the time now. I get so worked up in my head about the fact that they won't listen, and I just become this cauldron. I let out a 'shit' the other day that startled one of the secretaries -- she kind of half fell off of her chair. But she's really just a secretary in the trade mission, so why would she get it? All she's worried about is arranging the next lunch with the vineyard association from Bordeaux."

"Lucky her," I said. "Clueless and drunk at lunch."

When we arrived at Cafe Fessler, we walked in on what appeared to be a celebration. Gregory was popping open a bottle of champagne, and he and Henry and a couple of the fossils where grabbing glasses. Gregory saw us and shouted.

"Alex! Manon! Come here now. It is the greatest day."

"Liesl had the baby! A girl!" Henry shouted. And then we all hugged, together and in every combination. I even hugged a fossil and then suppressed the feeling that I really needed to wash my hands in the bathroom.

She was a little more than two weeks early, but mother and daughter were fine. Henry had driven her to the hospital and had seen the baby, but after a quick visit, Liesl was already asleep, and the nurses told him to come back in the morning.

"Seven pounds even," Gregory said. "A nice, big girl."

He was starting to cry. We had been there a few minutes before I realized that I hadn't asked the baby's name.

"Sylvie," Gregory said, and then he was bawling, just convulsed by tears, paralyzed by them. Sylvie had been his wife's name.

After a while, Henry was well past his customary one drink and in a silly fog. He stumbled off to bed early. The fossils sat around with Gregory and told him their Pop-Pop stories. I was going to stop in the bathroom and then head home with Manon when Gregory saw where I was going and walked along with me as if heading for the kitchen that shared a hallway with the toilets.

He reached into his pocket and handed me a folded piece of paper.

"This came last night from London, right at midnight," he said.

"Why didn't you tell me earlier?"

"I figured it could wait."

"And you wrote it down?"

"Read it. There's no danger."

The message was as devastating as it was short:

Information received and appreciated. Nothing here changes.

G

There were so many things I was feeling, so many things I wanted to say. Nothing here changes. With those three words, Groucho had expressed my helplessness and my hopelessness. Nothing here changes. The only good part was that it seemed as if he was on my side, on our side, and was as frustrated as we were. If your lot in life is to shout into the wind, I guess it was better not to be doing it alone.

I looked down at the paper again, then tore it into little pieces. I pushed open the bathroom door and then turned back toward Gregory.

"I'll flush this," I said. And then I hugged him -- as a thank you, and as congratulations, and because I needed to hug somebody.

"It is the greatest day." As the words escaped from my mouth, I immediately felt guilty. I wish I had meant them.

The decision to try my luck in Paris came slowly over the next few days, and then the drip-drip-drip just spilled over the rim of the cup. No one was listening. Time was running out. I had a friend in Paris, Leon, a journalist with journalistic connections. It might have been far-fetched, but it was all I had.

Manon's initial thought was that it was a waste of time.

"You're better off staying here," she said. "I mean, there's no way I could go with you. And I don't know how many connections Leon might have -- you don't know, either. It's just a complete shot in the dark."

"If you hadn't noticed, it's getting pretty fucking dark."

She smiled. "What do you think, you're going to crash Gamelin's dinner table at Maxim's and convince him that they're coming through the Ardennes? You're going to draw it all on the tablecloth, just push the dishes away and start sketching. It's mad."

"It's all I have." Then, after a minute, "But what about the gold? That's a story he could work on and write. Publicity might mean something there. You have to admit that."

"I'll concede there is a chance there," Manon said. "But based on my boss, the idea that my people would lift a finger to try to stop them is a fantasy. And the Swiss are so brazen, I really don't think it will matter. I don't think it's possible to embarrass them when you're talking about the family business."

"The family business?"

"Making money," she said.

"I still have to try."

"I know." She kissed me on the head, like a mother kissing her child before sending him off to school. Then we just sat there in her flat, side by side on her couch. We fell asleep there, my arm holding her, her head on my chest.

The next morning, I told Marta I was taking the night train to Paris. She grabbed the diary and her pen, expecting a few details for the record. I offered none. She waited.

"It's a personal trip," I said, finally.

"Then you'll be making your own reservations," she said.

"Already done."

"When will you be back?"

This was Monday, May 6th. I would be in Paris on the 7th and 8th, and probably the 9th -- but no later. I needed to be back here on the invasion date, whatever the outcome of my adventure.

"Back on the 10th, Friday," I said.

"Cancel everything between now and then?"

"I'm not sure there's anything to cancel," I said. She looked down in the diary and saw I was right. I wasn't sure I was going to be able to get there but, finally, I had the upper hand in the conversation. With that, Marta marched out.

I finished up a few things and then walked to my flat to pack a small bag. I took a quick trip to the MCMIX fountain, just to check, and there was no yellow chalk mark. Part of me thought I should contact Brodsky, to let him know I was leaving town. But he would just be even more cynical about my chances than Manon was, and I wasn't in the mood.

The taxi to the station left me there about an hour before the train's scheduled departure. The conductors and porters would start to allow people into their compartments about 30 minutes before it was leaving time. That left me some time for a coffee, which I was about to order when a familiar voice spoke over my shoulder.

"Two coffees, paper cups, please." It was Peter Ruchti.

I was oddly glad to see him.

"I can afford to pay in this place," he said. We took the coffees and walked into the massive train shed. Ruchti pointed to an empty bench, where we sat.

"You have time for a chat," he said. I looked at my watch reflexively, even though I knew I had nearly an hour.

"A few minutes," I said.

"I would ask where you're going, but I'm not in the mood to be lied to."

"Paris," I said.

"Business or pleasure?"

"I have a friend there."

"That doesn't answer the question but never mind. There's something I need to tell you."

I just looked at him, as expressionless as I could manage.

"Who's Werner Vogl?" Ruchti asked.

Suddenly, I don't think I was expressionless anymore.

"That bad?" Ruchti said.

"I don't know what you're talking about." A weak bluff.

"If that's how you want to play it, that's okay with me. Have a nice trip." Ruchti began to stand. I reached for his arm, and he sat back down on the bench, which suddenly felt a little colder.

"Vogl is a Gestapo captain, or at least he was," I said.

"Still is," Ruchti said.

"He and I have a...history."

"So I gathered."

"Is he here? In Zurich?"

"No," Ruchti said. "At least, not yet."

He pulled a folded piece of paper from his pocket. He said it was his transcription of a telegram that was received that morning in the German legation.

"One of their quote-unquote trade representatives walked it over to my office at lunchtime. He brought the actual telegram, let me see it and copy it, asked me if I could help."

Ruchti handed me the paper. It said:

Please facilitate inquiries into the whereabouts of Alex Kovacs, a Czech national. Believed to be in Zurich recently. Any and all information appreciated. Priority.

Capt. Werner Vogl, Gestapo HQ, Al. Szucha 25, Warsaw

Priority. Just great.

"I played dumb," Ruchti said. "Isn't very hard for me -- and besides, those assholes think we're all either incompetents or idiots or both. But that won't stop them for long."

"They already have me in their census book."

"One hand doesn't know what the other is doing sometimes, even in the great Hitler machine. But they'll be coordinated fairly quickly."

"But even if they figure it out -- when they figure it out -- I'm in Switzerland. There's nothing they can do to me, right."

"I wonder if the kid who got the bullet through the eye on Rennweg thought nobody could do anything to him."

"You still don't know who did it, though," I said. "Or why."

"No, not exactly. It's not as if it was some damned lover's quarrel, though. And you and I both know that it wasn't the good guys."

Ruchti stopped for a second. The coffee was already cold.

"Are you in that much trouble with this guy?" he said.

"Yeah. More than you can imagine." I thought about telling Ruchti the story, then decided against it. I just didn't have the energy. Besides, it's not as if him knowing why Vogl wanted to exact his revenge would make a difference either way in whether or not Vogl succeeded.

"Thanks," I said, and I meant it. Ruchti might just have been worried about keeping his playing field clean, but he didn't have to seek me out to tell me about the telegram. He might even help me out in a pinch if it came to that.

But that would happen later, if at all. Vogl was still in Warsaw, and I was getting on a train to Paris. It was an entirely alcoholic journey, as it turned out -- I even bought the last half-bottle of Hennessy from the bartender and took it back to my compartment. But if I slept, I don't remember.

PART IV

45

W e had spoken a few times over the telephone, but I had not seen Leon in nearly two years. So it seemed only natural when I spotted him there, sitting at a table at a sidewalk cafe, a bottle of wine already opened and poured, that the first words I would say to him would be, "A fucking beret? Seriously?"

"The mademoiselles, they like -- what can I say?"

"And glasses? Since when?"

"They're plain glass."

"The mademoiselles?"

"Oui, oui," he said. "Now come here and give me a proper hug, you fucking asshole."

Leon, Henry and I met during the war, fighting for the honor of the archduke, or something. We were just kids then, but came back to Vienna and remained the closest of friends. For years and decades, I could never manage to get serious with a woman, and I hated my father and brother back in Brno, so that left Leon, Henry and Uncle Otto as my only family.

Between female conquests, of which there were hundreds in the quarter-century I had known him, Leon had managed to carve out a nice career in journalism. He started covering cops and then society bullshit at one of the Vienna tabloids, Der Abend, the society bullshit consisting mostly of drinking free champagne at museum openings and spelling the rich people's names correctly. He managed to turn that into a job at one of the serious newspapers in Vienna, *Die Neue Freie Presse*, where his society connections morphed into political connections. The highlight of his career was the break he got on the story of the timing of the German invasion of Austria -- I was the source. Of course, within hours of its publication, he was slouched down in the front seat of a car, driven by Henry, that was speeding through a border checkpoint into Czecho-slovakia as Nazi bullets registered their disapproval. In the car, he had a copy of the newspaper with his big scoop bannered across the top, but he had no career anymore -- and no pass-port besides.

The Czechs then agreed to give Leon a passport and ship him to Paris as part of the deal I made with my former/current employers. His French was better than average -- the frauleins liked it as much as the mademoiselles, it seemed -- and he had a contact at a Paris newspaper, one of the correspondents who used to populate his favorite Vienna hangout, Cafe Louvre.

"What's the paper like?" I said.

"Better than *Der Abend*, not as good as *Die Neue Freie Presse*. But they let me have my head. They're even calling it a column now -- or a regular feature, with my name on it. It's called 'Fresh Eyes,' and it's supposed to be a foreigner's take on different aspects of French life and culture. Twice a week, no heavy lifting."

"What was the last one about?"

"Well, a lot of them are serious. I did one where a bunch of deputies tried to explain to me how having a government that falls every 10 seconds isn't such a bad thing -- that got a lot of attention. But the last one was about the history of the culture of perfume."

"I bet you did a lot of fucking sniffing around for that one," I said.

"My specialty," Leon said.

We drank the bottle and caught up. I told him about Henry and Liesl's baby, and about Manon. He told me about his latest, whom he claimed "can get both ankles behind her head without so much as a strain." Every few minutes, the reason for my trip popped into my head, but I kept forcing it out. We were in Paris in 1940, but we could have been in Vienna in 1930, and I didn't want to let that go.

"Come on," Leon said, after paying the bill.

"Where to?"

"The Paris version of Cafe Louvre."

We grabbed a taxi and, in a few minutes, were dumped out at a place called La Pluie, on Saint-Germain. The architecture was all different, as was the menu -- there was no schnitzel for two marks, for instance -- but you could just tell it was a newspaper bar. The foreign correspondents were all different but the vibe was the same -- lots of drinking, lots of half-formed opinions about the events of the day being tried out on each other, a wariness among competitors but also a collegiality.

"Does it work the same as Vienna?" I said.

"Pretty much. They're all scared of getting beaten on a big story so they tend to stick together and write the same shit. That protects them all. But the problem for them is, lots of newspaper executives show up in Paris. It was a haul to get to Vienna, and it was cold, so their wives didn't really want to go, which left the correspondents on their own a lot more. Here, they occasionally have to actually produce something enterprising for the boss. They can't just sit in here all day and rewrite the local papers. Although there's still plenty of that."

"So what do they think about the war?"

"That it's coming. Just look at them, all sticking together. You can tell they're getting worried about getting scooped."

It was time to tell Leon what I knew. We got drinks and took a table as far away from the correspondents as we could, and I began talking. I might have spoken for an hour straight, with barely an interruption from Leon. I laid it all out -- my increased role with Czech intelligence, my frustration with how they seemed incapable of acting on the information that we brought them, and the key points: that the invasion would come through the Ardennes, and that it would come on May 10th, this Friday, three days away.

In the midst of all of that, I also told him about the Nazi gold and the implications for the war. Leon seemed much more interested in that. He stopped me several times and went into reporter mode, asking me for clarifications and specific details, and to separate my theories from demonstrated facts.

"That would be a big fucking story," he said.

"But what about the invasion? Hitler's attempt to dominate the entire continent of Europe? Not big enough for you?"

"I could never write that one. First, they would never believe I had the proper sourcing for it. But even then, I don't know about you, but I'm not going to be the person responsible for panicking an entire nation. I mean, what if it's wrong? I believe what you're telling me, but Hitler is crazy. He could change his mind tomorrow. I can't touch that one -- but I know a military guy you can talk to about it."

It is what I hoped for all along, just an audience with someone who might listen and who maybe could make a difference. There was still time -- not much time, but still some. I don't know how long it took to move an army, but even a couple of days' head start toward the Ardennes had to help. I don't know -- it could be the difference between success and failure.

"But the gold story, that's dynamite," Leon said. "There isn't enough to publish yet, but I can start asking questions about it tomorrow. I know a guy who works at a bank. I helped him out of a jam, and he owes me a favor."

"What kind of a jam? A female jam?"

"Not important," Leon said. And then he smiled that fabulously wicked smile of his. It really did feel like 1930 again, for maybe a second.

46

The next afternoon, because this was Paris and mornings were for chumps, apparently, I met Leon outside the Saint Paul station. It was an easy walk for me from Le Meurice, on the Rue de Rivoli, across from the Jardin de Tuileries, because the bank was paying for this trip whether they knew it or not. And Saint Paul was a Metro station that was right in the Marais, where Leon lived. He was the least Jewish Jew that I knew, but the Marais was Paris' traditional Jewish neighborhood and, as he said, "Fuck it, I figure if I live there, I don't have to go to temple."

He had a friend he wanted me to meet. Over my late, ridiculously expensive breakfast, I fought my way through two Paris newspapers. My French was actually decent, with practice -- back-when in Brno, before I escaped as a teenager to live with Uncle Otto in Vienna, we had a French cook who taught me and left me with what one woman in Strasbourg once told me was "a charming Alsatian accent," which was good enough for a few kisses but also a very curt karate chop to my wandering right hand. So exactly how charming was it, after all?

Anyway, the papers were full of political intrigue. Most of it was about 200 former Communist mayors and deputies who had been exiled to internment camps on islands in the Atlantic after the party was outlawed. Military tribunals pronounced their sentences and put them on the boats, operating under the theory that you need to cut off the head of the snake first. But the papers were full of stories that quoted unnamed party members who said their members were never more motivated than they were when the boats pushed off from Fromentine with their former leaders on board.

France was crazily, and maybe fatally, unstable. The Communists hated the rightists and pretty openly smooched photographs of Stalin -- well, at least before they were outlawed. The rightists, whom the Communists called Fascists, didn't hate the Commies -- they feared them. Fear is a much stronger emotion than hate. And while the rightists couldn't smooch Hitler photographs in return -- some things just weren't done -- it was fair to say that said portraits gave them stirrings in places unseen behind their desks at the banks, and beneath the white linen tablecloths at their current favorite restaurant.

That left the people in the middle trying to govern, a group whose number seemed to shrink by the hour. They were like the people who ran for club president in every little club that you ever belonged to, the people who tended to win because nobody else wanted the job, or wanted to deal with the shit, and who spent their entire existence getting yelled at from a minimum of two directions. All of which meant that if a French government lasted as long as six months, they should have had a parade to celebrate. I'll never forget that they had no government when Hitler marched into Austria in 1938. Even if there had been some inclination to offer help -- and I'm not sure the phrase "offer help" has ever been in the French dictionary -- who was going to arrange it? The bell captain at the Ritz?

One thing there wasn't a lot of in the newspapers was war news, as in, none at all. Leon had warned me.

"They set up this Ministry of Information about six weeks ago," he said. "It's turning out to be the ministry of no information. Nothing in the papers, nothing on the radio -- you need to get a London paper to find out anything about Norway."

"How is Norway going, by the way?"

"Shitty," Leon said. "But like I said, you can't read about it here."

He was right. There wasn't anything. Thus fortified after breakfast, and assured that this place was as fucked up as ever, I met Leon. We were on the Metro's Line 1, the oldest line, and it soon became apparent that the friend we were meeting was going to be at the end of the line, the Chateau de Vincennes.

"All the way the hell out here? Why?" I said as we got off the train.

"Because this is where he works," Leon said.

"But what's out here? We're, like, how many miles--"

"About five or six from your hotel, probably."

"But what's out here?"

"Just that." Leon pointed as we took the last few steps up to the street. Just the chateau, perhaps the most fabulous combination of size and ugliness ever conceived by an architect.

"He works in there?" I said.

"They all do."

"Who's they?"

"The French high command," Leon said. He looked at his wristwatch. "We're a bit early. Let's take a lap."

As we walked, Leon played the tour guide. He said he knew all of the history because it was the subject of one of his newspaper columns. The headline was, "A Submarine without a Periscope."

"The press guy from the army was furious," Leon said. "I told him that the writers don't write the headlines. Of course, I didn't tell him that I suggested it to my editor. It came from an anonymous quote in the story from one of the junior officers on the staff who resented having to come all the way out here every day, to the ass-end of the Metro line."

"That junior officer wouldn't be the friend we're going to meet later, would it?"

"I'll never tell," Leon said. His smile, of course, gave it away.

The chateau was just odd looking, both wide and tall, with these massive battlements in the middle. It was the home of kings, going back centuries, obviously built more for defense than looks. There was even a moat to keep out the barbarians, only it was now dried out and beginning to sprout spring grasses.

"Based on what my friend tells me, he believes Gamelin would actually fill it with water again -- just one more barrier to keep the politicians outside," Leon said.

As we circumnavigated, we came upon a statue on one corner of the property of Louis IX, known to you and me as St Louis. But this also was a place known for death: Henry V of England died there, and the spy Mata Hari and many others had been executed there. As we turned a corner, we came upon a gaggle of school children, maybe 10 years old, about 30 of them being shepherded by two very outnumbered teachers. If they managed to get back to school on the Metro without losing at least one of those kids, they deserved the Croix de Guerre.

"You can go on a tour of the place if you are so inclined," Leon said. "Lots of big, dark, cold, damp rooms. A bunch of furniture from the 16th century that appears as if it couldn't survive a healthy fart at this point. A few suits of armor, if that's your thing. And they'll show you the courtyard, part of the barracks where they shot Mata Hari."

"I'll pass," I said.

"The truth is, it's nicer inside. These big walls -- it was built as a fortress, after all. They were trying to keep people out."

"And still are, it sounds like."

"Ask my friend," Leon said.

47

We waited at a cafe across the street from the chateau. If it had a name, it wasn't obvious. There was nothing written on the glass door, and nothing on the green-and-white awning, either. The menu was chalked on a small slate that the waiter dropped on the table with a mini-thud.

After a few minutes, Leon and I watched as an officer in uniform crossed the street and walked in our direction. He looked about our age, maybe a little younger. Leon introduced him as "the Captain."

"No names?" I said.

"Not for now," Leon said.

"Hell, I don't care," the Captain said, sticking out his hand. "Georges."

He ordered coffee, and I made conversation. I looked at Georges and said, "Well, how did you two meet?"

"Well, that's a story," Leon said. I loved it when Leon said, "Well, that's a story." I think the first time I heard him say it, our unit was a few miles outside of Caporetto, after the battle. I don't remember all of the details, but the tale that day involved a redhead and a scarf that doubled as a restraint. Whenever he pre-announced, "Well, that's a story," it was.

"So," I said.

"Well--" Georges said.

"We met because we were fucking two sisters," Leon said.

"And then we had a contest," Georges said.

"Let me guess," I said.

"Shut up, it's our story," Leon said.

"The contest was simple," Georges said. "Who would be the first one to fuck the other sister. Loser buys the winner drinks for a night."

"Ah, so it was true love," I said.

"I thought he told you to shut up," Georges said. I liked him immediately. He described the two sisters for me, just to round out the picture. His (original) sister was, as he said, "the more voluptuous of the two." When I arched an eyebrow, he said, "Not fat, voluptuous. Am I right?" Leon nodded.

"So how would the winner prove to the loser--"

"What do you think we are?" Georges said. "Our word is our bond. We're gentlemen, for fuck's sake."

His faux outrage was pitch perfect.

"So don't keep me in suspense. Who won?"

At this point, Georges actually stood up and raised his arms above his head, hands balled into fists. He looked like a boxer standing over a fallen opponent, splayed out on the canvas. It would have made for quite the scene, had there been anybody else sitting at one of the sidewalk tables.

"Leon, you're losing your touch," I said.

"What my worthy opponent failed to mention was that I lost by three fucking hours. I lost because I bought mine dinner and he only bought his a drink. Shows you where being a gentleman gets you."

"All's fair in love and war," Georges said. "That fits perfectly, doesn't it? Although, whoever said that, I kind of doubt he had our contest in mind."

The preliminaries aside, we began to talk about why I had traveled to Paris. Georges just let me speak, never interjecting, just nodding occasionally. I probably went on for a half-hour, my frustration with the leadership at every level of officialdom spilling out.

Finally, I was done. Georges shook his head. Then he cleared his throat, turned and spit on the sidewalk.

"Gamelin knows this -- or, should I say, most of it," he said. "I'm not sure he knows the Ardennes information is coming from three sources. I don't know if he knows the May 10th date comes from two sources. But he knows. Trust me, he knows."

"And what does he say?"

"We're, and I quote, 'awaiting events.'"

Georges sipped his coffee. It was cold. He raised his hand to get the waiter's attention. Waiters hated that, but he was wearing a military uniform, so screw the waiter. He pointed down at the table and drew a circle with his finger, for another round of coffee.

"Awaiting fucking events," he said. "I've personally heard him say that a half-dozen times, and I don't get into half of the big meetings. He must say it on the hour. Such a goddamned fossil. We are so doomed."

Fossil. I thought about the old men in Cafe Fessler, arguing about the positioning of FC Zurich's midfielders. They were as old as Gamelin. Hell, Gamelin was probably older.

"Why doesn't Gamelin believe it? Why don't his people believe it?" I said.

"Because of the plane crash." Georges began to tell the story, about the crash into Belgium and the original invasion plans falling into Belgian hands, a little scorched but readable. I stopped him midway.

"I know, I know. But that was months ago."

"But don't you get it -- it fits with what Gamelin knows, and what he knows is the last war."

"But--"

"There's no but," Georges said. "They have about two staff dinners a week. I get invited to about two a month. I've been at this post for seven months, so 14 dinners, give or take. And at every one of them -- every fucking one -- the conversation has turned at one point or another to the Marne. And Gamelin is always the one who turns it there."

I felt like crying. But Georges was wound up now and just spewing.

"He's such an odd little old man," he said. "I mean, what in the fuck are we doing out here? We had a nice normal head-quarters building at Les Invalides, left bank, almost on the Seine, near everything. But no, we have to come out here, away from the politicians, away from everybody. Do you know he lives in there, in one of the buildings in the back? It's like a fucking jail cell. The man in charge of the French army lives in this dark fucking room -- I think he sleeps on a cot, all alone--"

"With only the Marne to keep him warm," Leon said.

It was every bad thing that I had imagined, only it might have been worse. Still, I just couldn't believe that they were so calcified that they wouldn't listen to reason.

"All right, forget Gamelin for a second," I said. "Tell me what you think. Do you think it's crazy that he won't listen at all? Do you think the Ardennes is impossible?"

"It would be hard," Georges said. "Everything I know about reading a map tells me that. But I have to be honest -- I've never been there. I've never seen it first-hand. All I know about the Ardennes is what people tell me -- narrow, winding roads, trees hugging the sides, no way to get a tank through."

"But have they checked?"

"Checked?" Georges said, his tone mocking the question. "Checked? Like, actually gotten off of their asses? Of course not. All they know is what they remember from a family vacation to the Ardennes when they were 11."

Georges's voice was suddenly drowned out by a half-dozen soldiers on motorcycles, roaring out of the chateau and down the street. He waited until they were gone, past the Metro entrance, headed to who knows where.

"See that?" he said. "You can set your watch by it. That is our modern, 20th Century communication system with the generals in the field."

"What? What are you talking about?"

"That's it," Georges said. "No radios. No teletypes. That's what we have -- messengers on motorbikes. And they aren't even good motorbikes. We are so fucked."

"What does Gamelin say when people your age ask about bringing in radios?"

"Not just people my age -- the old colonels and generals on the staff can't believe it, either. But Gamelin says, 'This is preferable.' He isn't big on giving orders. He's more of a guiding-principles kind of general. I think that's a mistake because I think the generals in the field -- well, a few of them -- are a bunch of fucking donkeys. But that's his style."

"Well, what about the date?" I said. "I mean, it's the day after tomorrow."

"I know. They know. Like I said, we're 'awaiting events.' And what we're waiting for is a German re-run of the last war, a sweep through Holland and Belgium. That's where our best troops are. And the Maginot Line, well, I really do think the Germans will stay away from that."

"And in-between?" I said. "What is guarding the Ardennes?"

"Some divisions. Some shitty divisions -- you know, Uncle

Pierre and his buddies called up from the reserve, and a couple of canons pulled by horses."

"Armor?"

"Not there," Georges said. "Not really."

"Great place to attack, it seems to me."

"I'll bring this all up again at the next staff meeting." George looked at his watch. "In two hours. But nobody's really listening - - I have to be honest. I might be able to convince my boss to recommend that we move a few more battalions in that direction, but even if I do, they're all just Uncle Pierres -- the best troops will all be in Belgium.

"Let's just hope the Ardennes roads are as narrow as their vacation memories think they are," Georges said. "I mean, hope is all we fucking have at this point."

48

I spent the rest of Wednesday trying to convince myself that the trip hadn't been a total waste. Maybe one more plea at the French high command's staff meeting would move enough men, and move them quickly enough, to make a difference. If they could just slow the Germans down, it might matter. And as for the Nazi gold story, Leon was already in his dog-after-a-bone mode. He went to work after we got back from Vincennes and said he wouldn't have time to see me on Thursday.

So, maybe. My original plan was to take the night train back to Zurich on Thursday and get home Friday morning, the invasion day. But I changed to the morning train because, well, I just didn't feel like hanging around in Paris anymore. The morning train also took a more southerly route than the night train, and I figured the farther away from the Ardennes, the better.

I liked trains, but I didn't really like trains during the day. It seemed like a waste of time, where the night train was kind of fun and just more efficient. But, besides the route, I just wanted to get home and see Manon. As it turned out, though, an engine breakdown about an hour past Dijon left us stranded for 12 hours. I was glad I had taken a private compartment -- thank you, Bohemia Suisse -- where I could stretch out and sleep. The only upside was that the dining car and, more importantly, the bar car had fully provisioned themselves during the stop at Dijon. One of the porters told me that the railway company would have come rescued us in a lorry had it not been for that.

The passengers who filled the bar car for many of those 12 hours made for an ornery menagerie. I ended up spending a long stretch with a guy named Claude Montreaux, who worked for a company that sold threshing machines to farmers. I could care less about the machines, but enjoyed hearing about his life, which was not all that different from what my life had been in Vienna -- traveling a few days a month, tromping around farms, handholding farmers, hearing their complaints, trying to sell them on the latest, greatest model. And he had the best expense account story.

"Every four months, I put in for a new pair of shoes," he said. "On our expense forms, you have a line to write what the expense is for, another line to write the amount, and a third line to write 'explanation.' For the shoes, my explanation is always one word: cowshit."

"That's two words," I said.

"My story, my grammar," he said.

We eventually got around to talking about the war because, well, that's what you inevitably did, especially if you had been drinking. Claude had seen a London paper on his last trip up to Lille, and said, "Norway looks like a disaster."

I asked him if he had a sense of what was next, and he said, "I know this is lousy, but do you think there's any chance Hitler goes for England first before coming after us?"

"I don't know," I said, even though I was pretty sure I did.

"Yeah, I really don't think so, either," he said.

Claude said he had fought at Verdun and survived. "But I

won't take any clients near there -- I just won't go back," he said. "We have three salesmen, and the territories are drawn with pretty straight lines on the map, except that one." He stopped, took a long sip of his whiskey.

"I'll never go back," he said. And then another long pull. "Thank God my two kids are girls."

That's how it was with everybody. Actual information was barely available, but everybody had a gut, and everybody's gut was telling them the worst. It was human nature, 25 years after the last war, to expect the Germans to pull the same shit again -- especially with Hitler. They hated the Kaiser, but Hitler scared the hell out of them -- and, to repeat, fear is a much more potent emotion than hatred. Besides, nobody suffered like the French did in the great war. Whole villages were wiped out, never to be rebuilt -- and not just a couple. A generation of women had no husbands, no children. It's no wonder they needed Uncle Pierre in the reserve units.

I can't imagine what it must have felt like, to be a Frenchman and to know that the fucking Germans were coming again, for the third time since 1870. Then again, Claude's fantasy of a hope that they might turn on England first said a lot. As did the quiet, punctuated only by his sighs, that we fell into after a while.

Once we were moving again, most of the passengers seemed to shift to neutral corners. I went back to my compartment for a quick sleep. I would say that two-thirds of the passengers got off with Claude in Lyon. The stop there was long enough for me to stretch my legs in the station and buy a newspaper. It was early Friday morning, May 10th. There was nothing in the paper about an invasion.

Once we were moving again, headed toward Geneva, I finished the paper in my compartment and then walked down to the dining car for breakfast. There was only one other table occupied. The waiter was quick with a cup of coffee and a menu.

"Seems quiet," I said, looking around.

"Very," he said.

"Is this unusual?"

"Yes," he said. Then he leaned down. "But I was talking to a porter on another train while we were waiting on the platform in Lyon. He was on a run headed south, toward Limoges, and he said they were packed."

"Any reason why?"

"Rumors, I guess," he said.

In the absence of information, what else was there? Rumors. There wasn't much more to say. The waiter left me to put in my order. I don't remember if I ended up eating it or not.

Everything was slow. We sat forever in godforsaken places for no apparent reason. The stop in Geneva was supposed to be 15 minutes, but it lasted over an hour. The stop in Bern was supposed to be 5 minutes, but it lasted 30. Finally, the train limped into Zurich at about 2 p.m. A trip that should have taken 10 hours ended up taking nearly 24.

And in the station, in what was usually a quieter time between the morning and evening rush, a steady stream of people were coming in off of Bahnhofstrasse, striding with a purpose. The afternoon papers, the ones bannered with the headline that consisted of three enormous black words -- "Germany Invades France" -- were selling as quickly as the newsagent could untie the next bundle.

49

F or the next couple of days, I barely slept. My job, it seemed, was to read everything I could, see everything I could, and report back to London with as many daily updates as possible. I didn't have much, honestly. Army units seemed to be moving about and repositioning themselves from south to north -- I could see that much from the train station. I attempted to read divisional insignia from the uniform patches of soldiers grabbing a quick smoke on the platform during their stops, and even though it seemed pretty meaningless, Gregory and I passed it along to London every night.

I still had not seen or heard from Manon since I arrived back from Paris. She wasn't at home, or at work, or at the cafe, or with Liesl. Nobody knew where she was. And while I was worried, and a little bit mad that she hadn't found a way to leave behind some kind of message, I wasn't that worried. She was undoubtedly doing the same thing I was doing.

Still, I missed her, which fouled my mood even more than the daily updates in the newspapers. Because the story they told was the story that Fritz Ritter and the others had predicted. The invasion came on the 10th, as they had said. The attack went through the Ardennes, as they had said. Gamelin, the British, all of them had the roadmap -- but they all had crumpled it up and thrown it in the fire as if it were nothing more than kindling. And now the idiots were paying.

Three days in, the Germans were at the Meuse. If they managed to get across, they would take Sedan. And if they took Sedan, the entire country of France would have a collective nervous breakdown. In 1870, Sedan was the critical battle of the Franco-Prussian War, the decisive battle, and a thorough humiliation for France. This would be worse. Back then, France was forced to hand over Alsace and Lorraine to the Prussians, which was terrible but, well, it was only Alsace and Lorraine -- and besides, they got them back after the next war. Nobody who thought about it for even 30 seconds figured that Hitler would be willing to settle for a couple of provinces this time. And if he got Sedan, the road to Paris would be wide open.

By that third day, the Swiss were starting to panic -- not so much in Zurich, but more up near the French and German borders. I took a car ride and ran into paralyzing traffic from up there, all of it headed south. At one point, I was driving north with ease as the other side was jammed and not moving. Then a policeman blocked my path, waving two small white flags. He shuttled me off onto a side road.

"What do I do now?" I asked him, and he offered some very fast directions to Basel by taking secondary roads. He rattled them off too quickly to memorize.

"What's this about?" I said.

"We're turning this road into a one-way headed south," he said. "It's our only chance to clear this mess."

It was dark by the time I got back to Zurich. The streets were deserted. It was kind of like Vienna was in the days before the Anschluss, people burrowing in and saving their money before whatever was about to happen. I still didn't think the Germans would swallow Switzerland as long as the banks continued to play along, but who knew anymore.

I ate dinner at Fessler's. It was deserted. I saw Henry and Liesl and the baby for a minute, but they seemed intent on nesting in their flat, maybe even more intent than parents typically are, because of the war. They weren't in the cafe for five minutes. Gregory sat with me while I ate, and I told him what I had seen, and we composed the message for London. We did it right there at the table, and then he went upstairs to work out the code from the bible.

"What if they get Sedan?" Gregory said after we had received the confirmation back from Groucho.

"If Sedan falls, France falls."

"Look at a map -- it's a straight shot to Paris. And if the papers are right, the best French divisions are up in Belgium. So are the British."

"Maybe they can get it turned around."

"I don't know," I said. "It doesn't seem like these people react very quickly to anything."

"They have to wake up soon," Gregory said. "I mean, really. Don't they?"

Walking home, I kept thinking about what Gregory had said, and how he had always maintained more optimism than I had, despite how let down we had been. Yes, he was right. Yes, they did have to wake up -- and they probably would. Faced with a crisis, their eyes would be opened. France still had a big, fearsome army. The British would be some help, and they still had time here. The Germans were moving fast, but could they keep it up? Could their supplies keep up with their tanks?

There was still hope. I had actually talked myself into feeling pretty good, or at least better than I had been feeling, and then I opened the door and saw that Manon was there. We devoured each other, just about without words. Then we traded information, although neither of us knew much more than that the roads headed south were jammed. She didn't know anything more about Sedan than what was in the papers. But she agreed that it was the key to the whole thing. And she was more clinical in her assessment than I was.

"It might be too late for them to react," she said. "Idiots."

"Too late? It can't be. It's only been a couple of days."

"We'll know soon," she said. "Might not take long at all."

My hope had deflated again, and as I approached the confluence of despair and exhaustion, I fell asleep entwined with Manon. We were awakened a couple of hours later by a phone call from Liesl. I dropped the receiver in the dark and made her repeat what she had said because it had shocked me so. But the message was the same the second time as it had been the first time. Gregory had been shot in the cafe. He was dead.

50

The scene at the cafe was every bit as bad as I imagined it would be. Manon and I rushed over and found the police cars outside, jamming the narrow street, their lights flashing red and blue. Gregory's body had been removed by the coroner, but a puddle of blood remained as evidence of the spot. It was already drying, congealing on the wood floor.

Liesl was a rock, as was little Sylvie, wrapped tight in her mother's arms. Henry was catatonic. The three of them sat in a booth off to the side as the police detectives went about their business. We joined them, and I instinctively hugged Henry and didn't let go. But it was like I was embracing a lifeless form. He barely reacted to questions, or to a squeeze of his shoulder.

The drawer of the cash register was open and empty. A detective came over -- I didn't catch his name -- and said, "The lock on the door was forced, maybe with a crowbar. The till was empty. It appears, based on that alone, to have been a robbery that went horribly wrong. But what we don't get is why anyone would think there was a lot of money in the register at a place like this. Would there be?"

Henry didn't react to the question. I nudged him and said, "Henry," in almost a whisper, and he stirred as if from sleep.

"No, not much money," he said. "Nothing worth killing over."

"Was your father the kind of person who would resist an armed robber over a few francs?"

Henry shrugged, then fell back into his trance. But the cop was asking the right question. You never know how you're going to react in a given situation, but there is no way in hell that the Gregory I knew would have risked his life over that amount of money. Maybe back in the day, back in Vienna, when he had a crew to back him up and a reputation to uphold. But not here, not now, no, not at his age, not with little Sylvie there. It just didn't make any sense.

Which, of course, left...

I just couldn't entertain the thought. My mind literally could not process the possibility that this was somehow related to the radio in his spare room, and so it vanished from my consciousness before the thought even registered. The mind can be a fantastic organ sometimes, and it was for me that night, at least until Peter Ruchti walked into the cafe and began talking to a couple of the detectives who were still puzzling over the cash register and stepping daintily around the pool of drying blood.

Manon recognized Ruchti immediately and gave me a quizzical look across the table. I had not told her about Gregory because that was our deal -- we would share information but not sources or co-workers. It was just safer for everybody that way. But then, after this, I didn't know what I was going to do. I did know that I needed to talk to Ruchti, so I got up from the booth and announced to no one and everyone, "I need a breath of air," and walked out onto Oberdorfstrasse.

As I walked across the cafe, I looked at the window, my eyes having been caught by a blue-and-red flashing light. Across the street and a little bit down the street, a man stood in the shadow of a doorway. But he was lit, red and blue, with each cycle of the police car's light. He was lit just a little, though, and the colors distorted the picture, and I was a decent distance from the window, but the man standing in the doorway looked very much like Anders, the security guard at Bohemia Suisse.

But by the time I reached the street and had another look, there was nobody there. So I just stood there, leaning against the cafe, hoping Ruchti would take the hint. In about two minutes, he did. He offered his condolences.

"Do you think it was a robbery?" I said.

"No. But they do," Ruchti said, pointing vaguely inside. "And that's okay with me. But you have to be honest with me."

"About what?"

"About whether or not Gregory Fessler was working with you," he said.

I didn't answer for a second. I liked Ruchti, and I trusted him. He hadn't steered me wrong on anything, and he warned me about Vogl.

"Vogl." I spat the name out as soon as it came to me. "You don't think--"

"No," Ruchti said. "I don't think there's any way he's in Zurich. And I know he's Gestapo, but I don't think some captain in Poland has the ability to order a murder in a neutral country, hundreds of miles away. But you haven't answered my question."

I paused again, just looking at him. I didn't know what was right, but I had to take a chance.

"Gregory was working with me," I said.

"Doing what? Actually spying?"

"Well, no."

"Then what? Was he making radio transmissions? Because, you know, we're pretty sure that the German legation here now has a radio detection vehicle, a small lorry with an antenna on top that drives around the city. We've seen it a few times, followed it back to the German mission. It can detect a radio transmitter--"

"What? WHAT?" It was Henry. He had come out the door of the cafe and overheard the last bit of what Ruchti had said.

"No. Alex, tell me it's not true. Tell me you didn't get my father roped into this whole fucking spy business."

Ruchti looked at me, partly in a questioning way, partly in helplessness. When I started speaking, I addressed Ruchti's unspoken question first.

"Henry and his wife know about my role at the bank because they were part of the deal with the intelligence service to get out of Czechoslovakia after the Anschluss."

Then I turned to Henry.

"Mr. Ruchti here is with a Swiss police unit that has some intelligence aspects to it, and he knows some of my story," I said. "And Henry, yes, your father was helping me send coded radio transmissions to my Czech contact, who's living now in London."

"So is that it?" Henry was screaming, crying. His words pierced the night. "Is that why he was fucking killed. Goddammit, Alex. Is that why?"

Ruchti did his best to rescue me.

"The homicide detectives are experienced, and they think it was a robbery," he said. He looked Henry directly in the eye. "If they believe it, I believe it. The truth is that spies in this country have no reason to kill each other, and they don't because the Swiss government has made it quite clear that violence on Swiss soil will not be tolerated. Mr. Fessler, it just doesn't happen. And I would know."

The lie was stunning -- because, if not Gregory, there certainly was the fellow on Rennweg with the slug through his eye to consider. I wasn't sure if Henry bought it. He didn't say anything. Ruchti left with a shrug that Henry did not see, and a pantomime of a telephone receiver pressed to his ear. Call me, he mouthed.

Back inside, Henry began pacing near the kitchen. The police were packing up, and Liesl and Sylvie had already headed back to their flat. It was nearly 5 a.m. I asked one of the cops if he would escort Manon home. She looked at me questioningly, and I pointed toward Henry, and she understood that I would stay behind with my friend. Finally, when the door was closed, and we were alone, Henry looked at me in a way that scared me. It was a look I had never seen from him.

"Where's the fucking radio?" he said.

I led the way to Gregory's apartment, and then to the spare room, and then to the small table secreted behind the packing crates. The radio was there. I felt it, and it was cold.

"How could you?" Henry said. He repeated it, and then he repeated it again, and then he said "fuuuuuuck," the delivery more long than loud.

"Henry, he was a grown man," I said. "It was his decision. He felt the need to help."

"Alex, that's bullshit. Need to help? Fuck that -- what did he need? He had me. He had Liesl. He had his grandchild. Why did he need your fucking adventure?"

"I don't know," I was looking down at my hands at that point. I know I heard what I was saying, but I'm not sure Henry did. "I don't know why he needed it. But he did."

I paused for a second, then began babbling. "You know how much he loved you and Liesl, and how thrilled he was about Sylvie, and what a beautiful family you--"

"Get the fuck out of here," he said. "We're fucking done. And take that fucking piece of shit with you."

Henry stormed out. He slammed the door of the flat and stomped up the stairs. I heard him on every tread. Then I looked around for an empty box amid the clutter, a box that would hold the radio, and the sending key, and the bible. And I left, out of the flat and down to the cafe. I did my best to secure the broken door, jamming a chair beneath the knob to hold it in place. Then I found a menu and wrote a small sign on the back side of it and propped it in the front window:

C LOSED UNTIL FURTHER NOTICE

T hen I carried my box of shit and my bag of guilt and left through the back door.

51

I knew the Fesslers were Catholic, at least in name, but I had not known that Gregory had been much of a church-goer, not until his funeral, when the priest made a reference during his talk to "the friendly debates he and I would have many mornings after Mass, on topics ranging from the headlines on the front page of the newspaper to the latest disappointments perpetrated by his beloved FC Zurich."

The priest was the only speaker. Henry did not deliver a eulogy. He sat with Liesl in the front row on the right, next to the casket. They passed little Sylvie back and forth between them as they stood and sat and knelt. The only time she cried loudly was when the priest and the altar boys came down from the altar with the lit incense burner, gold on a gold chain, and the priest swung it back and forth as he walked around the casket. I almost never went to church anymore, but that smell always triggered something in me, something unsettling. I wondered if it would somehow be the same for Sylvie.

Besides the family, there were about 20 mourners. A couple of the more memorable fossils were prominent on the left side, and a kid in his 20's just might have been one of the guys I saw pissing against the wall at Hardturm before the FC Zurich game, but I didn't recognize most of the people. The truth was, I didn't know much about Gregory's life outside of the cafe. I didn't know he had much of a life outside the cafe, although the priest proved me wrong there. So maybe they were customers, maybe not.

I sat in the back of the Liebfrauenkirche. Zurich didn't have a lot of Catholics, but this was a beautiful church. High up on the walls was a riot of murals, bright and colorful representations of some religious thing or another. It was as if the Catholics were sticking out their tongues at the tight-assed Protestant churches that Zurich pretty much invented, and which seemed to set a tone for pretty much every aspect of daily life. Or maybe it was something in the Swiss genetic makeup that set the tight-assed tone, and the Protestants followed. Whatever -- I kind of liked the artwork, all splashed with red and blue and gold, even if I really didn't care what it represented.

I got to the church early and took my seat in the back, before the hearse and the family. I had not spoken to Henry since the night Gregory was shot, and I didn't know how I was going to be able to mend our fracture. My guilt had morphed over the few days into a kind of defiance -- it was Gregory's decision to get involved, goddamn it -- but there was no way I was ever going to convince Henry of that, at least not in the short term. But I wanted him to see me at the funeral, as a kind of unspoken opening. And I wanted to be there for my friend, Gregory.

When they opened the doors, the organ music began, and the priest and the altar boys led the casket and the family up the center aisle. The pallbearers were from the burial company. One of them was wearing white socks with his black suit.

Henry saw me immediately. He was walking not three feet from me, arm around Liesl. We locked eyes for what seemed like forever, but which was probably a second, maybe two. Then he averted his gaze. He did it with an exaggerated snap of his head to the left. There was no sign of recognition, no acknowledgment of my presence, and most importantly, no hint that my presence was appreciated. I did get a little of that from Liesl -- a quick, tired half-smile -- before she, too, looked away much quicker than she had to. But at least there was the half-smile. There was nothing from Henry, nothing other than dead eyes.

I had not expected anything more, but it still upset me. So did Manon. She didn't show up for the funeral. I don't know if it was the remnant of our latest argument, or what, but her absence might have bothered me more than Henry's reaction.

On the morning after, I went to her flat and told her about Gregory and the radio. Ruchti knew, Henry knew, Liesl undoubtedly knew, so Manon had to know. She was hurt that I had not told her earlier.

"But we agreed," I said.

"But this was different, Alex. Can't you see that? Gregory. I mean, it was just different."

"How? It was the exact reason why we made the agreement. Gregory had never agreed to have his identity shared with anybody. And besides -- imagine if I had told you, and he got shot. I'd always wonder if by telling you, he somehow had been revealed."

"If I had known, maybe I could have done something to prevent it."

"So you're absolutely sure it wasn't a robbery? Didn't you think it was a robbery until I just walked in here?" I said. And then Manon looked at me with eyes that betrayed nothing but disdain.

"Are you ever going to fucking grow up?" she said. And then, as if she immediately sensed her tone and tried to take it back, she said, "I didn't mean--"

"Yes you did," I said.

In the midst of the ensuing silence, I turned and left her flat. But I came back the next day, and when there was no answer to my knocks, I left her a note with the time of the funeral, and how I would be early, and where I would be sitting. Maybe she never received it -- there was a war on, after all -- or perhaps something between us was torn. After Gregory, after everything, I wasn't sure how I could deal with losing Manon, too.

As I worked this over and over in my mind, following along mindlessly with the standing and sitting and kneeling, not even attempting to listen as the priest droned on in Latin, I didn't know what to do. The only thing I was sure of was that I couldn't take another stare from Henry, so I got up and left the church when the family was kneeling at the railing between the altar and the pews and receiving communion. The sunlight shocked me when I opened the door. At least it was a nice day to feel like shit.

I needed to talk to somebody, and one of the downsides of the spy business is, there isn't a long list of somebodies available for consultation. But Brodsky was one of them. I had left a yellow chalk mark at the MCMIX fountain that morning -- and then, because of my inattention, I was forced to reach into the basin to wash some chalk dust off of my hand and also off of the pants of my black suit. After the funeral, after wandering for who knows how long, I walked by again and saw his mark of acknowledgment.

So that was where I would be headed after dark, one more time to the Barley House unless I could find Manon first. But there was still no answer at her flat. I got down on my hands and knees, pressed my cheek against the floor, and looked into the gap beneath her door. But on the other side, the entryway of the flat wasn't near any windows, and it was dark. I couldn't see if my original note was lying there on the floor or if it had been picked up.

52

W ar had done nothing to hurt the business of the Barley House, or dampen the din. Whether or not they were arguing about Hiter and Gamelin now instead of FC Zurich and Grasshoppers wasn't obvious, but it was still loud. And it still smelled.

"Fog of war," I said, upon encountering Brodsky at his usual table. I waved my hand and visibly moved the layer of smoke that had settled along the ceiling. I sometimes wondered if Zurich had health inspectors, and what the payoff must have been to keep this place open.

Brodsky was reading the newspaper.

"Morning or afternoon?" I said.

"Afternoon, just bought it," he said. "Still a few hours old."

"Are the Panzers in Paris yet?"

"No," Brodsky said. "It might be worse than that."

"What could be worse than the Germans taking Paris?"

"Look," he said. He folded the newspaper back upon itself and flattened the page on the table. The illustration was a map of the top half of France, with lines drawn on it to represent the armies' various positions. Brodsky began drawing with his finger.

"If you read the story, the Germans have turned north," he said. "Look," and he began pointing to spots mentioned in the text. "If they were going to Paris, they would go here instead." Again, more pointing.

"So what are you saying?"

"I'm no expert -- I can barely follow the map in a Michelin guide," he said. But then he began to explain that from what his sources in the Russian high command had been telling him, the Germans believed that all of the best troops, both British and French, were in Belgium. It was the same thing that Georges had said when we were at Vincennes.

"So what happens if the Germans sweep north like this instead of going to Paris?"

I looked at the map. The best British and French troops would be trapped between the Germans and the English Channel.

"You don't think?"

"I do think," Brodsky said. "Maybe Hitler is a genius after all."

"Fuck," I said. This was my considered military opinion.

"Yes, fuck."

"Do you think the French saw it coming?"

"Does it look like they saw it coming to you?" Brodsky said.

I was sure that they hadn't. I was sure that they were worried only about protecting their precious Paris and never dreamed that Hitler would unleash this kind of vise in the opposite direction.

"Fuck," I said.

"That all you've got?"

"Pretty much. But, I mean, what else needs to be said?"

We looked at the map for a while and played amateur Clausewitz, concluding that the only chance was for the French and Brits to try to bust out before it was too late. Of course, that would require some coordination between the two countries, and a bit of decisive thinking, and those old fools clearly had trouble deciding what to have for lunch.

We began talking about what we had seen in Zurich -- not out there, where the actual working people lived, but where we spent most of our time, within worshiping distance of the Paradeplatz. There were a lot of Germans in the center of the city, both permanent expats and workers -- mostly in the banks -- who were posted in Zurich for a year or two at a time. And most of those German were strutting, just a little louder in the cafes, just a little quicker with a laugh.

"Have you been out on the roads or at the train station in the last couple of days?" I said. Brodsky told me that he had and that the migration toward the south from places near the border like Basel had begun to reverse. He said that as soon as the Germans took Sedan, and then kept going, it looked to most people here that Hitler wasn't interested in causing Switzerland any trouble. So they packed up the cars that they had just unloaded, and left Aunt Marie's house in Geneva, and headed back home.

"Sedan," I said. "First 1870, now 1940. They ought to just blow it up, or at least change the name. Just call it Defeat. Or Disaster. Or Failure."

We got another round, and then I began to tell Brodsky what had happened, about Gregory and his involvement and his murder. He thanked me for the information about the German's radio detection lorry. And then he thought for a minute.

"You want me to clear your conscience -- is that it?"

I didn't answer him.

"I can tell you that you didn't rope your friend into this. I can tell you that he was a grown man, and he sensed a real purpose in his life by helping you, and that it was his decision, and that he knew the risks, and that you did nothing but support him, and that none of this was your fault."

I just stared at him.

"I can tell you that, and I believe it," Brodsky said. "But you will not shake this easily, or soon. That is just the truth. It is the danger of involving anyone who is close to you, or of becoming too close to a co-worker or a source."

He paused.

"Thank God I hate you," he said. Then he reached over and punched me in the arm. It was as close a moment as two grown men in a public place could permit themselves.

"Fuck you, asshole," I said. It was the only thing I could think of.

We had another drink. I didn't tell Brodsky, but I was pretty sure, right then, that I couldn't take this anymore -- not Zurich, not working for incompetents, not any of it. And if Manon and I were really done, again, and if Henry and I were done, I knew that there was no way I was staying. How could I? How could I even walk by the cafe?

53

B y the next morning, after another failed attempt to contact Manon at her flat, I decided that even if I didn't leave, I needed to be ready to go. That meant getting my money out of Bohemia Suisse.

Part of the problem was finding a destination as far away from all of this as I could. Maybe America made the most sense. I certainly had enough money to get there. But the way things were going, the only way out might have been through Spain, and then Portugal, with a flight or a boat from Lisbon. As long as the trains were still running to France, I would have a chance -- and they were still running, a couple a day. And even if I were to be stranded in, say, Portugal, I could survive that.

But, first, the money. It being Sunday, the easiest thing to do was just let myself into the empty bank and clean out my account and my safe deposit box. Between the two of them, there was enough money to live on comfortably for an indefinite period of time -- and Swiss francs were, as my banker friends liked to say, as good as gold but a lot lighter. You could exchange them in any big city. And if I wanted to make an even larger withdrawal than was justified by my account balance, there was nothing to stop me. I mean, what was Groucho going to do about it?

I let myself in and locked the door behind me. It was about 11 a.m., and I had not seen a person on the street outside. I decided against taking more than I was entitled to receive, but I did file a half-assed expense report for the trip to Paris and dropped it on Marta's desk.

That report, the withdrawal slip that emptied my account, and a note were now in a neat pile. I used Marta's typewriter to bat it out:

Marta,

I have resigned as president of Bohemia Suisse. Until a new president is appointed, you are to continue as before, paying yourself and Anders. As my final act, I grant you both a 10 percent raise, effective immediately.

Anything you cannot handle, and I don't imagine there will be anything, write to the address in London that is in the emergency file. In fact, write to London anyway and tell them that you have received this letter and are ready for any instructions.

Alex

I did not offer Marta any explanations, partly because I didn't think I owed her one but mostly because I didn't have one that I felt authorized to provide. So I pulled the letter from the typewriter's roller -- I always loved that sound -- and added it to the stack on Marta's desk. Then, after replacing the cover on her typewriter, I added one final flourish to my departure. Grabbing the diary, the sainted diary, I opened it and turned to today's page. Being a Sunday, it was blank. With my best penmanship, I wrote a single word and wrote it big enough to come close to filling the space. One word: Fin.

It was when I was replacing the cap on my pen that I looked up and first noticed Marta standing there. The second thing I noticed was the pistol she was aiming at me. I was honestly dumbfounded.

"Close your mouth and stand up," she said.

I complied as instructed, mouth first and then legs.

"Hands up, fingers laced behind your head," she said.

Done and done.

"Now let's walk into your office," Marta said. She looked down at the diary because she always looked down at the fucking diary. This time, she saw what I had written, the one word: Fin.

"Oh, that's perfect," she said. "That will fit in just right. I wish I had thought of it, but you made sure I didn't have to."

I walked ahead of her into the office and sat in my chair, as instructed. My hands remained on my head. Marta shut the office door behind her, the leather soundproofing panels now mocking me. They wouldn't eliminate the noise of a pistol, not entirely, but someone outside would likely just take the muffled blast for a car backfire a couple of blocks away.

"That a Luger? A Nazi gun?" I said.

"You thought you were so smart," she said. "Like anybody who didn't think about it for five minutes wouldn't see that you being president of a bank made no real sense."

I wondered if there had been signs about Marta that I had missed, but there hadn't been -- though, to be honest, it wasn't as if somebody working undercover for the Nazis was likely to have a swastika tattooed on her forehead. Still, I had never seen her out of the office doing anything, no less anything subversive. And in the office, she was just an overly-efficient pain in the ass, a perfect bank employee. The truth was, the fact that she and I sparred about stuff made her less concerning. If she had been an undercover agent trying to get close to me, she would have been fawning instead.

I had no idea what to do, so I opted for conversation in the hope that delay would be my ally.

"So how long have you known?"

"Almost from the start," she said. "You really are an amateur. I mean, that radio--"

"What radio?"

"Grow up, Herr Kovacs. Please."

Marta had killed Gregory. There, mystery solved, although it seemed likely that I would take the solution to my grave.

"But why? Why Gregory? If you knew so much about me, you must have known he was just the radio operator."

"He was involved," she said. There was no emotion in her voice, a matter-of-factness that was chilling.

"But that's bullish--"

"Enough. I have no problem explaining the operation now, given your current predicament. Herr Fessler had to die first. It had to look like a robbery so that the sensibilities of the Swiss police would not be offended. But they would know, deep down. Ruchti would know. And now you will be found to have committed suicide at your desk, overcome by the guilt of involving Herr Fessler in your venture and seeing him killed. I was going to force you to write a note, but your final addition to the diary will take care of that."

She actually smiled as she recounted the plan.

"Between now and tomorrow, my task will be play-acting a believable response to finding your body -- a scream, but not too much of a scream. I'm not sure Anders will be tough to fool either way. And then, when the police arrive, I will point out the latest entry in the diary, which ideally will be splattered just a bit with blood and brains. The homicide detectives will happily accept the story they have been handed. Ruchti will be the only one who figures out the guilt-about-Fessler part. It'll be the first thing he thinks of. You're an amateur, and you just couldn't take it."

Marta began to walk toward me, around to my side of the desk. The shot would have to be close enough to my temple that it appeared believable as a suicide. This would be my only chance.

As she approached, the telephone on my desk rang. It was likely Ruchti. I had left him a note, asking him to call me at the office around noon on Sunday, mostly because I thought he might have some advice about the best routes out of the country.

"It's Ruchti, I'm pretty sure," I said.

The phone rang. Twice. Three times.

"We're meeting for coffee. If I don't answer, he'll just come over. His office isn't a five-minute walk."

Four times. Five times.

"Okay, answer. Just get rid of him."

Six times. Seven. In one motion, I reached for the telephone receiver, picked it up, and clubbed Marta's arm with it. She screamed, and the pistol fell out of her hand, skittering along the desktop and then onto the carpet. I dove for it and reached it easily before Marta, her path blocked by the desk. At which point, I marched her out of my office and to her desk. I made her sit, put the diary beside her, and considered. I could just retype the letter, adding a passage about how it was never going to work between us. It wouldn't take five minutes. Then it would be her blood and her brains on the diary. It wouldn't be perfect -- what was she doing in the bank on a Sunday? -- but it would be good enough. Anders would find her body on Monday morning, and the case would be closed by sundown. They'd look for me for an interview, but I would be long gone. They would go to the emergency file and contact London, but at that point, maybe Ruchti would get involved and just shut it down.

All of this went through my head in about 10 seconds. Finally, my thought process was interrupted by Marta.

"You don't have the guts," she said.

At which point, I shot her in the temple.

For Gregory.

I couldn't believe how calm I was. Because there was splatter on the typewriter cover, I opted just to add a hand-written post-script to my note: "It never would have worked between us." Then I gathered the small piles of big bills that I had taken from the vault and stuffed them into a briefcase. I was looking back at Marta's desk -- the gun now in her right hand, her head on the blotter with plenty to blot -- surveying the grisly tableau. I had not disturbed anything, I was pretty sure. It was going to work.

It was as I turned to the door that I saw Anders facing me, with a pistol drawn. Two employees, two guns. At that moment, the boss of the year award seemed out of the question.

54

The oddest things can cross your mind sometimes. There I was, facing another pistol, and all I could seem to notice was that Anders was wearing a flat cap and a light gray jacket with a zipper. I was pretty sure I had never seen him without the blue blazer.

That he and Marta had been working together for the Nazis -- I couldn't believe it. Well, I could believe it, especially Anders -- but how had Groucho allowed his precious Bohemia Suisse to be infiltrated by Nazi spies, and how had he allowed me to be exposed? The incompetence at the head of this operation would be a story for the history books, provided that somebody other than Goebbels had a chance one day to write the history books.

It was so strange, being more consumed by my disdain for Groucho and his bosses and their bosses than by the pistol aimed at me. It was in the midst of that pointless reverie when Anders asked me, "Are you okay?"

I wasn't sure I had heard him correctly.

"Uh, yeah."

At which point, he lowered the pistol and placed it into his jacket pocket. So I had heard him correctly.

"Wait, what?"

Anders laughed -- another first. Then he told me his story. As it turned out, he had suspected that Marta was working for the Nazis -- "months ago," he said -- and began trying to keep an eye on her.

"But I couldn't do it 24 hours a day," he said. "And so I was late the night your friend was killed. I did get there after I heard the police radio, but it was too late. I have to believe she killed him."

I told Anders that Marta had willingly confessed when she thought she had me trapped and dead. I explained what happened after that. He took it all in, then walked over to Marta's desk and did a quick survey of the scene.

"It'll play," he said.

"What do you mean?"

"As long as you didn't track any blood or body parts around the carpet, I think the police will buy this. And I don't think you did."

He stopped for a second, folded his arms.

"Or we could go another way," he said. "You write up a new withdrawal slip for you, and another one for Marta -- she has a small account. Had. You leave them on my desk with a note that explains nothing, only that you were resigning as the president of the bank, and that Marta was resigning, and that I should contact London and all that. People will figure you ran away together, lovers fleeing the war."

"Or some such shit."

"Too hokey?"

"I don't know," I said. "It does take the police out of the equation."

"That's what I was thinking. She has no family, at least not here. I don't know if anybody would even notice she was gone."

"But what about her clothes? And her passport."

Anders slipped on a pair of gloves and walked back over to Marta's desk. Her purse was on the floor at the side of the desk. He made sure he wasn't stepping in any blood splatter, and then reached over, and opened it, and began to rifle through.

"Voila," he said, producing the passport with a flourish.

"But no clothes from her flat? No suitcase."

"It's not perfect, but it's good enough," Anders said. "Lovers in wartime. It'll play."

"And the body?"

"I can take care of that," he said. "And besides -- once I get the carpet cleaned up, it won't even matter. Remember, nobody's going to think she's dead. Nobody's going to be looking for a body. They figure the two of you for a villa outside Lisbon."

"But what about the age difference?"

"How old are you?" he said.

"40."

He paged through the passport. "She's only 44."

"That's a hard goddamn 44."

He laughed. The bullet and the blood had made it even harder. "I'll say it again -- lovers in wartime. Fuck it."

We talked a little about the logistics of dead body removal. He said he could get her out the back door, rolled up in a rug or something. I told him I didn't know there was a back door. He looked at me as if I were an idiot.

"Are you a Swiss spy?" I said.

"No."

"An anything spy?"

"No."

"Then why are you doing this, running these risks?"

"This might sound corny, but it's because I am a proud Swiss," he said. "My country is so worried about not offending anyone and staying neutral. All we seem to care about is doing what's best for business. We do that, and we convince ourselves that we're just doing it to protect our people, as a manner of self-preservation. But in doing it, in protecting ourselves, we ignore the assault on decency, and all that is evil that the Nazis represent. I just can't accept that trade-off. So this is what I can do."

At that point, I really felt like a shithead for all of the cracks I had made about the Swiss army when I first met him. I'm not sure I had been in the presence of true patriotism in all of my time in Switzerland, but now I was.

"Look, you need to go," he said. I rewrote the note again, this time by hand. I checked Marta's account balance from the master record book and withdrew what was in there. Cash in hand, I offered it to Anders -- "for cleaning expenses, if nothing else," I said. He refused, insisting that everything he needed was in the storage closet. For me to push any further would have been insulting, so I just added the stack to what was already in the briefcase.

For more than a year, I hadn't been able to stand being in Anders' presence. Part of me wanted to know if he really disliked me. He sensed the question without me having to ask it.

"I never hated you," he said. "After I figured out what you were doing, I actually admired you. But before that, I just thought you were a dilettante. I mean, come on? Being president of this place is like being the madam at a whorehouse. You just polish the brass and take your cut of everything that walks through the door, and--"

He stopped himself, mid-thought.

"Herr Kovacs -- I will call you Alex, this one time -- you need to go," Anders said. "And I mean, really go. Do you have any idea where?"

I didn't have an answer.

55

My flat was cold and dark. The light in the entrance hall had burned out. My first thought was to knock on the door of the superintendent in the basement and get a replacement bulb. Then I thought, no. I was leaving in hours, probably.

I almost didn't see the envelope that had been shoved under the door. It lay on the green checkerboard tile, with "Alex" written in a precise, tight printing style. It was from Manon.

I tore it open, and moved into the living room, near a window, and read:

My dearest Alex,

I don't know how to say this other than just to say it: I am leaving Zurich. By the time you read this, I will be gone. I am going home to Lyon.

There are a dozen reasons, but you are not one of them. You are the only reason that I almost decided to stay. I don't know if you believe me, but I have loved you almost from the very beginning. If I have not always shown it, that is because of the stress I have been under, and because of the profession we have chosen, and because I sometimes am not as nice as I need to be. But I have loved you, and I do love you. It is important to me that you know that.

At the same time, I must go. I cannot work for the fools in French intelligence anymore. I cannot risk my life anymore for idiots who cannot make a decision, who are too afraid to take any action, even when faced with a disaster created by that very indecision. When I told them, they replied that I could not resign, that it would be like desertion in the army. Well, the hell with that. My government deserted me a long time before I deserted my government. Hell, for all I know, my government won't even exist in another week.

In Lyon, I can be with my family again, and that seems more important now than ever. I also have been in communication with some old contacts there, and there already is talk of forming resistance cells against the Germans. If we are in a position where we are forced to fight for our city, house by house, I will. If our government capitulates and there is a German occupation instead, I will be there for sabotage, for resistance propaganda, for whatever. If I cannot again work for the French government, or its successor, or whatever old men are put in charge, I can still work for France.

My advice to you, my dear Alex, is to go to America. Go now. You have lost two countries already, taken too many risks, and now lost a great friend. You deserve to get away from this, from Hitler, from all of it. You have a good heart, Alex. It deserves a rest.

Just know that what we had was real. It is a love I will always cherish. The only thing wrong was our timing.

With all my love,

Manon

I cried as I read it a second time. Then I just collapsed onto the couch, barely moving, the letter stuck in my left hand.

She was right. The reason she was leaving was the reason I needed to leave. Like her, I could not work for these people anymore, leaders incapable of listening and acting. And she was right -- I was exhausted already, and the real fight was just beginning. Besides, this whole business had changed me. I had just killed a person and didn't even feel the least bit bad about it. That stunned me, in a way. It was self-defense, but not entirely. I might have thought of a different way out if I hadn't reacted so emotionally to her taunt. You don't have the guts. Well, fuck her. That was my reaction then and, for the most part, it was still my reaction hours later. That might have worried me as much as anything.

And on top of all that, there was Werner Vogl, my favorite Gestapo captain. Regardless of what Peter Ruchti said, I wasn't sure that I was out of Vogl's reach in Zurich. He might be in Warsaw now, but as the German army moved west and stayed west -- and that indeed appeared to be happening -- you had to believe that Vogl could be following. The idea of having Vogl occupy a permanent space in my consciousness was both tiring and terrifying.

Manon was right, too, that America made the most sense. Get the train and just keep going south -- to Geneva, to Marseille, to Barcelona and Madrid and Lisbon. Then to one of those Pan Am Clipper ships and to New York. To safety and calm. To a new life. To peace.

The problem, of course, was that Manon would not be in New York. I had never made a big decision in my life because of a woman. The truth was, I hadn't made many small decisions because of a woman, either. It was the trait I learned from Uncle Otto, for better or worse. He never married, and I had never been close. "Life's too short, buddy boy," is what he always said, and I tended to believe him. There was always another sales trip to Cologne, always another girl to charm with my travel stories.

But it all felt so empty, thinking back on it. So there I was, empty and exhausted, still angry at Groucho and Gamelin, unable to shake the thought of Vogl, the letter from Manon still clutched in my left hand. I eventually folded it carefully and put it back into the envelope, then into my suitcase, shoving some clothes on top of it, leaving enough room for the stacks of Swiss francs.

56

The train to Lyon was empty. Nobody was traveling into a war zone if they didn't have to, after all -- although the fighting was nowhere near Lyon. It was all much farther north. Still, you could see the families and their luggage crowded onto the platforms in some of the cities we passed through, all of them headed out of France and toward Switzerland.

The hotel across from the station in Lyon seemed empty, too.

"Quiet," I said to the desk clerk, trying out my French.

"From Alsace?" she said.

"Originally, yes. I live in Zurich now."

She looked at me a bit cross-wise, the face an unspoken question about why I would leave a safe, neutral country for France.

"I'm here on business," I said, and she shrugged. I think I might have ended up with the best room in the place. The water for the bath ran extra hot, and the mattress seemed extra soft. Or maybe it was just exhaustion. Whatever, I skipped dinner and slept for 13 hours.

I didn't know much about Manon's life in Lyon, other than that her last name was Friere and that she was from a family of silk manufacturers. The concierge had a telephone directory, and there was a Friere Brothers that manufactured silk in the Croix-Rousse neighborhood, a big hill on the north side of the city. Armed with directions, I decided to walk. Lyon was built up along two rivers, the Rhone and the Saone, and getting to Croix-Rousse meant crossing one of the Rhone bridges and then walking north, through the more downtown areas and then up winding, sometimes medieval streets. It was way up, too -- some of the way, you actually climbed 40 or 50 stairs to get from one road to the next. I stopped on a bench to rest about halfway up.

Finally, though, I reached Rue Dumenge, made a left, then a quick right, and saw the sign: "Friere Brothers. Fine Silk".

Suddenly, I was afraid to knock. I mean, I didn't even know if she was there. For all I knew, she had an old boyfriend who took her in. Like Anders said, "Lovers in wartime." When confronted with an opportunity to knock, what had seemed like such a good idea now seemed so risky.

I retreated to a cafe across the street, took a seat at the window, and watched the front door. At around 10:30, it opened, and Manon came out. She began walking in my direction. It soon was obvious that she was coming into the cafe where I was sitting.

I just watched her, heading in my direction. As she began to pass the window where I was sitting, oblivious, I knocked on the glass.

She stopped, looked. It seemed as if my face wasn't registering with her somehow. Maybe there was glare on the glass. Maybe she was just in shock.

One second. Two. And then she slowly raised up her hand, and put it flat on the glass, and kept it there while I did the same.

GET A FREE STORY IN THE ALEX KOVACS THRILLER SERIES

My interest is not just in writing, but in building a community of readers. My plan is to be in contact occasionally with news on upcoming books, blog posts and other special offers.

If you sign up to the mailing list, I will send you a **FREE** copy of "Otto's End," a story in the Alex Kovacs thriller series that explains exactly what happened on his trip to Cologne in November of 1936.

It's easy. **IT'S FREE.** Sign up here: https://dl.bookfunnel.com/kpuyzx4un8

ENJOY THIS BOOK? YOU CAN REALLY HELP ME OUT.

The truth is that, as a new author, it is hard to get readers' attention. But if you have read this far, I have yours – and I could use a favor.

Reviews from people who liked this book go a long way toward convincing future readers of its worth. It won't take five minutes of your time, but it would mean a lot to me. Just click the link below to leave a review on the book's Amazon page. Long or short, it doesn't matter.

Thanks!

I hope you enjoyed *The Spies of Zurich*. What follows is the first few chapters of the sequel, *The Lyon Resistance*. It will be available for purchase at https://www.amazon.com/author/richardwake

Thanks for your interest!

The small railroad bridge, our target for the night, was about halfway between Lyon and Saint Etienne, maybe 10 miles from each, give or take. The tracks ran close to the Rhone on one side and were hugged by farmland on the other. The land was relatively flat there, and simple grade crossings over the roadways were sufficient — except in this one place, where a dip in the land called for a little stone bridge to hold the tracks over an unnamed road dividing fields of hay. Although, on my scouting trips, it never seemed that big of a dip. This might have been one of those fortuitous occasions where a local elected official owned both the land that the railroad company needed and the little stone bridge construction company.

Railroad track demolition was one of the ways we annoyed the Germans. We had to admit, though, that it was mostly just that, an annoyance. If you blew up a few yards of tracks on a Wednesday night, you would screw up traffic in and out of Lyon on Thursday. If you were lucky, on Friday, too. But that was it — and it seemed that the Nazis were getting better at the business of repairing the blown lines. They also were bringing in an increasing number of men to perform regular preventative patrols.

So it was getting to be a lose-lose calculation — unless you were talking about a bridge. Because the destruction of even the smallest bridge, like the single stone arch I was looking at through my binoculars as I lay behind a hay bale, would put the line out of business for at least a week, and more likely two. The risk-reward suddenly tilted again toward reward, even while acknowledging that the German did the same cost-benefit analysis and kept a close eye on every bridge along the line, even the tiny ones. Which is why Rene, Max and I kept trading the glasses between us, staring at the back of the heads of the two German soldiers leaning on the fenders of their vehicle. They were smoking cigarettes. When they turned, you could see the tiny glow.

"How much time?" Max said. Rene looked at his watch.

"Still five minutes," he said. "No, six. Relax."

Max scooted away from us, crab-walking behind another hay bale to take a piss. If they gave tests to spies, or saboteurs, or resistance agents, or whatever the fuck we were, the adequate bladder test would have flunked Max out straight away. He was a good kid, only 17 and entirely cold-blooded — he very nearly severed the head of a German sentry he had already killed, just in a rage, during a mission to set a fuel depot on fire. But he had to piss as often as an old man, which was the only thing I could kid him about, seeing as how I was 42 years old and he called me Pops. As in, "Fuck you, Pops," which was pretty much his reply to everything I said.

If I was the brains of the operation — and in all modesty, I was — and if Max supplied the muscle and the balls, Rene was the demolitions expert. How he had acquired the expertise had never been explained to me, but Rene knew about the different types of explosives, and how to attach the detonator and the wires and, in this case, the windup alarm clock. I had been given a quick-and-dirty training session once, and I could wire an explosive charge to a plunger, but I would never trust myself with one of the timers. You have to know your limits, especially when you are talking about dismemberment.

Max had argued about everything when we set up the first charge, at about 10 p.m. It was on the tracks, maybe 300 yards from the little stone bridge.

"Pops, we're too fucking close," he said.

"We have to be close," I said. Then I explained to him for the fifth time that in order for this to work, the soldiers guarding the bridge had to be close enough to the first explosion that they felt it was their clear and obvious duty to investigate it themselves.

"But we need the time," Max said. "They could reach us with their rifles if they saw us."

"They're not going to see us," I said. "They're going to be running toward the explosion and then they're going to be staring at burning railroad ties and radioing back to whoever for instructions. As soon as they start heading for the explosion, we start heading for the bridge. We'll get where we need to be before they get to the explosion. And how much time do you need, Rene?"

"Two minutes, Alex," he said. "It's all packed in the cases. I just need to set the timers. Maybe less than two minutes once I'm on the bridge. The cases are pretty heavy for me to carry up that embankment, though."

"That's what Max is for," I said.

"Fuck you, Pops."

And so it went. We set the timer on the first charge to go off at 11. We still had three minutes. Now I had to piss. I could have held it, but I felt as if maybe Max needed to win one before the end of the night. So I crab-walked behind the same bale and listened to him mock me.

"Mine's just nerves, and I can always learn to relax," he said. "But your old man plumbing is shot forever."

As this went on, Rene continued to stare at his watch. He gave a one-minute warning, then 30 seconds. The three of us were ready to move when the explosion went off, piercing the night. I watched through the binoculars as the two soldiers jumped, then said something to each other, then hesitated, then began running toward the boom and what was now a fire of burning railroad ties. One of them was carrying a portable radio and holding it up to his ear as he ran. The other held his helmet down with one hand and grabbed his rifle with the other.

"All right, let's do it," I said. We all trotted, Max carrying the suitcases full of dynamite, Rene and I with pistols drawn. From there, it all went pretty much exactly as I had planned it out in my head. The embankment was not that steep, pretty easy for all of us, even Max with the cases. On my scouting trips — which were necessarily brief, to avoid suspicion — I had noticed that there was a space on each side of the bridge, between the rail-road bed and the keystone of each arch. I was pretty confident that Rene would be able to wedge the cases into the space, but you don't know until you know.

"They going to fit?" I said.

"Like a glove, Alex my boy. Like a fucking glove."

I don't think he took 90 seconds to get the clocks set and put the cases in place. The entire time, I could see the two soldiers, outlined against the fire on the tracks. We ran past our original vantage point to another, maybe 400 yards away. As we got set, Rene looked at his watch.

"Two minutes," he said, and then pointed to the binoculars. "May I?"

"Yes, the artist should see his masterpiece," I said.

We all stood now, not even hiding. It was a moonless night, chosen for that very reason, and cloudy besides. There was nobody looking at us. I took one more quick peek toward the first explosion and saw the same two silhouettes. Then I focused back on the little stone bridge, just in time to see it reduced to a little stone pile. The two explosions came about 10 seconds apart.

As Rene stared into the binoculars — "Ah, it's beautiful," he said, once, then twice — Max and I instinctively hugged each other as if we had just assisted on a game-winning goal during stoppage time. But then we had to go, three men dressed like farm laborers to three different farms in the area. From there, we would be transported back to Lyon.

"You both memorized your directions, right?" I said. "And stay off the roads."

"Fuck you, Pops," Max said.

My farm was in Chassagny. Our plan was to sleep rough in the fields behind the three farms where we were headed, the assumption being that the Gestapo would be knocking on doors before dawn in their search for the bridge saboteurs. I didn't think I would be able to sleep, but I did, the adrenaline rush long past and leaving only exhaustion in its place. It was the rising sun that woke me, and then the slamming of the back door of the farmhouse in the distance as Marcel Lefebvre headed to the barn and his cows. I followed him in, a minute or two later, and I startled him. He fell off of his milking stool and came within inches of compounding the indignity by landing in a pile of cow shit.

"You missed them," he said. He was on his feet now and embracing me.

"Missed who?"

"Your friends in the black leather coats," he said. "They were banging on the door at 3:30. They searched the house and the barn with torches and warned me to be on the lookout for some resistance saboteurs."

"They're just paranoid," I said.

"I hope they have something to be paranoid about," Marcel said.

I told him about the little stone bridge, and he dropped a teat to thrust his hand toward the sky. Then he continued milking. I watched in silence as he filled a pail. It didn't take long.

"Everybody's OK, right?" he said. When I assured him we were, he motioned for me to follow him into the house — "Quick, quick, just in case," he said, and we scampered inside.

From a barrel in the corner of the kitchen, he poured us two tumblers of rough red wine. I looked at my watch theatrically. It was 7:15 a.m.

"Hell, we're celebrating," Marcel said, shoving the glass at me.

"I wasn't complaining," I said.

"You better not be — this is a good batch."

Marcel was in his 50s, a widower with no kids — which meant he did everything on his little hay farm, including delivering the hay to his customers. That is how I would be returning to Lyon, secreted in his hay wagon. For fun, and for some extra money, he made wine. There were some real wineries nearby, but his was a grapes-in-the-bathtub-sized operation. He sold mostly to friends, or at local farmers' markets. He had some beautiful old oak barrels, and the wine he made was significantly better than crap, an everyday wine that was noticeably tastier than typical everyday wine. Of course, given the rationing, even crap wine was very much in demand.

He worked hard at it, as a kind of profitable hobby, and had about 25 barrels in the barn. As it turned out, those barrels were why he joined the resistance. With petrol in low supply, and a lot of car motors converted to burning wood, the Germans did a different kind of conversion. They had engines that would run on alcohol, that would run on wine. And so, they traveled the countryside and went about the business of requisitioning all the wine they could get their hands on.

"It's bad enough they wouldn't pay for it," Marcel said, when he first told me the story. "But Alex, I could live with that. I understand pigs. But when they dumped motor oil in with the wine, I just couldn't take that."

The problem wasn't that the oil spoiled the wine for drinking, because it did. That was the Germans' purpose. The issue was the barrels. The oil ruined them, too, leaving behind a residue that soaked into the old wood and could not be cleaned out. They couldn't be used for wine anymore.

"I cried when I had to break them up," Marcel said. He used them for firewood.

"How many did they get?"

"Twelve."

"How many did you manage to hide from them?"

"Fourteen," he said. Then he laughed. "With these assholes, the way I figure it, I'm still ahead of the game, 14-12. And now, I help you guys out here and there, and the wine I have left tastes that much sweeter."

He pulled two empty bottles out of the cupboard, filled one with wine and one with milk, and stoppered them. "Here," he said, handing them over. "We need to get going."

With that, me and my bottles climbed into the wagon. He had square bales already loaded — three layers of bales, five in a row, five deep, 75 bales in all. Except it was really 73, as I found out when I crawled into an empty space in the middle of the hay structure and then sat as Marcel sealed me in.

He had asked me ahead of time if it was necessary, and I admitted that this was exercising an insane level of caution. I mean, it isn't as if every other wagon headed into town with farm goods was manned by a single person.

"So you're my helper — what's the big deal?" Marcel said.

"You're probably right," I said. "But what if you get stopped by a German who knows you live alone here, and work alone? I'm sure they're really on edge, really jumpy, and it's just not worth the risk, even if you just told them I was a day laborer helping with a big load."

So I sat in darkness, save for a tiny shaft of light — and, presumably, oxygen — that made it through the immense pile. And, as it turned out, Marcel was stopped by a German patrol, and one of the soldiers did jab a bayonet into the hay bales two or three times for show. If the steel had struck flesh, it would have been a lot harder for Marcel to explain than a strange day laborer sitting next to him in the passenger seat. But the bayonet hit nothing besides hay, and we made it to the Lyon municipal stables by 10. Yes, I was being smuggled into the place where the city police boarded their horses.

"Don't worry," Marcel said. The wagon was parked behind the barns. No one was around. "Besides," he said, "now you can be my day laborer."

"It's worth it for the wine and the milk," I said. We had the truck unloaded within an hour. Then, Marcel made sure to pull every stray bit out hay out of my hair and pockets and cuffs. If I walked fast, I would be home in another hour.

The walk home took me past the old army medical school, which was now Gestapo headquarters in Lyon, which was just one more bit of evidence of God's twisted sense of humor. What once had been a place where men were taught to save the lives of those who had been thrust into hell was now a place where the hell was manufactured instead.

The Gestapo had been in Lyon for four months. We were all in church when they arrived — literally. It was November 11, 1942, and we were praying for the dead of the first war on the anniversary of the armistice. And if everyone in the church was praying for the French war dead, and I was praying for the friends I lost fighting for Austria-Hungary, so be it. We were on the same side now. When we walked out of the church together, the German columns were arriving. We were in the Free Zone for the first two years of the war, the part of France where the Germans couldn't be bothered and left it to the fucking Vichy to run things. But then, seemingly overnight, we were worthy of their attention. The brass piled into the Hotel Terminus, across from the train station, and attempted to operate from there for a while. But the business of torture and terror, a booming industry, quickly outgrew the hotel's accommodations. So while they continued to use the Terminus as their dormitory, the Gestapo had taken over the old medical school on Avenue Berthelot, a block and a half from the Rhone, for their hijinks.

I could have avoided it, but I liked walking by — big and solid, Nazi flags flying, black-uniformed sentries at the gate. It reminded me why I was doing this. I made Manon walk by with me the last time we were close. And while she didn't object, she did say, "You know full well that I don't need a fucking reminder."

Manon was my wife. We met in Zurich in late 1939. I followed her to Lyon, her home, after the German invasion in 1940. We had fallen in love despite a rather unconventional romantic beginning — unconventional in the sense that she was a spy for the French intelligence service who seduced me because she was trying to figure out what I was up to, me being a spy for the former Czech government in exile and all. As it turned out, we possessed not only a physical and an emotional attraction. We also bonded over a professional realization that became clear as the panzers sped through the Ardennes: that we worked for idiots, for blind men married to the past, for cowards incapable of action.

So now we worked for the resistance, and for each other, and against the black uniforms and the swastika flags. We published an underground newspaper, one of a half-dozen in the city, called "La Dure Vérité." It was really a sheet or two run off on a Roneo machine, once or twice a month, but we were convinced it made a difference, maybe even more than the sabotage — railroad tracks, telephone lines, whatever would disrupt the German terror machine. We were sure that the 1,000 copies we produced were being read by 20,000, passed secretly from hand to hand. Of course, there also were days when we were convinced that nobody was reading anything and that nothing mattered. Those were the days I went out of my way to walk down Avenue Berthelot, to watch the red flags starched in the breeze, to see the sharpness in the creases in the black SS uniforms. And, maybe to see Barbie.

Klaus Barbie was the man in charge, and I had never seen him. There already were stories of his brutality, but how much was true and how much was an urban legend was unclear. It seemed as if everybody's horrible story was third-hand. If he really was torturing and killing people, and doing it personally, they wouldn't be around to tell the tales, after all. I didn't know anybody who had been in his presence for more than a few seconds.

Max had seen Barbie on the street, arriving at Avenue Bertholet one day, and said, "He's fucking short. He's not one of those big, tall blond assholes." He guessed Barbie was maybe 5-foot-6. Another friend had heard his voice once, outside the Terminus as he was waiting for a car. "He speaks French — he was talking to the valet at the front door, and he was doing OK with the language. Just really slow."

But as for the rest, the rumors of torture and brutality, they were just that. Still, I was dying to put a name to a face, maybe just to give myself a more vivid nightmare. On this day, though, as on all the others when I walked by, I didn't see him. And now that I thought about it, maybe that was what made the nightmares worse.

I crossed the Rhone and then walked north, up to our neighborhood, the Croix-Rousse, up the steep hills, so steep that sometimes there was a stone staircase to take you up from one cross street to the next. Our house, a tiny single with a tinier patch of grass out front, was a few blocks away from Manon's family business, a silk manufacturing factory that her uncle ran by himself since her father's death a few years back. Manon helped with the bookkeeping and used a store room in the back as the base of our underground publishing empire. Our resistance cell was tiny — Manon and I, and a couple of others — and we met in the factory when it was necessary. Which meant twice in the last year, and one of those times was just an excuse to get drunk together after I came into possession of a case of bootleg wine. The other time was to tell them that the various resistance groups had been forced to come together into a kind of confederation after Barbie and his pals arrived, and that our sabotage work would have to be coordinated. That's how I ended up working with Rene and Max, who were with Liberation, a much bigger resistance group than ours.

As I approached the house, Manon was sitting on the little front porch, taking a bit of the afternoon sun. Eyes closed, face upturned — God, she was beautiful. She greeted me in the time-honored fashion, and after we were done, we lay naked in the bed and she whispered softly, "Enough of this. I'd kill for a glass of that milk. And then a glass of the wine."

I feigned annoyance. She reached down and grabbed me there. "The milk and the wine are rationed," she said. "This isn't. Not yet, anyway."

We pulled on robes and sat at the kitchen table and drank first from the milk bottle and then from the wine bottle, just passing them back and forth, not even using glasses. I recounted what I had been doing the last two days, and Manon kissed me on the forehead and called me her "little mad bomber." She told me a funny story about her uncle and the half-deaf old woman who ran one of the looms, screaming at each other about a botched order. The sun felt warm through the front window. Winter was done now.

Both bottles were about half-empty, maybe a little more, when the knock on the door signaled the arrival of three Gestapo men, two of them with guns drawn. One of them came into our bedroom and watched me get dressed, and then it was into the backseat.

The Lyon Resistance, the next book in the Alex Kovacs thriller series, will be available for purchase at https://www.amazon.com/author/richardwake

ABOUT THE AUTHOR

Richard Wake is the author of the Alex Kovacs thriller series. His website can be found at richardwake.com. You can connect with Richard on Facebook or you can send him an email at info@richardwake.com.

f

Made in the USA
Middletown, DE
07 May 2020

94188596R00177